HONEY
TRAP
JJ MARSH

PREWETT
BIELMANN

Honey Trap

Cover design: JD Smith

Published by Prewett Bielmann Ltd.

All enquiries to admin@beatrice-stubbs.com

First printing, 2019

ISBN 978-3-9525077-6-6

For Gilly, Jane, Liza and Kat, aka Triskele Books, whose influence on Beatrice and me cannot be overestimated

Chapter 1

The expression on Agusto's face made his feelings clear. He was not going to change his mind. His white coat, spattered with red stains, was sweat-marked and creased after a long stressful night but his eyes were as sharp as a skewer.

Still, Rami had to try. After all, it was a matter of honour.

"No need, Agusto. I have my Harley and a raincoat. It's only a fifteen-minute ride."

"You think I want to call a cab for *your* benefit? Do not flatter yourself, you young mule! Tell me what happens if you get wet and catch a cold. No, I'll tell you. The number one restaurant in Naples loses its second chef because you are damn well staying away from this kitchen with any unhealthy bugs. I am protecting my investment. Now I am sick of arguing with you. All I want is to rest my feet and drink a grappa. Take a cab, go home and leave me in peace. See you tomorrow."

Rami gave in. His exasperated head shake disguised a smile. "Up to you if you want to throw money away on taxis. You're the boss."

"I am. And if you remembered that more often, we could save ourselves a lot of hot air. Goodnight."

"Goodnight. Give Isabella my best wishes."

"I will." Agusto unbuttoned his tunic and pulled off his bandana. "And, Rami, if the weather is as shitty as this in the morning, get a cab back. NO arguments! Just keep a receipt. Go, you stubborn goat, have I not suffered enough?" He hurled his chef's attire into the laundry bin in the alcove and bounced his way through the doors to the dining area.

In a second, the kitchen became a haven of calm. The stainless steel surfaces shone, empty and sanitised. The ovens, now cool and silent, gaped at him with sooty mouths. The room was as soothing as church. Rami reflected for a moment on how the source of all the tension and bustle which accompanied every service had only just left a few seconds ago. Agusto's presence was a whirlwind, filling every space with a charge of energy so ferocious, one's senses could scatter to the four winds.

After retrieving his raincoat, Rami let himself out of the back door. His Harley was parked in the open garage, next to Agusto's Ferrari, but one glance at the raindrops pounding the pavement convinced him a taxi was indeed the best choice. The wind lashed his cheek as he stood under the awning and he hoped he wouldn't have to wait too long.

"*Buonasera*," said a voice behind him.

Rami turned with a start. The man wishing him a good evening had come from the garage, but his face was unfamiliar.

"*Buonasera*," he replied. "This is private property, you know."

"I know. I'm your driver, here to take you home."

"Ah, I see. I was trying to hail a taxi, I didn't realise he'd already ordered one."

"The car is over there. Shall we?"

They dashed across the road, heads bowed against the vicious weather. The driver opened the back door and Rami got in. It was a luxury limousine, with wide leather seats and a divider between driver and passenger. Trust Agusto to choose a high-end service.

Rami wiped his face and watched the restaurant disappear as the car pulled away into the traffic. Weariness crept over him. It had been a long and tiring night, and the yearning for his own apartment intensified. Home. Car horns and sirens competed with the thundering sound of the rain on the roof. Street lights and shop signs melted into an indistinguishable blur through the windows and the scent of furniture polish made him think of his grandmother.

After they passed the entrance to Galleria Borbonica, the car turned left instead of right and Rami frowned. He rapped on the glass divider.

"*Scusa!* We're going to Miracoli. You need to take a right."

The driver looked into the rear-view mirror and gave him a thumbs-up. But he made no effort to turn right, passing several other opportunities to join Via Toledo. With no indication, he pulled into the kerb, causing other drivers to hoot furiously.

The rear passenger door opened and a man in a long coat slid in beside Rami. His face was handsome and young, although not one Rami knew. His Italian was formal and he had an odd accent, as if he was foreign or from the north, which amounted to much the same thing.

"I apologise for this interruption, but it is imperative I talk to you."

"What about?" Rami's voice gave away his mistrust.

"Let's call it your annual appraisal." The man smiled and offered Rami a cigarette.

"I don't smoke," he lied. "Who are you and why are you in my taxi?"

The man leant forward and tapped an extraordinarily long fingernail on the divider. The driver glanced in the mirror and with his right hand, drew open the small communication window.

"Did you tell him this was a taxi?" There was a nasty smile in the newcomer's voice.

"No. My exact words were 'I'm your driver, here to take you home'. No one mentioned a taxi." The car turned right. Finally.

Rami's fellow passenger laughed. "*Perfetto!* We are indeed

here to take you home." The driver made no comment and closed the divider once more.

"Signor Ahmad, no need for alarm. This is just a friendly conversation."

"Again I ask you, what about?"

The man continued smoking, as if he had not heard. Rain hammered on the roof and the driver continued in the direction of the city centre, far from Rami's own neighbourhood. Ahead of them at the lights, a man ran across the road, a newspaper over his head, splashing through puddles and soaking his trousers.

The man beside him rapped on the divider and when it opened, he spoke in a cheerful tone. "Dino, you hungry?"

"Always got room for some of grandma's cooking, Luca."

Ice trickled down Rami's spine. They knew. He swallowed, feeling the noose tighten. "Thank you for the lift, but I think I would prefer to walk from here."

Neither man reacted. The man called Luca continued to smoke while Dino navigated the traffic and the foul weather. Rami guessed where they were going. The Spanish Quarter. Luca opened the window and tossed out his cigarette. Without warning, he lunged at Rami, grabbing a fistful of his raincoat and pulling him close. His breath smelled sour and of smoke.

"You can't have the foot in both stirrups. Time to make a decision."

"What are you talking about?" Rami tried to prise the man's hands off him. His question was genuine, borne of confusion rather than innocence. He needed to know which organisation these guys represented.

Luca released his coat and pushed him backwards, leaning on top of him as if coming in for a kiss. His forearm pressed against Rami's throat. "Listen to me, *sfigato*. You're not the first to try this trick. It happens when people get greedy. Not anymore. We know what you're doing and it stops right now.

How it stops is up to you."

Rami sensed the car coming to a halt and Dino switched off the engine.

Luca increased the pressure on Rami's windpipe. "No more last chances. Tell us who you're working for and where the money's going. Otherwise, I'll let Dino off the leash."

"I work for Agusto Colacino at Ecco. You know that!"

The door behind his head wrenched open and Dino dragged him out of the car by his hair. Rami's torso hit the cobbles, knocking the wind out of him.

Dino placed a foot on his chest and actually snarled, like a Doberman. Rain smeared Rami's glasses so that he sensed rather than saw Luca loom over him, blocking out the street light.

"You think we have any interest in a *stronzo* like you? Grow up. All I need is the name of your boss. Fair warning: if you say Agusto Colacino one more time, Dino will kick your teeth out. Who are you working for? Just give me his name and you can go home."

Rami heaved in some air. "*Her* name," he rasped. That earned him a few seconds. Dino removed his foot and Rami managed to scramble onto all fours, still gasping for oxygen.

He took several breaths until Luca's rain-stained brown shoes stepped into his sightline.

"The name."

Rami said three words.

That was all it took. The shoes disappeared, doors slammed and the car drove off. If Rami hadn't rolled away as fast as he did, he would have been under the wheels.

He struggled to his feet and reached in his pocket. Phone and wallet both gone. Thankfully, he'd left nothing incriminating in either. With no cash or cards, he would have to walk. He made for the lights, checking over his shoulder several times. No one was around.

At one in the morning, soaked, physically and mentally

exhausted, he turned into Via Vergini Crocelli which housed his apartment block. His long, wet walk had not helped him find a solution. Still he found himself between the devil and the deep blue sea. He would need to sleep on it, and hope against hope that a solution came to him in his dreams.

He trudged the last twenty metres home to his apartment, unlocked the gate and stepped into the courtyard. His mind fogged by his fruitless mental circles and glasses blurred by raindrops, he neither saw nor heard his assailant. The first thing he felt was a blade piercing his ribcage.

Chapter 2

The noise began before dawn. First one moped clattered across the cobbles, followed moments later by two more. Both riders were forced to splash into puddles by the kerb to dodge a taxi driver reversing down the narrow street. They expressed their displeasure by beeping their horns and questioning the driver's parentage and sanity.

A wooden rumbling reminiscent of mediaeval times bounced off the tall buildings lining the street. Two thickset men manoeuvred a cart onto the marketplace, bringing with them a scent of ripe strawberries, peaches and apricots. One threw off the protective tarpaulin and began tucking hand-written signs saying *3€ per cesto* into the strawberry punnets. The other retreated into a recess for the second stall, singing a ribald version of 'Musetta's Waltz' from *La Bohème*. A third market vendor drove his three-wheeled van to park opposite and carried on a semi-shouted conversation with the fruit vendor as he unpacked his selection of slippers and housecoats for display.

Signora Emilia heard it all from her penthouse at the top of the palazzo, visualising every aspect of the scene below. The same routine as every day. If there was a single note of the street symphony missing, she would know. She slipped her arms into a robe and opened the shutters to look out at the view she knew so well.

The sky lightened to a pure, constant Virgin Mary blue. Yesterday's rain had washed much of the dog mess and litter into the gutters and steam rose from the small squares of earth around the trees. Pigeons scattered as a battered truck made a three-point turn at the junction, then returned to peck at crumbs beneath the tables outside the Polish supermarket. Beer-bottle tops trodden into the tarmac glinted like fish scales under the morning light.

Signora Emilia began her toilette, listening and watching through the lattice of lemon trees on her balcony. The sound of flesh slapping onto marble ricocheted around the square, telling her the butcher's shop was taking delivery of the day's stock. A two-tone police siren could be heard from Via Foria. The fishmonger hosed down her counter, adding actual fish scales to join the bottle tops. Two older women with hair the colour of a fox pelt were already queuing outside the bakery, calling up to the apartment above.

"Leave that poor man alone and get down here. You're not the only one with an appetite!" They cackled together, handbags swinging from the crook of their arms.

A metal shutter rattled up to a general cheer. The *pasticceria* had opened and the smell of coffee permeated the air. Signora Emilia sat by the window to apply her make-up and choose her jewellery while keeping an eye on the café. As always, the first customer was the squat, elderly Sicilian with a huge nose and a tiny Chihuahua. He drank his *macchiato* alone, but shared the *sfogliatina* with his dog. The pigeons stood by, strutting and cooing like gossipy security guards.

Spaces for market stalls filled up fast and the number of vehicles already double- and triple-parked gave rise to a discordant loop of impatient horn-blowing and curses. Pedestrians threaded their way through the traffic with insouciance, phones pressed to their heads, ignoring the exhaust fumes. Children walked in gaggles to school, some still eating their breakfast pastries wrapped in a paper tissue. Stray dogs skulked under the market stalls, scooping up anything edible or napping in the shade.

Prepared to face the public, Signora Emilia descended to the courtyard of the palazzo, checking her reflection one last time in the neighbours' window. A well-dressed woman in her sixties, fingers glittering with rings and carrying a faux-Gucci bag, her make-up was nothing short of sculptural. She unlocked the metal gate with a nod to Signor Melle, caretaker in name only.

With a breath to steel herself, she joined the chaos of the morning market. She crossed the street with an imperious hand to stay the idling vehicles and began her morning shop. From the butcher, she purchased two chicken breasts with a polite enquiry after his wife's health. Chicken bagged, she moved up three stalls to acquire artichokes and asparagus, with a few quibbles over the price. After a brief stop for an espresso and head-shaking conversation with the café owner, she returned home, stepping daintily over a trickle of water flowing from the fishmonger.

Only twenty minutes later, she unlocked the gates to her sanctuary. Once inside the courtyard, she purged the exhaust fumes, fruity scents and whiff of unwashed bodies from her sensitive nostrils. She glanced down at her heels, concerned the fishy water had come home with her, and noted another trail of liquid, like brown paint, had traced its way across the mosaic floor. The source was the ugly metal trash container she had persistently campaigned to have removed.

One of her lazy neighbours and their rotting waste again. Instead of using the correct bins, they tossed any old leaking bags into the main receptacle, forcing their neighbours to endure the stench till refuse collection day. Pressing her nostrils closed, she opened the dirty metal lid with forefinger and thumb, and then dropped it with a strangled shriek.

She backed away in the direction of the street until she saw the eternally angry face of Signor Melle, at the window of his ground-floor apartment. She couldn't speak but pointed a shaky finger at the bin.

He lifted his shoulders and shouted, "*Cos'é?*" but Signora Emilia had lost the power of speech. The caretaker took in the dark seepage across the courtyard and disappeared, only to be replaced by his wife, openly gawping. Their apartment door opened and he came out, scowling and muttering about having better things to do than deal with more complaints about the bins.

Without a word to her, he marched across to lift the lid. He dropped it with the same speed and yelled at his wife.

"*Chiama la polizia! Abbiamo un cadavere!*"

Chapter 3

Friday mornings weren't usually Adrian's favourite time of the week. But today was especially precious. Will had been working on a major case for twenty-three consecutive days and Adrian had seen his husband for no more than an hour in the evenings before the exhausted detective fell asleep. Now it was all over. DS William Quinn's investigation into a modern slavery network had been resolved, the perpetrators arrested, paperwork filed and Adrian had his husband home again.

A three-day weekend stretched ahead of them. Ideally, it would contain a lie-in, maybe breakfast in bed, and a browse around Borough farmers' market, followed by a walk along the Thames before returning home for a lazy lunch with whatever goodies they'd sourced. Bliss.

In addition to all these delights, they would be entertaining a guest for dinner. His ex-neighbour and dear friend Beatrice Stubbs had arrived in town yesterday for a girls' night out with an old mate. Today, she would attend an appointment with her therapist before joining them this evening for dinner, gossip and some excellent wine. Adrian had already made up the spare bedroom, which they all referred to as 'Beatrice's Boudoir'.

The morning exceeded Adrian's expectations. They luxuriated in bed till nine and chose to have breakfast at the market – coffee and fresh bagels with cream cheese and salmon at a pop-up café. Appetites satiated, they wandered through the stalls, senses overloaded by the sights of glistening olives, steam rising off golden pies, pyramids of multi-coloured peppers and wafts of black garlic and truffle threading the air like lures. Will stopped to taste a selection of chillies while Adrian engaged the lady on the fish stall in conversation about the best cuts for New England chowder. The bump and jostle of dawdling bodies, which on the Tube or in the street would have been irritating, simply made him feel embraced and a part of things.

On their way back from Old Street station, the clouds thinned and a pale sun broke through to hint at spring. It lifted Adrian's spirits from light to almost giddy. He caught Will's hand as they turned into Boot Street towards home and pulled him close for a kiss. They continued, hand in hand, to their squat apartment block and stopped in surprise.

Someone was standing on the threshold. A tall woman in a leather jacket with an electric-blue bob was pressing one buzzer after another, waiting for a moment and pressing the next.

Adrian shot a quizzical look at Will, who shrugged and strode up the path.

"Hello there. Can I help?"

The woman swivelled to look over her shoulder. "Hello! Yes, I hope you can. I'm looking for Beatrice Stubbs." Her accent was Southern European, perhaps Spanish or Italian. She was striking to look at, not necessarily a natural beauty, but well-groomed with a statement style. In Adrian's opinion, few women over forty could get away with shocking blue hair.

A police officer to his bones, Will asked questions first. "Beatrice Stubbs? Can I ask why are you looking for her?"

The woman turned and came down the path, her hand outstretched. "My name is Isabella Lopez. I met Ms Stubbs a couple of years ago, in Spain. At the time, she told me she was a food writer. We had lunch together and I gave her as much information as I could about white Rioja. After the Castelo de

Aguirre scandal broke, I recognised her face in the newspapers. Not a food writer at all, but a British detective!"

Adrian gasped. "I remember that! I was there, actually in that building!"

Isabella's face broke into a dazzling smile. "You were? Really? So you *do* know Beatrice Stubbs?"

Will pressed his fingers to his brow and shook his head. "Yes, we do. My name is Will Quinn and Mr Lack of Discretion here is my husband, Adrian Harvey. Would you like to come in for a cup of tea?"

Before the kettle had boiled, Isabella demonstrated she could fit more words into a minute than the fastest speed talker Adrian had ever met.

"At first I was shocked that someone would lie to me about being a food expert but then I said to myself, what else would an undercover detective do? Of course she lied because she had to get the information somehow. It never even occurred to me to suspect she was not who she said she was and that's because I was so busy showing off about Spanish cuisine and impressing on her my expertise with wine ..."

Adrian lit up. "You're the wine expert? Could this get any better? I'm the owner of Harvey's Wine Emporium and I would love to pick your brains."

Her eyes widened for a second then Isabella threw back her head and laughed with such abandon, Adrian and Will could not help themselves but join in.

"Pick my brains?" She dabbed underneath each eye with the first joint of her finger. "The things you British say. I must write that one down. 'Pick your brains!' That is wonderful and disgusting at the same time. Where was I? Yes, I am a wine expert and you can pick my brains as much as you want. I would like to visit your shop while I'm in London. Is it open today? Because I have a flight home on Sunday and if I can find Beatrice

Stubbs, I will spend tomorrow with her, but tonight I have no plans so I ..."

Will interrupted. "Milk and sugar, Isabella?"

"No, thank you, black is fine."

"The shop is open today. If you like, I could take you there?" offered Adrian, before she could resume her flow.

"Wonderful! I would love that! But first I must ask you how I can find Beatrice Stubbs. I had terrible trouble trying to locate her. She's no longer in the police force, her mobile number doesn't work and it was only by luck I discovered her address by means of some bribery at a hotel in Vitoria. Then after travelling all this way to visit her at home, there is no Beatrice Stubbs on the doorbell. Does she have another name?"

"No," said Will. "She doesn't live here any longer. There are new tenants in her old apartment. She moved to Devon to live with her partner."

"Where is Devon? Is that far from here?"

"About five hours away. But ..." Adrian stopped, aware of Will's warning glance. "But we might be able to track her down. In fact, Will could do that while we visit my Wine Emporium. Let's just finish our tea before we go."

"Oh yes, the tea. This is very nice. It is so important to me to find her. I need her to investigate a case of espionage and she is the only person who can help me. That much I am sure. No one else has such a combination of skills. No one I have ever met. It is not important if she is working for the police or working for herself. She is the right person for this job." She took a sip of tea and Adrian seized the moment.

"Beatrice has retired, Isabella. She's no longer solving crimes; she's growing vegetables and writing a book. Obviously I can't speak for her but I don't think she'll be interested in a case of spying in Spain."

Isabella set down her cup with such force, Adrian feared for the saucer. "She must! And it is not Spain but Italy. Let me explain because this is complicated and very emotional. I am now married since two years. My husband is a chef who owns a high-class restaurant in the centre of Naples. His food is the talk of the whole country. His cuisine earned him a Michelin star and the restaurant boasts a *Tre Torte* from the *Gambero Rosso* for our desserts. A table at Ecco is incredibly hard to get because there is a waiting list of three months and a table reservation fee. Last month, two rival restaurants revealed new specialities. Specialities they had STOLEN!"

Her shout startled Adrian, who dropped his teaspoon.

"Not only that, but they are taking our staff. When they cannot take or force our employees to spy for them, they ... they ..." She pressed her fingertips to the inside corners of her eyes and wiped away tears.

Will handed her a square of kitchen paper which she took but did not use, digging through her handbag instead. She brought out a photograph of a young man, laughing in the sunshine, wearing chef's whites.

"This is Rami Ahmad, who was Ecco's sous chef. Last month he was killed on his way home." She pressed the kitchen paper to her eyes. "He was thirty-one," she whispered.

"You think he was killed by a rival restaurateur? That's going a bit far to stay one step ahead of the competition," said Will, his disbelief evident. "I assume you reported this to the police?"

Isabella gave a dismissive snort. "The police? Useless. They said it had all the hallmarks of a drug-related killing. No imagination. Rami was killed because he would not defect or turn traitor, I am sure of it."

Adrian gazed at the smiling face with eyes as brown and rich as figs. "That's horrible. He looks like such a good person," he said.

Isabella clutched his forearm. "He was the best person. A success story of a Syrian immigrant who everybody, EVERYBODY, loved. Listen to me. Someone is trying to break us. They have spies in our kitchen who know everything we do and sell the information to our enemies. We don't know who to trust, the ambience in the kitchen is toxic and my husband is so stressed he cannot create. We have to fight back. We need a spy of our own. Someone who knows food, who understands human nature, who is a good liar and a brilliant detective. The only person I can think of is Beatrice Stubbs."

Adrian clasped her hands. "Leave it to us. We will find her for you, I promise. Come along, let's go and talk wine."

As they left, he gave Will a meaningful look.

Chapter 4

The sound of traffic on Clapham Common woke Beatrice just before eight. Used to countryside peace in Upton St Nicholas and little more than snores from man and dog indoors, London's taxis, buses and motorcycles seemed like a horrendous discordant racket that could wake the dead.

She got up and showered, with a sense of freedom. Dawn and Derek had left for work over an hour ago. Once dressed, she cleaned up the kitchen, washing glasses, throwing away takeaway containers and reliving the warm conversational cosiness of the previous evening. The scent of Chicken Tikka Masala still hung in the room, so Beatrice opened the windows while she packed.

Her mind turned to her afternoon appointment with her counsellor. James would want an honest appraisal of her mental health. What exactly was she going to say? She switched on Radio Four to distract herself. It did such an admirable job she found herself shouting at a politician in less than five minutes.

After three rounds of the flat to make sure everything was spotlessly clean, windows closed, bed stripped and thank-you note propped on the kitchen table, Beatrice wheeled her case outside and closed the door behind her. Time to face the streets of London.

She walked up Cedars Road and took the No. 77 bus to

Waterloo. It would take far longer than the Tube or train, but the pace suited her. That way, she could soak up the sights of what used to be her home; the Thames, Lambeth Bridge, MI6, the Houses of Parliament and Big Ben. A tourist in her own past. The sensation was both melancholy and elating. At Waterloo, she parked her case in Left Luggage, hopped onto the Tube to Charing Cross and went shopping.

"Shall we start with how you've been feeling since our last meeting?" James began.

Beatrice took a moment, although she had rehearsed at least a dozen replies. As so often happened when faced with her counsellor, her prepared spin and polish evaporated like warm breath in cold air. James would see through it all in a moment.

She inhaled and blurted it all out. "I am a failure, James. I cannot write this book and I don't know what on earth persuaded me to try. It's a daily misery, looking at what I've put on paper and cringing with embarrassment. Everything else in my life is a source of joy – Matthew and his family, my friends, our animals, and I love being in the village. I really do. That feeling of missing out on what's happening in London has almost completely gone. There's only one thing getting me down and it's the bloody wretched book."

James didn't reply and made a few notes.

"Right. I appreciate your honesty on that score and would like to address it in a moment. As for your overall well-being?"

"I'm fine. I take my stabilisers, I see you once a month, I keep my mood diary religiously even though it's rather boring because nothing massively up or down has happened since Christmas. The countryside is doing me good. It's only now that I've changed down a gear I realise how much the pressures of the job and living in the city actually aggravated my mental health. Now there's only one constant thorn in my side and it's making me miserable."

He wrote for a long time and Beatrice waited, fidgety and impatient. Eventually, he looked up.

"I am going to ask you a question and I will give you a full minute to think about it. Acknowledge your first response and question that with the mental rigour we agreed is necessary to get at the truth. The stronger your initial assertion, the harder you should examine its impulses. Please do not reply until I tell you the time is up. My question is this: Beatrice, we have often discussed your tendency towards displacement activity. To what extent are you placing responsibility for your dissatisfactions onto a particular endeavour? In this case, your book. Please, consider my question carefully."

Moments ticked by as Beatrice suppressed her indignation. She conducted a whole conversation with herself, staring at the reproduction of a David Hockney, a path leading away into a lurid forest. It gave her time to think and argue with herself. James too gazed at the print, not at her. A pattern they had repeated over years.

"Take all the time you want. I'm in no hurry, but the restriction of one minute is now up." James's voice, a cool hand on a hot forehead, unleashed the torrent.

"I'm not. Really, I am not dissatisfied and won't tempt fate by saying so since the dramas of Christmas. I'm enjoying peace, routine and lack of life-threatening situations. That said, I am increasingly unhappy and defeated by this inability to turn my life experiences into fiction. Turns out I'm not half as interesting as I thought I was."

"Who commissioned this book?"

Beatrice's gaze snapped from the picture to James and his expression of mild enquiry.

"No one commissioned it, you know that. I just decided to write a fictionalised memoir for myself. I thought it would be fun and even more than that, therapeutic. But it isn't. It's the opposite."

"So in effect, you are the commissioning editor. Let's imagine for a second that your client comes to you and tells you the book you commissioned is not working. How would you react?"

Beatrice thought about it. "I suppose it depends why I wanted the book in the first place."

"You mentioned a moment ago that the original objective was to entertain the client and perhaps provide her with a therapeutic activity. Yet the client describes the project as 'a thorn in her side' and 'a daily misery'. Does that affect your viewpoint?"

Beatrice was silent for a long time. When she finally spoke, she was hesitant. "If writing the book is making the client unhappy, she should stop. But ..."

James waited.

"But, my concern for my client would be this. If she has no project, what will she ... do with herself?"

"Many writers are procrastinators, finding any other task to do before sitting down at the desk. Might your client have any other activities she prefers over writing?"

"She certainly does. Cooking has always been an interest of hers, and since moving into the cottage, she has discovered the delights of gardening and walking the dog. She also has a great passion for books, so long as that is only reading them. She enjoys travelling to historical sites and trying out new restaurants and loves nothing better than pottering around an art gallery."

James nodded slowly. "All of which are available to her now, because she has the time, financial means and if she feels like it, companions with whom to share her experiences."

Neither spoke for several minutes.

"But that's not enough, is it? She needs to feel useful." As always, James put his finger right on the problem. "She could always volunteer as a community support officer. Still keeping the neighbourhood safe but no longer in the line of fire."

"That's a thought," said Beatrice, although the idea of going from Acting DCI to a glorified lollipop lady was underwhelming. "So, in your view, should I tell my client to drop the book?" she asked, unable to keep the smile from her face.

James smiled back at her. "Do you think she will be dreadfully disappointed?"

"I think she'll be bloody delighted!"

The cheesemonger was in full flow on the merits of Jersey cattle when Beatrice's mobile rang. She instructed him to cut her four ounces of Llangloffan and answered the call.

"Hello, Will. If you want me to bring some fresh Parmesan for this evening, your timing is ideal."

His laugh warmed her. "We don't need you to bring anything, least of all cheese or wine. Farmers' market all done and dusted before lunchtime."

"Too late for the wine. Matthew smuggled two bottles of Châteauneuf du Pape into my suitcase while I wasn't looking and if you think I'm lugging them all the way home to Upton St Nicholas, you can think again." She inhaled deeply, all the competing odours of pungent cheeses filling her nostrils.

"In that case, it would be rude to refuse. No, the reason I'm calling is that someone came here today, looking for you. Does the name Isabella Lopez ring any bells?"

"Hang on a sec." Beatrice paid the cheesemonger and thanked him for his recommendations, then left the shop to devote her attention to Will. "Sorry about that, I'm still here. What was the name again?"

"Isabella Lopez. Apparently you met her in Spain while investigating the white Rioja fraud."

Beatrice frowned in concentration. "The thing is, I met a lot of people at that time so it's hard to recall each individual."

"This one is a wine expert with blue hair. She said you had lunch together in San Sebastián."

"Oh yes! I remember her. Fabulous smile and talked my ears off over one of the best meals I've ever had. Her hair was pink then, if I remember correctly. Isabella Lopez, yes, I've definitely not forgotten her. Lovely woman and a great deal of help. What is she doing in London?"

"Searching for you. She wants you to do a job for her and her husband in Italy. Adrian has taken her to his shop, sorry, emporium, but I wondered if we should invite her to dinner this evening."

Beatrice crossed Seven Dials, dodging between two black cabs. "I'd say that's a marvellous idea! She is quite fascinating and I think she and Adrian would get along famously. But I wouldn't want you to go to any trouble on my account. I can always bring extra provisions ..."

"No need. I'll call Adrian and ask him to invite her for dinner at eight. But I suggest you get here early for a martini so we can catch up. Because when Isabella arrives, no one else will get a word in edgeways."

"Excellent! See you at seven then! Have to go now or I'm going to be late for my hair appointment."

Thus it was that Beatrice dragged her suitcase along Boot Street and gazed up at her old flat with curious mixture of nostalgia and relief. The nostalgia was due to the happy memories and the person she had once been. The relief was that she no longer had to fight with herself, her job and London on a daily basis. No need to get back on a Tube till tomorrow lunchtime, and even then, only to start her journey home. Best of all, she enjoyed the anticipation of an entertaining evening with friends.

Although Adrian had given her a key, she rang the bell out of politeness. The buzzer permitted her access and there, in the doorway of the first flat, was Adrian Harvey, looking dashing in a black shirt. From behind him came scents of fish, spice and citrus, accompanied by the uplifting tones of Ella Fitzgerald.

"You're here!" He drew her into his embrace with one arm and took her wheelie case in the other. "Come in quick, we have so much to discuss before Isabella arrives. Shall I take this into your boudoir?"

"Thank you. How come you look even more handsome than last time I saw you? What is your secret, please?"

He threw a look over his shoulder as he wheeled her case to her room. "Love. And good genes. Go into the kitchen, Will's making martinis."

Beatrice kicked off her shoes and hung up her coat, then took her tote bag with wine and gifts into the kitchen. Will came around the kitchen island for a hug.

"Your hair looks lovely! How are you doing?"

"Thank you. I'm very well, if at least seventy quid worse off for a hairdo which will last all of four hours. How are you?"

Will motioned her to a stool and began pouring the brine from an olive jar into three cocktail glasses. "I'm feeling better than I have done in a long time. Since we wrapped up that slavery case, I have my weekends to myself again." With a practised air, he measured gin and vermouth into a silver container, added ice and shook the mixture for ten seconds. "Not to mention signs of upward mobility."

"Yes, I wanted to congratulate you on that case. Dawn said it was a massive operation. Well done, DS Quinn." Beatrice watched as the crystalline liquid flowed into the olive juice, creating a muddy blend of beauty. Will added an olive speared with a toothpick to each, just as Adrian returned.

"I appreciate that, ex-DCI Stubbs. Dirty Martinis. I hope you approve."

"Anything with dirty in the title appeals to me." Beatrice admired her glass. "When you say 'upward mobility', are you referring to the crocuses coming out or the possibility of promotion?"

Will's face broke into a wide smile and he raised his glass.

"Next month, I have a date for my assessment and interview for the position of DI. Let's not count our chickens, but I'm optimistic. Cheers!"

"Cheers, you lovely couple, and I'm very happy to see you both again."

They toasted and Beatrice savoured the kick of salty water, delicate vermouth and hit of gin which stayed with her long after she'd swallowed the first sip.

"Delicious! This might be my first, but I already know that I love Dirty Martinis and always will. Listen to me, Detective Sergeant Quinn, you would make a brilliant DI and if your supervisors can't see that, there's something wrong with them. Would it help if I put in a word?"

Will replaced his glass on the counter. "It probably would. The thing is, I'd actually like to do this on my own merits. Don't get me wrong, I am grateful for the offer. If I crash and burn this time around, can I ask again?"

"For an officer of your calibre, the offer is always there."

"I appreciate that." He returned to the hob while Adrian hopped up to sit on the stool beside her.

"So?" he asked.

"So what?" she replied. "This Lopez female, the wine, the general opinions on politics and weather and country living – what do you want first? By the way, what's for dinner? It smells divine."

"One of Will's specials. New England chowder with a side of potato wedges with honeymoon sauce. We picked it up on, well, our honeymoon."

Beatrice lifted her nose into the air and sniffed. "And what exactly is 'Honeymoon Sauce'? As an elderly lady, I have a sensitive palate, you know."

Adrian laughed. "You are far from elderly and you're going to love this. It has all your favourite flavours. Though had we known we would be cooking for a Michelin-starred chef, we might have chosen a different menu."

"Like battered cod and twice fried chips from Pavel and Miki on Old Street?" called Will, grinning at his husband. "Anyway it's not Isabella but her husband who's the chef. Don't worry. The food will be fine. My only concern is whether you've chosen the right wine to go with it."

Adrian faked outrage. "Don't get chippy with me. And you can stop smirking, that pun was intentional. Isabella is here to meet Beatrice. We could serve her pasta with a jar of supermarket sauce with wine out of a box and I doubt she'd notice. Her aim is to get Beatrice to accept this job, one hundred per cent."

Beatrice took another sip of martini and released a sigh. "Tell me a bit about this job."

"Oh no, you don't," said Will, pointing a wooden spoon at Adrian. "I knew you'd try to get your oar in first. It's not your place. Shut up and let Isabella explain when she gets here. This has nothing to do with you. Or me."

Adrian wrinkled his nose. "He's right, much as I hate to admit it. It's just that I know how to tell a story so much better than most. Well, you'll have to wait for her to explain and use our time to catch up on the important stuff. How's Matthew? How's the book?"

"Matthew's fine and sends his love. Those French wines are from him and he recommends enjoying them with cheese or charcuterie. As for the book, it is no more. It is an ex-book."

Will and Adrian both stared at her, their respective actions of herb-chopping and martini-sipping interrupted.

"No big deal and let us not have a pity party over a project that simply didn't come off. Turns out I'm not a writer. I saw my therapist today, as you know. James pointed out the escape route I'd been seeking. No one commissioned me to write the thing, no one is eagerly anticipating its arrival in bookstores, no one insists on my writing this book other than me. I can give myself permission to desist. So I am abandoning ... no, that's negative language. I am walking away from an endeavour which makes me feel inadequate and brings me no fulfilment."

She could hear the question reverberating around this tasteful modern kitchen with all its chrome, marble and slate. *So what will you do instead?* Thankfully neither of these sensitive souls gave it voice.

"OK, that makes sense," said Adrian. "Tell us about your girls' night with Dawn yesterday. How's she doing?"

Conversation guided onto safer tracks, martini hour was over before they had even realised it. At ten past eight, the doorbell rang and the personality of Isabella Lopez burst into the room.

"Beatrice Stubbs! I look for you everywhere and now, finally, you are here!"

Dinner, as Beatrice had known it would be, was a delicious triumph. A fish stew cooked with fresh vegetables in a rich stock, accompanied by sweet potato wedges with a hot peppery sauce, satisfied every taste. Adrian made a point of explaining his and Isabella's wine pairings and the atmosphere was genial.

Yet the conversation revolved around one topic. Isabella's problem and how only Beatrice could solve it. At first she was flattered and simply sought a polite way to refuse. But after Isabella had shown her the picture of the murdered star chef, explained her husband's sense of honour and expanded on the restaurant's standing in the community, a familiar curiosity tugged at her gut. Her resolve to retire from the business of detection was weakening and she needed a buttress.

"Will, in your professional opinion, wouldn't an undercover job in a high-end Neapolitan restaurant be better suited to someone who speaks the language and can actually cook pastries and desserts? A fifty-something ex-copper whose speciality is toad-in-the-hole is going to stand out like a sore plum. I'm sure we could point Isabella in the right direction of some suitable private detective agencies."

For a few seconds, no one spoke and the only sounds in the room were cutlery on china and some smoky jazz.

Will chewed the last mouthful of sweet potato and put down his fork. "Possibly, yes. On the other hand, the situation could benefit you both. Here's what I think. Isabella is right. You have all the skills to work such a case and it would be something you'd enjoy. The flip side is you have none of the skills to pass yourself off as an Italian expert on puddings. That would have to be Isabella's call. The thing is, if the book is not to be, you could take this opportunity to set yourself up as a private detective. Think about it. You could take the jobs you want, refuse those you don't and only work when a case appeals to you."

That was not the response Beatrice had expected.

"Oh my God!" gasped Adrian. "That is perfect! Your own detective agency? I love the idea and starting with a case of culinary espionage is so very you. Will's right, Beatrice, you could do this! With your contacts, your experience, there is no one better qualified. You know what? I could ask Jared to design you a logo. Beatrice Stubbs P.I. – Detective for Hire!"

"Beatrice, listen to me," implored Isabella. "Our restaurant employs staff from seven countries. With so many languages, English is our lingua franca. My father-in-law made every one of his children and grandchildren spend a year abroad to learn English. You don't need to speak Italian to work for us; I'm not fluent. Most important is you need to understand the cooking." She knocked her knuckles against her forehead. "I have it! You are a winner of a competition. Your prize is to learn from the best chefs in Europe. Not an expert but learning on the job and bringing your own skills. Yes, this works! Beatrice, please, we need you."

The idea of a private detective agency thrilled Beatrice to her bones. The idea of telling Matthew she was off to Naples, working undercover to combat organised crime, less so. She needed time and all her powers of persuasion. Because paid investigative work beat voluntary community support hands down.

"Will, that was a lovely meal and I wouldn't mind copying the recipe for that sauce. Isabella, thank you for the offer. I will give it serious consideration, but it must be a decision taken by my partner and myself. Now that I have finally retired from the force, I suspect he might look most unfavourably on the idea of putting my health at risk once again. Leave it with me and I will do my best. I promise to give you an answer by Monday. Now I'd prefer to change the subject. It's Matthew's birthday in a few weeks. Would either of you two wine experts have a top tip for a lesser-known vintage?"

Chapter 5

A heron stood in the river, shoulders hunched so it resembled a little old man. Beatrice and Matthew stopped to watch it as they crossed the stone bridge. Reflections of overhanging trees shimmered and fractured in the fast-moving water and the sunnier of the two riverbanks sported a clutch of daffodils. Such cheerful yellow flowers always brought a smile to Beatrice's face.

Huggy Bear came running back to see what had delayed them, so they moved on with their walk, pointing out to one another primroses and unfurling leaves in the brightest green. The sun shone through the trees, creating little spotlights on the ferns and mosses beside the path. One could almost see the earth warming, waking and bursting into colour.

A bark made them look up.

"I hope she hasn't gone chasing after rabbits again," said Matthew. "I was searching for over an hour on Saturday morning."

They rounded the corner to see the terrier with her front paws on the trunk of a tree, looking up into the canopy. She barked again.

"Squirrels," said Beatrice. "You won't catch one, pooch, they're far too quick for you. Come on."

The trio made their way out of the woods and across the field, heading back to the cottage. Despite the sun's best efforts, the wind was chilly and Beatrice's nose and ears were numb with cold. Thoughts of the fireplace and a mug of coffee encouraged her to pick up the pace.

Matthew spoke as they crunched their way up the drive. "I've been thinking."

"About our conversation last night?" asked Beatrice.

"Partly. And partly about Tanya."

Beatrice couldn't see what the offer of a private detection job in Italy had to do with Matthew's youngest daughter. She waited for him to offer a link.

He said nothing and unlocked the front door to begin the process of kicking off wellingtons, taking off coats and drying a dirty Border terrier.

She decided to give him a prod. "Did you come to any conclusions on either subject?"

Matthew pulled off his hat and hung it on its hook. "Not conclusions, exactly, but I do have the beginnings of an idea."

Once the dog was at least slightly cleaner than she had been when they got home, Beatrice released her out of the hallway and into the house. Huggy Bear raced over to her food bowl and sat down. Beatrice put on her slippers and headed into the kitchen to make coffee, allowing Matthew to get to the point in his own time. Dumpling unfurled from his position on the kitchen chair, blinked his Pernod-coloured eyes, and with tail held high wandered out in search of breakfast.

The pot was bubbling and the milk warmed by the time Matthew had finished feeding the animals and continued his speech.

"Yes. As I said last night, I think the private detective agency is an inspired idea. However, I'm not at all keen on you going off to Naples on your own to investigate a situation which has already claimed one life. It might be different if I were there to keep you company and ensure you're not walking the streets alone. The fact is, I have a great deal of affection for Naples and its history. Which led me to Tanya."

Beatrice poured the coffee, opened the biscuit tin and selected a chocolate digestive. "Still not quite making the connection," she said.

"You see, if we were going to Naples, it would be the perfect opportunity to take Luke along. At six years old, he can appreciate seeing his history lessons come to life. Imagine taking him to see Pompeii, for example. Not only that, but I would like my grandson to learn a little about other languages, cultures and cuisines. As a single mother, Tanya has not been able to afford many holidays abroad. Last year when they joined us in Portugal was only the second time he's been out of the country."

"So you're proposing we go to Naples with Tanya and Luke?" asked Beatrice, surprised at this turn of events.

"No. I'm proposing you and I take Luke, leaving Tanya with some time to herself for a change. Firstly, we should get Luke into the habit of travelling with us a few times a year and secondly ..."

"Tanya can have some time alone with Gabriel!"

"Precisely. Their friendship may date back to primary school, but the romance is relatively young. It is short notice, as Luke's holidays start next Monday, but what say we suggest taking him away with us for a fortnight? You can pursue your investigation, I can show Luke the city of Naples and when you're not on the job, we can enjoy exploring the Amalfi Coast. Meanwhile, Tanya can have some quality time with her new boyfriend."

Beatrice beamed at him. "You are quite brilliant, you know."

When Beatrice called Naples, Isabella was ecstatic. "I am putting everything in place today. I make the story. You are a reality TV winner, on tour of European restaurants, learning Italian pastries. You stay two weeks only and we have an apartment you can stay in with your husband. No one knows who you are really. Only me and Agusto. We all play our roles and you sniff out the spy, yes?"

"As I said in my email, I can guarantee nothing," Beatrice repeated. "However, I promised to put all my energy and expertise into finding the leak in your operation. My partner and I may well be travelling with a young child. Is there a sofa bed or spare mattress we can use?"

Isabella hooted. "There are lots of bedrooms, a dining room and a roof terrace! You will have enough space for guests. Email to me the flight details and I will arrange a car. I am so excited you are coming to Napoli! A week seems too long to wait. There is much to organise, I must go now."

"Um, about the question of payment. Our agreement was ..."

"Of course! I will make the first payment today, as we discussed. Oh, Beatrice?"

"Yes?"

"You can learn a lot about pastry in one week. Do your homework, eh? *Ciao, arrivederci* and see you very soon!"

The phone went dead before Beatrice could respond. She sat by the telephone table and thought about *Masterchef, The Great British Cake Off* and that other programme with annoying men in cars. A grey shape appeared from the kitchen. Dumpling's mouth was making the shape of a miaow, even if no sound emerged.

"Hello, old fellow. What do you say to a saucer of milk before the hooligans return? Come over here and meet Italy's Next Top Pastrychef."

With the cat curled up on Matthew's kitchen chair, Beatrice made up her mind to go the hard way. Choux pastry, one of the most difficult recipes a person could attempt, according to her mother. She researched methods and rooted about the cupboards until she had assembled the ingredients, then set to work.

Two hours later, when Matthew returned, the kitchen table was laden with assorted desserts, some more successful than others. Most of the choux buns had collapsed, causing the profiterole tower to lean further than the one in Pisa. The biscotti looked exactly as they did in the recipe book picture, but the crunch factor was harder than expected. The amaretti were edible, if a touch on the soggy side. But chilling in the fridge was Beatrice's tiramisù, a long-practised favourite, lightly dusted in cocoa powder, much like herself.

Huggy Bear dashed around the kitchen in excitement while Matthew blinked at the scene of devastation. Pans, bowls, sieves, spoons and forks filled the sink; the floor was patterned with cocoa powder, flour, sugar, and some spilt pistachios and beside the slowly cooling oven stood a pile of eggshells.

Matthew turned down the stereo, muting Mario Lanza. "Are you going for full immersion Italian?" he asked.

Beatrice caught hold of the dog to stop her vacuuming up the nuts. "Isabella said I should practise my pastry skills. My mother always played operas while she was cooking, so I fancied a bit of 'O Sole Mio'. Don't look like that. I've got two Pavarotti albums lined up for tomorrow so you'd better get used to it. Take this animal out of here till I've cleaned up. And another thing."

Matthew took Huggy Bear outside and closed the door. "What's that?"

"We're going to need a food processer. Beating dough is exhausting."

"You do look as if you've done three rounds with Mr Kipling."

Beatrice brushed a stray hair out of her face. "Tell me what Tanya said. Can we take Luke to Italy?"

"She's all for it. But she says he must decide for himself. She's going to ask him when he gets home from school."

"That woman is a natural mother. Now then, which one of these would you like to try first?"

After consuming three different desserts for afternoon tea,

neither had much of an appetite for dinner. Beatrice curled up on the sofa with various cookery books to continue her research, Huggy Bear stretched out in front of the fire, Dumpling tucked himself into a ball on an armchair and Matthew retired to his study to browse flights to Italy.

The doorbell woke Beatrice. Her legs were weighed down by a small dog and her chest compressed by recipe collections. A high-pitched voice in the hallway indicated that Luke had arrived. She disentangled herself from canine and cookbooks and got to her feet, patting her hair and blinking away sleep. Before she could reach the door, it burst open and Luke ran towards her, his face shining. Huggy Bear started barking, Dumpling slunk away into the shadows and Beatrice crouched to receive Luke in outstretched arms.

"We're going on holiday!" he said, squeezing her tight and releasing her instantly to make a fuss of the dog. "Can Huggy Bear come too?"

"And leave Dumpling all alone?" Beatrice replied. "That would hardly be fair. No, they will stay home while we go the pizza capital of the world!"

"Yay!" yelled Luke, running back to the hallway with Huggy Bear at his heels. Beatrice followed him to greet Tanya and her brand new beau, Gabriel.

"You were napping," said Tanya, as they hugged hello.

"Pensioner's prerogative," Beatrice retorted, turning to embrace the impossibly handsome Gabriel. "How's the forest?"

He grinned. "Bursting out all over. It's a great time of year. But I reckon you'll have a whole lot more sunshine in Italy."

Matthew herded everyone into the kitchen for tea and more cake as they made arrangements. The combination of sugar and excitement had Luke fit to burst, so Tanya suggested he take Huggy Bear for a run around the garden before it got dark.

Beatrice closed the kitchen door on the barks and childlike shouts, returning to the kitchen table, the hub of their home.

"You're sure you're comfortable with us taking him away?" she asked, pouring more tea.

Tanya picked up a biscotto. "Absolutely. He adores the two of you and will probably be on his best behaviour the whole time. Dad's right, he needs to travel a bit. Ow, are these supposed to be this hard?"

"Yes. They're for dipping in coffee. Gabriel, another profiterole?"

He shook his head. "Never had much of a sweet tooth, Beatrice, but they look impressive. You'll fit right into a posh Italian restaurant."

Beatrice laughed. "I wish I had your confidence. Anyway, I shall be here all week, whipping up Italian confections, so do feel free to come over and judge. Anyone for tiramisù?"

Chapter 6

Trattoria della Nonna ****

Review by Luciano Rigiani

An ambitious concept which doesn't quite hit the heights it aims for. The ambience in the restaurant is cheerful and welcoming, the staff efficient and the decor has enough rustic touches to hint at a genuine grandmother's kitchen.

The problem is the unevenness of the food. The first course of bruschetta and salad was serviceable but nothing out of the ordinary. Fresh bread with garlic, basil and tomatoes; rucola with shavings of Parmigiano and black olives? This is something I would make at home for a quick lunch.

The *primo piatto* was certainly out of the ordinary and not in a good way. Of course, ways to cook pasta range from the practically raw in Puglia to al dente in Rome, but here, the *orecchiette* were soft to the point of breaking up. Over-seasoned and heavy, the porcini sauce could not redeem it. My companion praised her angel hair spaghetti with pesto, describing it as delicate and fragrant.

The *secondo piatto* took my breath away. *Vitello Vero alla Nonna* was one of the best dishes I have consumed this year. The thinnest slices of veal simply scattered with the lightest golden crumb and fried for mere seconds, accompanied by a sage and truffle risotto that had me moaning aloud. A blend of flavours which work so well you want to eat nothing else. My companion devoured her beautifully presented *Frutti di Mare alla Griglia* with great enthusiasm.

Opinions on desserts differed. The consistency of my panna cotta was perfect, but the orange coulis seemed a distraction to the firm vanilla cream. The *Torta alla Nonna* seemed to be nothing more than *panettone* stuffed with a sauce anglaise. The portions were generous, the prices startling and the wine selection was surprisingly diverse.

There's talent here and I will be interested to see how that develops.

If the team can raise their game to the standards of the main courses, they would make Nonna proud.

Comments

miki_mangia: super dinner! main courses AMAZING!!! desserts so-so la-la. wine selection best ever!

John Collins: My family and I ate here last month and I can recommend it on every level. Great team, all English speakers, friendly and pretty fast service, portions typically European so make sure to order sides of bread or salad. Really delicious food! If we're ever in Italy again, we're going back. 5*

GiannidiRoma_67: Surprising to see such quality food in such an out of the way restaurant. I am impressed.

illeonedormestasera: Sisters took me to Ecco in Napoli – most fantastic dinner of my life! But this place comes pretty close. That vitello con risotto – I will never forget you.

HungryHippo: Food here is exceptional and the atmos is cozy. Grandma's kitchen is right. Even have those bottle lights which make it feel like Christmas.

Zara-n-Zed: Loved this place SO much we went back THREE times. The fish, the zabaglione, the wine, even the coffee is to die for. Best restaurant ever!

ragazzagialla: BUONISSIMO!!!!

FoodBlog404: Several 'house specialities' are quite clearly efforts to copy first-class restaurants such as L'Albergo Luigi in Ostia and Ecco in Naples. The difference is that at those 5* establishments, everything they serve is of the finest quality. At Nonna's, you will get a five star main course and a three star experience. That said, staff helpful and what they lack in knowledge, they make up for in charm.

JustAnotherJoe: Hit and miss. If I were you, I'd give this a miss.

Chapter 7

It wasn't intentional, but Adrian did spend a lot of his week after Beatrice and Isabella had left researching wines from the region of Campania. There was a great deal to learn. It was an extraordinary area he knew little about and would really like to delve into deeper.

While the shop was quiet and Catinca could cope, he slunk into the office and browsed the vineyards, the wholesalers, the soil and the breathtaking range of wines. Oh those wines! Occasionally he would have to get out front and assist his assistant with a sudden rush of customers. He smiled and served and advised, while wishing them all gone.

He sensed Catinca watching him as he straightened a few labels and picked up a discarded receipt. Her latest look was 1960s gamine Parisienne. Yet again, she pulled it off effortlessly. Turquoise mini skirt, opaque black tights, black roll-neck sweater and a French manicure. Her earrings were crystal studs and her lipstick one shade paler than her skin. She had wound her hair into a chignon which accentuated her cat-like, kohl-rimmed eyes. On her feet, as always, was a pair of black Converse trainers.

He sidled back towards the office, but she followed him.

"Whassup?" she demanded, coming to stand in front of his desk.

"Nothing, nothing at all. Just doing some research for the shop."

She narrowed her eyes in suspicion and hooked two mugs from the shelf with one finger. "Coffee break. I'm going over John's for a couple caramel lattes and then you and me gonna have a chat. You got a bug up your bum, I can see that. Wanna Danish?"

Adrian refused and watched her skip over the road like a pixie. That short-arsed little Romanian knew him better than almost anyone. He served two customers while she was gone. A Pinot Noir for the dithering young man who wanted 'to impress someone but in like, a casual way?' He sold the harassed woman in the hijab a bottle of cava, assuring her that a light fizz was perfect for an office leaving-do. Then he gazed out of the window. How long did it take to get two takeaway coffees?

Eventually, Catinca trotted back across the street to Harvey's Wine Emporium with two full mugs and a tube under her arm.

"Did you have to make them yourself?" he asked, aiming for dry and sardonic but coming out as petulant and sarcastic.

"Bit of small talk, keeping friendly with the neighbours, that's all. John gave me a print of Chet Baker!" She unrolled the poster, revealing the distinctive face of the jazz trumpeter in his younger days.

"When did you get into jazz?" asked Adrian, taking in the black and white shot of a cool and chiselled face.

"Since working here. Drink your coffee and tell me what's bothering you because you are doing my nerves in. Moping about the place like you just come back from a funeral? Killing the atmosphere, mate."

Adrian took a cautious sip of the sweet and milky drink, and then released a deep sigh. "I had a row with Will."

Catinca's gaze did not falter. "A fight?"

"No. A difference of opinion with some heated exchanges."

"So a fight," said Catinca.

"No. You watch too much American TV. A fight means physical violence in British English and that would never happen between Will and me. We just had a row over the fact that I want to go to Naples over Easter with Beatrice and Matthew. He wants to stay here and put in some overtime to impress his superiors. He might be up for promotion to Detective Inspector."

Catinca's eyes widened. "Like Beatrice was? Awesome!"

"Yes, well, it all depends on his appraisal next week."

"Tell me about the figh... difference of opinion thingy."

Adrian sighed. "Will and I never argue, but this time, he just wouldn't budge and I got upset and he said I was being selfish and this morning he just got up for work and left without even a kiss goodbye. I sent him a message at lunchtime and he hasn't replied. I hate rows, well, any kind of confrontation really, and I can't help thinking it's far too early in our marriage to have this kind of communication breakdown."

Catinca rolled her eyes. "Drama queen. OK, so Will don't wanna go to Naples but you want."

"Yes, we could make it a working holiday, research the vineyards, taste the wines of Southern Italy, spend time with Beatrice and Matthew, and explore a new city. Normally Will loves those kind of city breaks." He sipped at his coffee, picturing the four of them in a taverna with some sort of effusive Italian matriarch insisting they try her homemade lasagne.

Catinca sniffed. "Working holiday? Might be for you, mate, but what about Will? When is his interview?"

"A week tomorrow. But then it's Easter and we could go for the weekend or even longer. If you'd look after the shop, of course."

The bell rang to announce a customer and Catinca jumped to her feet. Adrian only faintly listened to her chirpy small talk, picking at a thumbnail and hearing the echoes of Will's flat refusal.

I said no. I cannot afford to go flitting off to a European city on a whim when my career is at stake. Stop being so selfish and think about other people for a change.

The customers departed, apparently satisfied, and Catinca plonked herself on the stool in front of him and finished her coffee in two noisy gulps.

"Three options. One. You stay here and sulk because of missing out. Bad for you, bad for Will.

"Two. You lay on emotional blackmail and you both go to Naples. Bad for Will, good for you, bad for the marriage in long term.

"Three. You go to Naples. Will stays home to prepare for interview. Good for you two, good for your jobs and compromise always good for a marriage. Bonus? Good for me 'cos I get to manage shop." She folded her arms with a feline smile.

Adrian thought about it, his eyes fixed on a rack of Bordeaux. Option Three had all the advantages and the only risk being whatever design concept Catinca would impose on the shop while he was gone.

He focused on her immaculately made-up face. "How does one of such tender years get to be so wise?"

The bell rang again, admitting a middle-aged couple. Catinca bounced up with a huge grin and picked up both coffee mugs with one hand.

"Outside, young and well stylish. Inside," she slapped her palm to her sternum as if swearing allegiance, "old soul."

Chapter 8

Sitting by the window on the plane, Luke had plenty to command his attention and the flight landed without incident. Matthew was still fretting about cat, dog, Aga, greenhouse and cat again as they waited for their luggage. Beatrice had long since tuned out, her mind on the case. True to her word, Isabella sent a car. A muscular man in a suit with a sign saying BEATRICE STUBBS was waiting at Arrivals.

The moment they stepped outside, the heat struck them. Somehow mellow and relaxing, the southern Italian climate appealed to Beatrice in an instant. The driver was an affable sort, and on discovering this was their first trip to Napoli, took on the role of guide, indicating various points of interest along the route.

The poorhouse, an enormous crumbling edifice which looked much like a prison, stretched for what seemed like a mile on their right. They had time to take it all in as the traffic stopped and started, either movement accompanied by a blasting of horns. Piazza Garibaldi and the main train station, with people swarming in all directions and a solitary police officer standing in the street attempting to impose order on chaos. Churches watched over by marble statues, army officers patrolling with dogs and guns, washing fluttering from balconies, children clamouring for ice-cream, graffiti and posters adorning stone walls, old men smoking at cafés and millions of mopeds sped by like some kind of slideshow.

Compared to Upton St Nicholas and its sleepy village routine, this was absolute mayhem. Sandwiched between Matthew and Luke in the rear seat, Beatrice responded to each nudge and point and exhortation to look with exclamations of delight. Every one of them was genuine as she succumbed to a sense of optimism and excitement. She was back on the job.

Luke hurtled at least five times around the breathtaking apartment Isabella had provided while Matthew and Beatrice took in the scale of the place. Over two floors, the palatial residence had four bedrooms, two of which had ensuite bathrooms, a kitchen, dining area, living space and on the top floor, a magnificent roof terrace with incomparable views across the Bay of Naples. Luke chose his own room, which coincidentally happened to be next to the master bedroom, housing Beatrice and Matthew. Beatrice took several pictures to share with Adrian including the text: *Your choice of rooms. You are going to LOVE this! Bx*

They unpacked and freshened up before a stroll around the local quartier. The most striking thing was the noise. People shouting from balconies, drivers impatiently hooting their horns before the lights had changed to green, conversations in cafés, into phones, across streets. Mopeds buzzing up streets so tall and narrow they were practically mediaeval. Graffiti decorated many walls and the scent of food seemed to chase them everywhere.

They succumbed to a pizza lunch in an unprepossessing place halfway down a grubby alleyway. Matthew struck up a conversation in Italian with the owner who welcomed them with real warmth. The sense of being an alien subsided. Beatrice and Luke chose a Margherita, the simplest pizza on the menu, so they could judge the essentials. Matthew opted for a *calzone* with an egg, which Beatrice found rather indulgent in view of their upcoming five-star dinner.

After lunch, they wandered as far as Il Duomo before getting lost on their way back. Eventually, they arrived at the sanctuary of the apartment. At six o'clock, washed and changed into their formal wear, the party regrouped for an aperitif on the roof terrace as the sun began its descent into the sea. A contented expression settled on Matthew's face as he pointed out geographical features to his grandson and expounded on their history. The man was a born teacher. Beatrice listened and learned.

Ettore, the same genial driver from the airport, came to collect them that evening. He assured them the restaurant was not far and that he would take the scenic route along the bay. Listening to his cheery chatter, no one spoke, absorbing the dusky pink to indigo shades of encroaching night and city lights reflecting off the sea around the fortifications. Neapolitans strolled the seafront in family groups or couples; the scents of sea and grilling smoke teased through the open windows, and on one of the boats, someone was playing a guitar. Beatrice squeezed Matthew's hand. She had a good feeling about this.

Isabella greeted them at the door with evident enthusiasm, kissing everyone twice, even a bemused Luke. She ushered them to their reserved table and promised to return with her husband as soon as the kitchen was prepared. Two Aperols and an orange juice appeared courtesy of a young waitress, and everyone found their aperitif exactly to their taste.

Matthew's attention was drawn to the menu and he took out his reading glasses with intent, murmuring his approval as he perused the dishes on offer. Beatrice was talking Luke through the choices when Isabella returned with a tall imposing man in chef's whites.

"Agusto, this is Matthew, Beatrice and Luke. Everyone, this is my husband and the genius behind this restaurant, Agusto

Colacino."

Agusto shook Matthew's hand. "Welcome! Thank you for coming!" He crouched down so he was at eye level with Luke. "*Ciao*, Luke! Is your first time in Italy?"

"Yes. I went to Portugal last year and I liked it. And when I was small, I was in France with my mum, but I can't remember much about that."

"We must give you an unforgettable experience of Napoli. Starting tonight." He stood up again. "And this is the famous Beatrice Stubbs. Our saviour." He took both her hands in his. "I thank you with my whole heart for helping us."

Beatrice flushed. He had an extraordinary aura, an intoxicating energy and charm which were futile to resist.

"Pleased to meet you, Signor Colacino. As I said to Isabella, I can't promise anything, but I will do my best."

He squeezed her hands and let go. "If my wife has faith in you, so do I. Let us sit and I will tell you the background. Maria, drinks!"

Once the waitress had poured three glasses of Prosecco and two sparkling waters, she retreated to the bar, leaving them in peace.

Agusto raised his water and proposed a toast. They joined in, chinking glasses, wishing each other a successful week.

"I will start at the beginning. Ecco is here for six years now, same age as you, Luke! We have a Michelin star for three. My clients tell me my *vitello* recipe appears on another menu, but I am not concerned. Replications can never reach the standards of the original. Then I hear a new restaurant is reproducing most of my menu at lower prices. So I go, I taste the *piatti* for myself. These are not replications but the exact same dishes. They produce MY dish exactly the way I do. They are not even ..." He frowned and looked at Isabella. "*Come se dice sottile*?"

"Subtle."

"Yes, subtle. They are not even subtle. Even the presentation is the same as if I had sent the dish out myself. But this is a local restaurant, quite new, with financial support from some well-known people. It is better if I don't shake the boat."

Isabella nodded. "We don't want any trouble."

"Instead, I take the dish off my own menu and create something original and delicious. Venison and chestnut-stuffed ravioli with a rosemary butter and wild garlic cream. The recipe sounds simple but it is not. It was my signature dish of the season last autumn, until a friend of mine, also a chef, came back from Piedmont and told me that he had eaten the exact dish in a restaurant there. He took photographs. It is my dish, even to the shape and size of each raviolo. How is this possible? Only I and my chefs know how to create this plate of food. Someone is selling my secrets. It is the only explanation."

Isabella chimed in. "Since last summer, we have huge staff turnover. Normally, we keep people for years. But now, someone is offering higher wages and taking the people we train for their own restaurants. We know this. But spies in the kitchen, this is too much. Agusto has inspiration no longer. Everyone is suspicious. This will destroy us if we cannot stop the leaks."

Beatrice sensed the heat in their impassioned speeches. Their clasped hands and tender looks between the chef and his wife gave evidence of loyalty, love and deep frustration at whatever was thwarting their dream. "Thank you for the context. When I come to the kitchens tomorrow, I will need a list of current staff, duration of employment and if possible, details of those who have left since last summer. I'd also like any information on the recently deceased chef. Can I interview both of you separately at some point?"

Isabella flicked her blue hair behind her ear. "I will organise the personnel files for you. No one in the kitchen knows who you are except Suhail. We had to involve one other person, you understand? He is the pastry chef and we need him to make your story work."

"I see. You think he can be trusted?" asked Beatrice.

Agusto checked his watch and got to his feet. "We have no choice but to trust him. I must go now as the first covers are due. Tomorrow Ecco is closed and Suhail and I will train you on desserts and pastries. He will be your sous chef for desserts. You can speak to me, Isabella and interview Suhail also. He was a good friend of the man who was stabbed. They come from the same town in Syria. Enjoy your meal and I will see you tomorrow. *Buonasera a tutti!*" He placed his fingertips to his mouth and blew a general kiss at them all, before charging back through the kitchen doors.

Isabella gazed after him, a softness in her eyes. "He is happy you are here. He is optimistic again." She clapped her hands together. "Dinner! Luke, would you like to try our risotto with buffalo milk for your first course? The ricotta tortelloni with our own ragù is my personal recommendation for you, Matthew. But, Beatrice, I remember how much you enjoyed a particular dish in San Sebastián. I want you to try the blue lobster salad with smoked beans and anchovy dressing. Maria, the wine list please!"

She flashed her brilliant smile at them all and departed. All three of her guests ordered exactly what she suggested and Matthew accepted the wine waiter's recommendation of a Greco di Tufo.

Luke followed Beatrice and Matthew's example and poured a little olive oil and balsamic vinegar onto his side plate. Each tore off a chunk of ciabatta from the bread basket and dipped it in. City lights reflected off the blue-black sea through the windows, delicious smells emanated from the kitchen and the party settled into a relaxed silence. Until Luke asked a question.

"Beatrice? Did that man say someone got stabbed?"

Matthew's eyes switched from the boy to Beatrice, but gave no indication of how to respond. Beatrice opted for the truth.

"Yes, he did. One of the chefs at this restaurant was killed a few weeks back. As Isabella and Agusto told us, someone is trying to poach their staff or persuade them to spy. It seems this particular man refused to do either and ended up dead. Which is why I've come to investigate."

Luke chewed his bread. "OK. The other thing ..."

Beatrice steeled herself. "Ask whatever you want. I will always tell you the truth, Luke, even if you might not like it." Her noble position was instantly deflated.

"I didn't want to say in front of that lady but I don't know if I like buffalo milk."

Matthew coughed and took a sip of his wine, leaving Beatrice to reply.

"I suppose it does sound a bit strange. Let's look at this another way. Do you like pizza?" asked Beatrice.

"Yes."

"What about the cheese on pizza, mozzarella?"

"The stringy stuff? That's one of the best bits."

"That is made from buffalo milk. So I'd say it's a safe bet that you will like buffalo milk risotto. and now's your chance to try it."

A waiter approached with three perfectly arranged plates, placing each in the correct place and wished them *buon appetito*.

Beatrice picked up her fork and looked into Matthew's smiling eyes. "I think I might enjoy Naples," she said.

Luke piped up before Matthew could reply. "Me too!"

Chapter 9

At ten the next morning, Beatrice reported for work at Ecco's staff entrance beside the garage. Agusto, already in his whites, opened the door and hurried her inside, glancing around the courtyard. Once the door closed, he seemed to relax.

"Good morning, Beatrice. How are you? Would you like coffee?"

"Thank you but I already had breakfast. I'm ready to start when you are."

"You have the right attitude! Isabella is printing the personnel files ready for you. Suhail, come here. I want you to meet Beatrice Stubbs."

A thin young man emerged from behind a fridge. Also in kitchen whites, he wore round spectacles and had a droopy moustache. His long-lashed eyes were deep brown and somehow sad. He attempted a smile, holding out his hand.

"Hello, Missus Stubbs. I am happy to meet you. I look forward to working with you and helping you in this investigation. Please call me Suhail."

Beatrice shook his hand, noting the firm grip, and returned his smile. "Nice to meet you too and thank you for allowing me to shadow you. Please call me Beatrice."

He gave a respectful nod. "Do you want to start now?"

"Yes, I do, but not with the cookery. First, I want to sweep the entire restaurant for listening devices. To be honest, I think it's unlikely the copycats are getting your recipes through bugging the place, especially with the amount of background noise. But I would be remiss in my duties if I did not check. It would also save us a great deal of time if that were the route through which the information is leaked. Do you mind?" she asked Agusto.

He shook his head with emphasis and thrust a hand around the room, inviting her to go ahead. She had the impression Agusto came to life in the evenings and was not what she would call a morning person.

She got to work with the new devices she had picked up in London and scanned all work surfaces, serving hatch, restaurant and waiting staff station. Not a single blip. Next she should check the security status of their telephone calls and emails, but that could wait till Isabella joined them. Now, to learn all about puddings.

While undoubtedly a brilliant chef, Agusto was a dreadful teacher. He spent too much time telling her what not to do and getting distracted by anecdotes and outrage at his imitators to guide her step by step. So when she made an error and his patience exploded, both tempers frayed to breaking point. Three different attempts at a Savarin had gone into the bin before Isabella took Agusto away to look at some new glassware, leaving Beatrice with Suhail. His quiet, diffident manner of teaching was a simple demonstration of one stage with an invitation to repeat. His corrections were gentle suggestions and in one hour, she had achieved a complete Savarin, glazed with apricot jelly and filled with cream and fresh fruit, along with a dozen rum babas, shaped like mushrooms and soaked in a rum glaze.

They broke for lunch and Suhail went outside to pray. So it was only the chef, his wife and the private investigator who sat in the empty restaurant to eat pasta and discuss the case.

After working all morning with food, Beatrice was surprised to find she still had quite an appetite. She tucked into the *tagliatelle alla verdura* with gusto, while quizzing her hosts on exact locations where they might have discussed menu ideas and the level of communications security.

Isabella was completely convinced their emails were secure but could not guarantee either mobile had not been hacked. With a shake of his head, Agusto dismissed her concerns. He never wrote recipes down, insisting staff learned them by heart. His mobile could only be relevant in his telephone orders to suppliers.

"I always meet all my suppliers in person so I can trust the product and the person. Some of these farmers grow crops especially for me. It was impossible to get baby courgettes until Signor Bertolino agreed to pluck them very young and keep the flowers. Now, everyone wants them and I must move on."

He was still gesticulating at Beatrice when there was a knock at the window. A darker version of Agusto pressed his face to the window.

"Gennaio!" exclaimed Agusto. "Beatrice, this is my little brother!"

Beatrice glanced at Isabella. "Should I leave? I mean, how do we explain my presence?"

Isabella rose to her feet and moved to unlock the door. "No, no, Gennaio is family. I know you will like each other."

"I thought it was only ..." Beatrice trailed off as the big man entered the room and made a bee-line for her, grabbed her by the shoulders and kissed her on both cheeks. He smelt of tobacco and cloves, a pleasing combination.

"*Benvenuto in Italia*! So happy you are here! You will be the one to save Ecco! My name is Gennaio and I am your servant. Anything you need, anything at all, I am here for you."

Before she could reply, the large man kissed Isabella's cheeks and embraced his brother. When they were side by side, Beatrice saw Agusto was slimmer, greyer and a few centimetres taller than his younger brother. Gennaio's dark curls and heavy frame made him seem squatter and more bullish than the chef.

A shadow crossed the corner of her vision and she spotted Suhail back at his post, waiting for his pupil to return.

"Lovely to meet you, Gennaio. The lunch was most welcome, Isabella, but perhaps I should get back to work. We have more pastries to perfect and I'm a slow learner despite Suhail's excellent instruction. Can we have a quick word before I return to the kitchen?"

Isabella's hand snaked into Agusto's huge paw. "We are at your service. All of us. Anytime you want, you can pick our brains!" She burst into laughter, causing an expression of puzzlement on the faces of the two men. Beatrice was none the wiser. She dropped her napkin on her plate and followed Isabella into the office.

"Take a seat, Beatrice. What can I do for you?"

"That's all right. I'll only be a minute. Do all restaurants close on Sundays?"

"No, many are open over the weekend. Why?"

"I wondered if you could call those who have copied your recipes and ask them where they got them from. Not as Agusto's wife. Pretend you are a journalist, say you're doing a review of their restaurant and see how they react to your questions."

"That is a brilliant idea! I will do it this afternoon."

"Good. Now I'm off to work."

Next on the menu, zabaglione, white chocolate mousse and candied fennel sauce. Truth was, rather than learning new culinary skills, Beatrice quite fancied a nap. Standing at counters, whisking, beating, folding, stirring and piping was quite hard on the arms, not to mention the feet. All the bending over plates with a pair of tweezers to position a mint leaf just so and heaving pans on and off the heat took their toll on her back. Suhail noticed her wince and gave her a kind smile.

"On a normal day, we don't work as many hours as this. But we work much faster. When the kitchen is full, it is very hot and noisy and stressful. Running shoes are a good idea."

"Thank you for the advice. I will make sure to wear trainers next time."

"You're welcome. Are you ready to present these dishes to Agusto?"

Beatrice looked at the three plates. A perfect chocolate heart filled with white chocolate mousse in a circle of upended strawberries. Panna cotta with an almond and fennel coulis sprinkled with candied mint leaves and sliced almonds. Amaretto poached peaches with zabaglione and Amarettini biscuits. She'd gone right off fussy puddings.

She huffed. "I suppose so."

Agusto had plenty of criticisms and pointers about the presentation, but seemed satisfied with the quality of the desserts. Then he dropped his bombshell.

"Good. Once the kitchen is clean, we are finished for the day. Tomorrow, we will do two things. Suhail will teach you the pastries and I will create your signature dessert. What is it?"

"What is what?"

"Your signature dish! This is the story we tell. Competition winner and British pastry chef comes to Ecco for two weeks, with special dessert created just for us. You tell me the idea, I will design it. No?"

"Um, well, I don't really ..." The expression on Agusto's face stopped her short. "Let me think it over and I'll give you a couple of ideas in the morning."

"No, no, no. That is too late. I need to think about this overnight. Creativity is not a flash of inspiration. It is hard work and practice and years of technique, understanding of ingredients and storytelling. Give me an idea. Anything I can work with."

Beatrice's mind froze. How could she pull an idea that would meet Agusto's artistry out of a hat?

He placed his palms together and dipped his fingers up and down, an imploring gesture with a touch of impatience. "What do you make for dessert at dinner parties? What is your favourite after-dinner sweet when you go out to a restaurant?"

In a panic, she told the truth. "Brown bread ice-cream. There's a pub near our house which serves the most delicious brown bread and honey ice-cream. It's like breakfast in a bowl."

"Brown bread ice-cream?" Agusto's eyebrows shot up to his hairline. "At Ecco?"

"Sorry, it was the first thing I could think of." Beatrice's voice trailed off.

"Chef?" Suhail spoke in little over a murmur. "What if we make the ice-cream part of an *affogato*? The story is already there. Beatrice described it as 'breakfast in a bowl'. What goes better with brown bread and honey than coffee? A classic London combination with a sophisticated Neapolitan twist."

Agusto's eyes gleamed. "An *affogato*? Let me think about this." He paced off around the dining room tapping a forefinger to his lips.

"What is an *affogato*?" whispered Beatrice.

"It means 'drowned' in Italian," answered Suhail, *sotto voce*. "At its simplest, it is a ball of ice-cream with a hot espresso tipped over it, usually served in a glass with biscotti for some texture."

"But here we already have texture," boomed Agusto, from the other end of the room. The man must have the hearing of a bat. "The caramelised breadcrumbs give crunch and the ice-cream gives sweetness. The hot rich coffee over the top makes the ice-cream melt a little and accompanied by a digestif, is the perfect way to finish a meal. But the twist? What is the twist? I must think. You clean the kitchen and I will empty my mind. The answer is there, I feel it. *Ciao, a domani!*"

Chapter 10

Thanks to Suhail's constant efficiency throughout the day, the kitchen was returned to its pristine condition in under ten minutes. Ettore sent Beatrice a message informing her he would wait for her outside. Despite her desire to rush home and relax, she hadn't finished the job. After Suhail had gone, Beatrice went in search of Isabella and found her in the office, poring over a spreadsheet.

"Beatrice! How was your day?"

"Tougher than I expected. I have two concerns. If I am going to be that busy and actually working as a chef, how on earth do I get to observe the rest of the team? Secondly, the personnel files you gave me only include kitchen staff. What about the front of house people? Surely they are aware of what they are serving? I know from personal experience your sommelier and maître d' are highly knowledgeable about the contents of the food."

Isabella rolled her shoulders and yawned. "Timing is everything in this business. It is not so difficult. You prepare the desserts. Make everything ready, then you have time to watch the other chefs. Work only when dessert orders arrive. You can have the waiting staff files if you want, but they don't really know what goes on in the kitchen. Maybe Alessandro and Maria have a better understanding, as you say. I will print their files for you.

Are you in a bad mood?"

Beatrice thought about the question. "Not a bad mood, exactly, just realising that this is a bigger job than I thought. Plus I am really worn out after today."

"Go home and rest. Is your driver here?"

"He's waiting outside. Did you call any of the copycat restaurants?"

"Yes, and the reaction was very interesting. I called three and found some things in common. All the owners are new to the restaurant business, with almost zero experience. Very strange. They talked about their style, their chef, their branding and their location with passion and enthusiasm. Only when I asked about how they create their dishes, they avoided the question. One made an excuse, the other gave me nothing but bullshit and the last one hung up." Isabella wrinkled her nose.

"Hmm. OK, I need to think this over. Can you get me the personnel files on the waiting staff for tomorrow? I'll be in early for my baptism of fire."

"No problem. How did you get on with Suhail?"

"The man has the patience of a saint. I'm very glad he's got my back. Have a good evening and see you tomorrow."

By the time she got back to the apartment after Ettore's enthusiastic questions and erratic driving, she was so tired she could barely drag herself up the stairs. Only the thought of the new arrival spurred her on.

She could hear his voice the minute she opened the door.

"Which just goes to show how important it is to end a relationship on good terms. A mantra I live by whether it's work or love."

Her breath caught and not just because of the stairs. He couldn't have split up with Will already! Not after a marriage of only four months.

He stood up as she came into the room. "Here she is! The

Nigella Lawson of Upton St Nicholas! Give me a hug."

She held out her palms in rejection. "Just wait a minute. Have you left Will?"

"What? My God, why on earth would I do that? No, we're in this for at least as long as you and Matthew."

"Thank heavens for that. I could do with a bit less domestic drama." She embraced Adrian warmly, kissed Matthew and planted a peck on Luke's head, which was bent over his games console. She dumped her bag onto the coffee table and flung herself into an armchair.

"Tired?" asked Matthew, with a sympathetic smile.

"Shattered. And I have to do it all again tomorrow. What do you think of the apartment, Adrian?"

"Utterly glorious. I've taken photos in every room but only sent about half to Will. I don't want to make him jealous. Much. How was your day?"

"Eye-opening. Turns out I know nothing about cooking and I am frankly terrified about learning how to be a five-star chef on Tuesday. What about you lot? Been exploring, Luke?"

He looked up. "Yeah. It was good." He returned his gaze to the screen.

Matthew elaborated. "We walked around most of the historical centre and visited two museums. We lunched on pizza in Piazza Dante and Luke learned how to order for himself in Italian. He was quite the star attraction, I can tell you. Then Luke had a rest in his room and I had forty winks on the sofa. So we were fully restored by the time Adrian arrived. Tell Beatrice about your flight while I check on dinner."

Adrian sat up, looking stylish and well-groomed in a button-down blue shirt, cream trousers and deck shoes. "I was just telling them that the steward on my flight was an ex-boyfriend. Do you remember Giacomo? I'd completely forgotten he worked for British Airways until I boarded the plane. Not only did he get me upgraded, but kept me plied with wine the whole flight!"

Beatrice laughed. "Trust you. How's Will? Is he really all right about you coming away alone?"

"He was till I told him about Giacomo. Ha! No, he's fine. Really. It was the best solution as he has no distractions and can prepare for Monday's interview. I am so excited to be here and I cannot believe we are actually going to dine at Ecco!"

"Are we?" Luke's head shot up. "Again?"

"Yes. They have fixed it so that the four of us can eat there on Saturday night. Though to be honest, I've already had enough of haute cuisine."

"Yay! That place is wicked!" Luke grinned.

"That's exactly what the Michelin reviewer said." Beatrice accepted a cup of tea from Matthew.

"We thought you'd probably be worn out after a full day in the kitchen and perhaps not keen on going out to a restaurant, so I'm making *ribollita*. Cannellini bean and vegetable soup. Comfort food which is full of flavour, yet not too heavy and classically Italian. I'll serve it with toasted ciabatta, parmesan and lemon oil."

"Matthew Bailey, I adore you. Even when you talk like a menu."

Luke put down his console and looked at Beatrice. "Are you hungry?"

"Oddly enough, after craving over a hot stove for hours on end, I actually am. Now tell me how to order my pizza in Italian."

The party moved up to the roof terrace, Adrian carrying wine, Matthew heaving the huge tureen, and Beatrice managed the bread. They ate and drank and exclaimed over the sky, which changed tone from golden through burnt orange to streaks of silver and black, as if they were watching the embers of a bonfire.

Beatrice went downstairs to tuck Luke in at ten, fully intending to return and finish her glass of wine and voice her opinions on European politics. But the door to their room was ajar, the bedside lamps on and her willpower ran out. She brushed her teeth, washed her face and was asleep by twenty past ten.

Chapter 11

In an honourable attempt to repay his hosts' hospitality, Adrian rose early and did the dishes from the night before. He popped out to the nearby bakery, wrinkling his nose at the overflowing bins, and stopped for a moment to enjoy a glimpse of the seafront. When he let himself into the apartment, Beatrice was sitting at the kitchen table, reading some paperwork. She was still in her dressing-gown, her hair wild.

She eyed the paper bag in his hand. "Good morning, Mr Fresh-as-a-Daisy. Are those pastries?"

"Yes, but I will also make a fruit salad with yoghurt for anyone sick of baked goods. When do you have to leave?"

"In about an hour. I'll jump in the shower and join you in a bit. Matthew's having a lie-in. Yesterday just about wore him out. And he wasn't even being a pretend chef." She shuffled off down the corridor humming 'At the End of the Day' from *Les Misérables*.

Adrian snorted with laughter, opened the windows and listened to the bustle of a Neapolitan Monday morning as he chopped apples, oranges, kiwis and grapes, brewed coffee and warmed the pastries in the oven. He was just putting a milk pan on the hob when PI Beatrice Stubbs came in and sat down. She wore a long-sleeved T-shirt, loose trousers and a pair of trainers.

"You look more like a jogger than a chef," he said, pulling out a tray of *sfogliatelle* with an oven glove.

"That's because it's bloody hard work. Honestly, I ache all over from yesterday and that was just three of us in the kitchen. I am dreading Tuesday. Why on earth would I put myself into one of the most stressful, overheated and pressured environments in the world to do someone a favour?"

"Don't tell me they're not paying you! I'd never have encouraged you to do this if I thought it was a freebie." He poured the coffee.

"Of course I'm being paid. I'm not completely mad. But the effort this job requires is a bit more than poking around on the Internet. Listen, I can't face those fiddle-arse croissanty-things but I know Luke will love them. Give me unadulterated fruit as Nature intended. Then I must haul my sorry self to Ecco and endure another day of feeling inadequate."

Her pout made Adrian laugh aloud. "Drink your coffee and eat your fruit. I am even happier to be here now I know how busy you're going to be. I can support Matthew, entertain Luke, cook, clean and ensure our hard worker returns home to a decent meal every evening. All you need to do is concentrate on the job. Aha! The boys are up."

Washed and dressed, Matthew looked ready to take on the day, albeit with a few more wrinkles under the eyes. Luke was still in his pyjamas, hair awry and face puffy. Beatrice hugged and kissed them all, took two mouthfuls of fruit, drained her coffee and left for the restaurant.

After her departure, the three males ate in silence, each absorbed in iPad, guidebook or games console. Finally Matthew set down his cup.

"The weather looks pleasant, so how would you feel about a boat trip? Over to Capri to potter around the island, grab a spot of lunch, then back across the bay to buy something scintillating for Beatrice's dinner. Can I get a show of hands?"

Adrian and Luke both shot their right hands in the air.

"Good choice. So it seems only one of our party is yet to get dressed. Luke, off you trot while Adrian and I clear the kitchen. Please apply Factor 50 everywhere and bring your hat."

The speedboat bounced across the waves, jolting the passengers perched on the plastic benches. Adrian found the spray and speed exhilarating, as did Luke, but Matthew's posture remained stiff, as did his smile. The leathery boatman reached out a muscular forearm to assist them as they clambered onto the quay.

Adrian spotted the subtle transfer of Euros as Matthew shook their pilot's hand. They all waved goodbye and gazed up at the colourful peak of Capri. The weather was warm enough to turn pale British skin pink, clusters of purple heather and yellow broom seemed to erupt from each corner and the cheerful chatter of the quayside lifted everyone's spirits. Too romantic for words. Adrian was glad he'd re-watched *The Talented Mr Ripley* before leaving London. Now he knew exactly what to expect.

Luke ran ahead up the steep narrow street, pointing out ice-cream shops, souvenirs and on every other doorstep, reclining cats. Basil, oregano, thyme and marjoram grew on most windowsills, adding a herbal note to the lemon-scented air. They strolled uphill, snapping pictures of one photogenic panorama after another: small coves changing colour with each wave and cascading terraced gardens. On the winding streets, tiny one-person utility vehicles carried suitcases, their drivers hooting to clear a path between the tourists. Of those there were plenty. Adrian guessed the nationality by dress sense before he could even hear the accents. He took a decision to stop being judgemental and admire the beauty of this little island with its celebrated history.

Luke's energy took him further ahead than Adrian deemed comfortable, while Matthew's slow progress stretched the distance between them to a worrying degree. Adrian caught

Matthew's eye, indicated Luke and made the motion of a grabbing claw to indicate he'd catch the boy. The ex-professor rested against a wall and nodded his permission. Ducking groups of tourists dawdling up the congested little street and taking selfies, Adrian loped after the six-year-old, scanning both sides for a small blond head. With a surprising sense of relief, he spotted Luke watching a street vendor waving beribboned sticks to attract young eyes. Right behind him stood an older man in a black beret, equally absorbed in the display.

Adrian drew Luke away with a gentle hand on his shoulder. "Let's stick together. Your granddad isn't as fast as you and we shouldn't spilt up. Now I'm not sure what you think, but I wonder if it's too early for an ice-cream?"

After much deliberation, Luke chose a double scoop of stracciatella and chocolate, Adrian tried the lime sorbet and Matthew chose to drink a glass of mineral water in the shade of an umbrella. His face was grey and weary. Adrian put it down to seasickness. Not everyone liked speedboats as much as a six-year-old boy and an excitable wine merchant. Perhaps by the time they had reached the summit, Matthew would have regained his appetite.

The island charmed them all, despite the throngs of equally charmed day-trippers, so that photo opportunities were a question of queues or jostling for prime position. The steep cliffs cascaded into the Mediterranean Sea, every single house, shop or hotel seemed freshly painted and the pragmatic chaos of Capri seemed to embrace the visitors with such warmth, one would always yearn to return.

After many delays, mostly instigated by Adrian in order to allow Matthew rest stops, the trio arrived at Casa D'Anna, with its terraces overlooking the Bay of Naples. Adrian tried out his perfectly accented Italian and was mildly irritated when the waiter answered in English.

"Yes, we have a table for three. Inside or out?"

With a longing glance at the divine balcony, Adrian considered Matthew's sweaty brow and Luke's damp shirt. "Inside please."

Two hours later, they boarded the ferry back across the bay. Filled with good food and delightful views, all three were in great spirits. The steadier, slower trundle of the ferry suited Matthew, who gazed out at the afternoon sunshine with a peaceful expression.

Adrian helped Luke assemble a photo-montage for Tanya, so she could experience their day virtually. They added a selfie at the end, both pulling faces with Matthew's half-smile in the background.

By the time they reached the apartment, Adrian could see his companions were in need of some quiet time alone. He offered to go shopping for ingredients and cook for them all after they had rested. The suggestion was well received, and both wandered off to their rooms. Adrian sprang down the stairwell, planning roasted Mediterranean vegetables with a parmesan crumb and tomato-basil sauce. His mind was on wine when he opened the door and noticed a figure on the opposite side of the street, wearing a black beret.

The man was absorbed in his phone and only when he looked up did he realise Adrian was staring at him. He swivelled on his heel and paced away into an alley.

"Hello, love of my life, star in my firmament!"

Will's laugh filled Adrian with a bubbly joy no Prosecco could match. "Hello, you. I've been waiting for your call. How's it going in Naples?"

"Marvellously! We went to Capri today and I cooked the most divine vegetarian dinner with a Sangiovese. Beatrice is all ready for her big debut tomorrow and the rest of us are going up the volcano. But that is not why I called. How did your appraisal go?"

Will paused and Adrian's stomach clenched in anticipation. He could hear ice tinkling against glass. Celebrations? Or drowning his sorrows?

"The feedback was 99 per cent positive, but I'm not going to make DI this time. They're promoting someone else. Apparently I lack experience in management roles."

"That's such crap! How can you get experience unless they give you a management role?"

"Yep, I know."

Adrian could hear the defeat in his husband's voice. "Can you appeal or something?"

"Nah. The only thing I can do is work harder, get my face seen, attract more approval and put the effort into being Mr Popularity. In other words, more crap."

"Will, I'm sorry. I know how important this was to you. I wish I hadn't come to Italy. I should be there with you right now."

There was another silence. Adrian waited, trying to gauge Will's mood.

"I admit I wish I had your shoulder to cry on or swear at. On the other hand, that's the end of the process. I have no further interviews, so why should I volunteer for extra shifts over Easter? They can stuff it. Tonight, I'm drinking whisky and getting shitfaced. Then I have to work till Thursday evening but I could take next week off and join you all in Italy."

Adrian took an intake of breath so sharp it made him cough. "Really? I would love that so much and we have a gorgeous apartment with a roof garden and views and we could be together and I miss you more than I thought I would." Emotion welled in his throat and prevented further speech.

"I miss you too. Let's do it. I'll book a flight tomorrow and we can spend Easter together. See, I feel better already." He paused and Adrian could hear him take a drink. "Hey, listen, after I left work, I was pissed off and in need of a friendly face, so I stopped off at the Emporium to say hello. Let me tell you, Catinca has excelled herself."

Adrian's pulse raced. "What does that mean?"

"Full-on Evita. Argentinean wines, soundtrack from the musical, dress code for all staff and snack samples of chocolate insects and mini-empadillas. The place was packed."

"Did you take pictures?"

"No, sorry, I was having too much fun. Just relax and appreciate your assistant is kicking wine-selling ass. I love you."

Adrian sighed. "I love you too. See you next week."

"I can't wait. And that is no exaggeration."

Chapter 12

Eight years earlier, Beatrice had been in charge of a Police Support Unit during the 2011 London riots. It had been the most exhausting and stressful night of her life. Wave after wave of emergencies shredded her nerves and just when she thought the pressure would crush her, it increased yet further.

The closest thing she had experienced since was the Tuesday lunchtime slot backstage at Ecco. Had she been in the main kitchen, with Agusto's constant shouting, orders flying about in all languages, the intense heat and clattering of cookware and crockery, she would have buckled.

Her saving grace was the fact she and calm, unflappable, efficient Suhail had an alcove to themselves to prepare the desserts. Their service was slow, although Suhail produced three times as much as Beatrice. Agusto came round the fridge twice, chivvying them to speed up. She did try to go faster and he sent back two dishes immediately, as her presentation was sub-par. Suhail binned them and started again, with a patient smile at Beatrice's apology. As diners approached the end of their meals, dessert orders rang through on the computer display at such a pace, Beatrice began to panic.

The salad chef, a pretty girl called Chantal, joined them to help out, her competent hands steady and reassuring. Beatrice recalled her public role as British wannabe chef and disguised her less-than-rapid performance as devotion to quality control.

Eventually, three o'clock came around and the computer screen showed no more orders. Sweaty and dehydrated, she set to clearing up.

Suhail shook his head. "That's my job, chef. Chantal and I can manage. You take a break."

"Thank you both very much. You are both excellent professionals." She made her way through the kitchen, trembling from the stress and at a loss as to where to go. The restaurant was still occupied by the last few diners, the kitchen was still a nightmare of bangs and shouts and she couldn't hide in Isabella's office. She opted for the little courtyard outside the kitchen door, greeting two other chefs having a cigarette. They appeared relaxed and clean, whereas her chef's coat was splattered with coffee, chocolate and raspberry coulis, and her hands still shaky.

One of them offered her a cigarette.

"No, thank you. I don't smoke. Although right now, I wish I did."

The young man smiled. "Your first day at Ecco? The pressure is high."

The cool spring breeze soothed Beatrice's red face and she took the opportunity of a casual conversation to learn a little about her co-workers. "I'm Beatrice. I know Agusto introduced everyone at the start of service, but I was in such a panic, I couldn't even remember my own name."

The cigarette-offerer held out a hand. "Marcello. I'm now Agusto's sous-chef. This is Bruno, who is doing his apprenticeship. He started last week. Your first day was also high pressure, eh, Bruno?"

The handsome young man rolled his eyes. "Crazy! Worse than military service. Hello, Beatrice. Pleased to meet you." His accent had a US twang.

Beatrice shook with them both and leaned against the wall, shoving her hands in her pockets. "Do you work both lunch and dinner shifts? It must be incredibly tiring."

Marcello shrugged. "After a while, it is normal. You don't work the evening service?"

"No, one shift per day is all I can handle. Yes, I won a competition on TV, but that's a million miles from holding my own in a professional kitchen. I've got two weeks to learn. If I survive that long."

Both men laughed.

"What do you think of my uncle?" asked Bruno.

Beatrice tilted her head in puzzlement.

"It's OK, you can be honest," he grinned, blowing out a stream of smoke. "Agusto terrifies all of us."

"Oh I see. You're his nephew. I think I met your father yesterday. Gennaio?"

Bruno shook his head and stubbed out his cigarette. "No, Gennaio is also my uncle. My father died when I was a child. Both my uncles are always very kind to me. I did the first part of my apprenticeship with Gennaio, and the second part with Agusto."

Beatrice squeezed her eyes shut for a second in embarrassment. "I'm sorry. I shouldn't make assumptions. You're training to work in the food industry?"

Bruno coughed a laugh. "Please don't be offended, Beatrice, but that's the last thing in the world I want to do. I have to accept my uncles' offers because they are family. But as soon as I finish, I'm setting up a start-up business as an app developer. I got confirmation of funding just this week."

"Do your uncles know?"

"Not yet. I want to tell them both together and Gennaio is on a business trip this week. When he gets back from Hungary I plan to break the news over Easter, when everyone is in a good mood. Wish me luck."

"Good luck!"

Marcello turned to Beatrice. "Isabella says you live in

London. Great city."

"Yes, I'm based in London, but now exploring Europe to learn international cuisine. Some would say I'm too old to try a new career, but I'm enjoying the experience even if it scares me to death. Learning something new keeps me young."

"And you bring something new to us. The *affogato al colazione* is wonderful. A fantastic idea with the ice-cream and the tuile," Marcello smiled.

Beatrice opened her mouth to protest that the tuile, or brandy snap as she would have called it, was Agusto's addition. Plus Suhail was the one who suggested pouring coffee over the ice-cream and designing it as a breakfast dessert. But she simply nodded modestly and wondered if she could request the personnel files again but this time with an entirely new column. Who was an employee and who was a relative?

"Judging by the number of orders we had today, it was quite the novelty," she said. "Do you have a signature dish, Marcello?"

"He is the King of the Sea!" laughed Bruno. "If it swims, he'll cook it."

Marcello finished his cigarette and ground it carefully into the wall-mounted ashtray. "Bruno exaggerates. My speciality is seafood, fish, soups, fillets, patés, gratins, brochettes and sushi. When you live by the sea, why not make the most of it?"

The door behind them burst open and Agusto thrust his head out. "What the hell are you doing out here while there's still food to be refrigerated? I don't pay you to lounge around smoking! How the hell you expect to train your taste buds while dragging on those terrible things, I don't know!"

All three scurried up the steps and past the nerve-wracking figure of Agusto, who glared at each of them like a Minotaur.

Alessandro, the maître d'hôtel, stalked around the restaurant, ensuring its restoration to pristine condition was complete. He checked glasses and adjusted cutlery, inspected napkins and ran a finger across the surface of the bar. He agreed to Beatrice's request for 'a bit of a chat' with a smooth smile.

"I hoped to talk to Maria as well, but I assume she's left for the day."

"Yes. She will return at six for the pre-service briefing. Would you like to sit here?" He indicated the table behind the greeting station, the one kept in reserve for emergencies. It was not laid for service, bearing only a laptop computer and a selection of little silvery shapes.

"Thank you." She looked down at the shapes. A fish, a cresting wave, a tiny little toast rack, none larger than her thumb.

"Cutlery rests," he explained. "I need to make a choice. Which one do you like?"

Beatrice picked up the fish, running her finger over the engraved scales and dorsal fin. The toast rack had three wide gaps, perfect for resting your knife and fork, but reminded her somehow of missing teeth. The cresting wave was more delicate, arching like a bass clef. It looked the most attractive but least practical. Surely your knife and fork would simply slide off? As if reading her mind, Alessandro turned it over and placed a pen inside. It rested securely and the wave transformed into something resembling the palm of a hand with curled thumb.

"I'd go for that one. Pretty, functional and rather intriguing," she said.

"Yes, I agree. It has balance. Thank you for your help. What would you like to know about the front-of-house operation?"

Beatrice studied him. His eyes, unlike her constantly distracted driver, seemed to be constantly watching, alert to every detail.

"My fundamental question is how the two parts work together. How far do you and Agusto collaborate to ensure the guests get the experience they anticipate?"

"That is a good question. The restaurant has a mission. We think big with ideas and imagination. We also think little, and that means attention to detail. Every element combines to deliver a sublime dining experience. Come, I will show you." He stood up, with an air Beatrice recognised. A man eager to share his knowledge, exactly like Matthew in a lecture hall. She followed him across the room, the willing pupil persona not merely an act.

"Look out of the window. You see an ancient port welcoming cultures from all over the world. Napoli has a proud heritage, a culture all its own. This forms the foundation of Ecco. We are proud of our Italian roots. Our ingredients are local and seasonal and the freshest you will find. But we are also a port, open to new tastes and influences. We incorporate all this into our menu. Sometimes, we explore spices from Malaysia or fermentation from Japan. Ecco looks to the future, but remembers its past. This way."

He led the way to the centre of the restaurant. "We have room for only sixty guests, so it is not so large. One table, one party, so only sixty diners per service. Look around. Tell me what the ambience of this room says to you."

Beatrice took in the Mediterranean blue of the walls, painted so the colour lightened from intense lapis lazuli at the bottom to pastel forget-me-not at the top. Along the bottom of two walls were glass bricks allowing sunshine to enter. Above, sunken spotlights cast yellow pools or drew attention to eclectic works of art, each representing some maritime scene. Gold-coloured tablecloths covered each table with white napkins folded into sail-like peaks. The terrace design, where the tables at the back were on the highest level and those at the front on the lowest, meant that every diner could appreciate the panoramic view of the Bay of Naples.

"It's a reflection, isn't it? The colour scheme echoes the view. Sea, sand, sky and those glass bricks create an effect like ripples of water round your ankles. As if you're paddling on the beach."

Alessandro patted the fingers of his right hand to the palm of his left in muted applause. "Very good. Do you see a difference between today and your experience as a diner on Saturday evening?"

Beatrice recalled her first impression of the restaurant atmosphere. "It was darker, somehow. Now I see yellow and peony, like a beach in the daytime. The other night it was more orange and navy. The napkins were blue, not white. So it *is* a reflection of the exterior and changes with the time of day."

"And ...?"

"There's plenty of room between each table. People aren't crammed up against each other fighting for space." She examined the nearest table. "Are those for children?" she asked, pointing to the dumpy little stools which looked like something from an upmarket kindergarten.

"No, no. These are for the ladies' handbags. Waiters place one to the right or left of our female guests, depending on which arm she carries her bag. One cannot expect designer accessories to be placed on the floor."

"You've thought of everything, haven't you?" Beatrice gave him an appreciative nod.

"We try. Come, let us sit. You asked me how the kitchen and restaurant work together. In my experience, each establishment operates differently, but I will tell you about Ecco. The heart of the place is Agusto. He changes the menu at least once a month, sometimes more often. When an ingredient is out of season, he replaces it with something else. That may mean an alteration to a dish or removing it entirely and introducing a substitute. We meet every Monday morning to discuss the menu. This is not a matter of ingredients and correct accompaniments. It is a question of story."

Beatrice tugged at her earlobe. "Agusto keeps saying the same thing but I confess I'm not sure what he means. Why does each dish need to have a story?"

"Miss Stubbs, if you want to become a professional chef, you need to understand where flavour is created."

"I can see by your face you expect the wrong answer. You look like a card shark with all the aces."

Alessandro rested his chin on his knuckles, waiting for her answer.

"Right, here you go. Flavour is created in the kitchen, from the imagination of the chef, his knowledge of food and the best combinations of ingredients to maximise the experience."

Alessandro reached behind his greeter podium and withdrew a briefcase. He tilted it towards him to enter the combination and drew out a document.

"Read this. Then we can continue our conversation. I think you will enjoy it."

Chapter 13

CONFIDENTIAL
Consultancy advisory paper for management of Ecco
This paper draws on research carried out in the University of Naples Federico II Science Department, first published 2011.

The Essence of Taste – Professor P. Bonardi
Summary
Introduction

Taste as a gustatory sense can be defined as the ability to determine flavour. Traditionally, we associate this ability with our taste buds, located in the mouth and more specifically on the tongue. At the time of writing this paper, we are able to distinguish five distinct flavours: salty, sour, sweet, bitter and umami.

If the experience of taste is as simple as that, how do we account for the multi-billion-dollar industry surrounding food? Not simply manufacturing, but consider cookery schools, celebrity chefs, recipe books, personalised diets, specialised shops, the range of restaurants and cultural cuisines.

It is only in this millennium that a significant body of research by neurophysiologists and cognitive neuroscientists has investigated the profoundly multisensory nature of human perception. The relationship between olfactory receptors (our sense of smell) has long been recognised as an effect on what we experience as taste. What then of the other three senses: visual, tactile and auditory?

Interestingly, major food companies are far ahead of the scientists. Their awareness of the role of colour in what makes the food or packaging around it more appealing gave rise to a whole industry of additives. Food advertising reflects the importance of sound: 'crunchy', 'crispy', 'Snap, Crackle and Pop'. Companies like Häagen-Dazs changed the view of ice-cream as a child's treat to a sensual experience as much about touch as taste.

At the core of all our cerebral processes is what the marketing industry terms 'the lizard brain'. This part of the cortex can be described as the most animal element, where raw sensations are experienced. Above that is the area which is responsible for perception, by assembling those sensations into meaning. Up another level and we see cognitive thought process, assessing the meaning in relation to ourselves. Here we see language, memory, expectation, creativity and logic.

Essentially, as this paper will prove, taste is not what happens in the kitchen, but what happens in our heads. Gordon Shepherd, author of *Neurogastronomy* says, "A common misconception is that the foods contain the flavours. Foods do contain the flavour molecules, but the flavours of those molecules are created by the brain."

Findings

Extensive tests over three years on paid test subjects with some expertise, such as wine-tasters, perfumers, flavour-developing companies and food scientists, and volunteers with no particular aptitude or interest in the topics, gave us the same results.

All five senses in addition to language, culture and expectation make a difference to how we experience flavour. Each is closely intertwined and difficult to isolate.

For example, seafood with lemon is perceived to have less flavour when served on a warm white plate. Tasters confirmed an increase in intensity when exactly the same dish is served beside crushed ice on a black plate.

Crudités in primary colours are judged to be fresher, crunchier and more likely to be organic when listening to upbeat, recognisable, popular music rather than background muzak and presented upright in painted flowerpots rather than horizontally in a dish.

When the menu described a dish as Mexican Mole: game birds accompanied by a dark chocolate sauce, it scored very poorly. Exactly the same ingredients and presentation but entitled Secrets of the Forest: game birds accompanied by a dark chocolate sauce, was far better received.

Conclusions

By appealing to all the senses and transmitting subtle ideas through careful selection of ingredients, presentation and association, the potential purchaser requires the following pattern. This is the same for a kebab stall as it is a five-star restaurant. Set up expectation: desire, atmosphere, satisfaction. A kebab stall does this with lurid pictures of its wares with a clear price tag. This is what you get. A restaurant does this by telling stories. You choose your own adventure.

What does this mean for a five-star restaurant such as Ecco?

Ecco needs a story. An overall 'history' even if it is invented. Clients want meaning, authenticity and something to tell their friends. The interior décor must reflect this narrative. Designed by local architect Gianni di Napoli, the restaurant represents tomatoes/discovery/history, or whatever you think appropriate.

What is the chef's story? What drives him to create these culinary experiences? The staff must know all these tales and relate them as if for the first time.

Recommendations

In practical terms, once you have made decisions regarding the conclusions above, it is all about detail.

Study how the restaurant fits into its environment. If outside is noisy and chaotic, the restaurant should be an orderly haven. If outside is dull and uninteresting, the restaurant offers life, colour and beauty.

Test all your dishes for the most suitable presentation. Test, test, test. Heavy dessert bowls persuade the diner to feel fuller, light wine glasses suggest sophistication. Use what works best for your dishes – be prepared to change the concept with the season.

Pay attention to the cleaning chemicals used on tables and floor. The environment must be neutral in terms of scent. Fresh flowers are a mistake. Air conditioning should be someone's job. The air is the tablecloth of the room. It must be clean.

When planning the menu, give as much thought to the soundtrack as anything else. Think of your tasting menu as a symphony with different movements and select the correct music for each course. Atmospheric contemporary composers encourage diners to focus. Restricting yourself to classical limits your mind and their sensations.

Scent is a delicate and easily disturbed route of appreciation. Sorrel, thyme and watercress can be drowned by strong perfumes. On your website, along with the dress code, suggest diners wear nothing stronger than deodorant.

Second-guess your guests. Provide finger-bowls, handbag hooks, choices of table and suggestions based on their preferences.

Take as much information as you can when they reserve. Occasion, allergies, ages, special requests, languages spoken? Assign the appropriate waiting staff and let them know you were expecting them. Train employees how to describe unusual ingredients.

Tell stories. Ensure every waiter knows the provenance of the dish, why it's special, and the myth behind it. Make them more than consumers, they are the audience. Your job is to entertain all of their senses.

For your diner, this is a special experience. You make 50 *tagliatelle prosciutto e funghi* every night, but for your client, this is the first time. Make each meal incredible and each client the centre of the universe.

Stories, detail and constant maintenance of standards. This, and only this, will make Ecco the best restaurant in Napoli.

P. Bonardi, 29 Juni 2015

Chapter 14

Something woke Adrian with a start. He rolled onto his back to listen. Car horns, scooter engines and loud voices created the usual clamour in the street outside, but there was another fizzing tone. Tyres on wet streets. It was raining.

He slid his legs out of bed and opened the rococo curtains. Seal-grey clouds blocked the sun and threw an arrhythmic scatter of raindrops at the window. Streams had formed between street and pavement, carrying debris towards the drains. The citizens of Naples continued about their daily business with umbrellas or newspapers over their heads, shouting, cursing and laughing as usual. As he watched, the scene fluoresced as if someone had taken a flash photograph. A moment later, an enormous sequence of booms echoed across the city, like rocks rolling down a mountain.

Adrian wasn't scared of thunderstorms. Not any longer. As a child, he used to tremble and cry, cowering under the bedcovers. Even as a teenager, he'd been unable to hide his nervous reaction to the terrifying display of light and noise. Only when he met a wonderful Scottish keyboard player in Lanzarote had he learned to appreciate the majesty of a storm, curled up with someone he trusted, protected against the wrath of Nature.

A thought popped into his mind. He might not be afraid of Nature's fireworks but he was a fully grown man. He dressed in the nearest items of clothing to hand and hurried along to Luke's room. After knocking twice, he opened the door to see a compact bundle under the duvet.

"Luke? Are you awake?"

His blond head appeared, his expression unhappy but not yet tearful. "The thunder woke me up."

"Me too. Listen, it's still early, but what do you say to getting dressed and watching the storm from the roof garden? Over the Bay of Naples, the view will be spectacular. We could make ourselves some hot drinks and toast and drag a couple of blankets upstairs to keep us warm. You could even try and catch the lightning on your iPad. Imagine sending that to your mum!"

"OK." Luke hopped out of bed like a rabbit and started putting on his fleece over his pyjamas. "Are Granddad and Beatrice coming?"

"I think they'd prefer a lie-in. Let's leave them in peace and tell them all about it later. Do you want hot chocolate and honey toast?"

"Yes, please!" Another crack of thunder sounded across the city and Luke's eyes widened.

"Quick then, because we don't want to miss it. Put your warmest things on and I'll make our breakfast."

Twenty minutes later, each tucked under their blankets, Adrian and Luke sat side by side on the roof garden sofa. They consumed toast, coffee and hot chocolate between exclamations of ooh, aah and did-you-see-that? Adrian overdid the wow factor, determined to turn every moment of alarm into awe, even if he did gasp when the thunder exploded directly overhead like a gunshot. Luke soon matched his excitement and tried time and again to capture the lightning forks hitting the sea.

After some startlingly close booms and strikes, the storm receded south and the observers finished their breakfast, exhilarated by their shared experience. Adrian was just about to suggest more toast when Beatrice appeared at the top of the stairs, looking eager and ready for work.

"There you are! Have you been watching the storm?"

"Beatrice, it was amazing!" said Luke, his face shining. "We saw the whole thing! I took photos and videos of the lightning and I can show you, if you like?"

"I like. But now it's over, I want to sit in a warm kitchen and drink coffee while I relive the event vicariously. Come downstairs, Matthew is making porridge."

After Beatrice left for the restaurant, the menfolk took a unanimous decision. In view of the inclement weather, today was not the right day to visit Pompeii. They would save that for Sunday when their party would be completed by Will and Beatrice.

Matthew made a proposal. "All the tourists will want to get out of the rain but enjoy the city. So they'll either head to the museums or the subterranean systems. As we're all up early, why don't we head for *Galleria Borbonica* and see underground Naples. What do you say to exploring some tunnels, Small Fry?"

Luke thought about it. "Will it be very dark?"

"No, no, this is sort of like a museum but a bit more real. An architectural and physical record of the city's history. With plenty of lights. I think you'd like it."

"OK," said Luke and picked up his device to scroll through his lightning photographs once again.

Adrian smiled at Matthew. "I must say I'm relieved. If we had pressed on with our plan to visit the ruins, I'd have got soaked. Umbrellas and cameras are a tricky combination and there is no way on earth I would be seen dead in one of those awful rain ponchos. Why don't I clear up while you check the map? Luke, unless you plan to show your pyjamas to the whole of Naples, you might want to get changed."

Forty minutes later, they arrived at the entrance to The Bourbon Gallery, paid their entrance fee and met their guide, Davide. During the taxi ride across the city, Matthew had already explained why the tunnel had been built (an escape route for the French royals), its various uses across the centuries (car pound, air raid shelter, hospital) and the complexity of its waterway systems. Adrian began to wonder what on earth poor Davide might be able to add.

Prepared for a damp scramble through mouldy brickwork, Adrian was stunned by the scale of the subterranean network. Beautifully lit and well-maintained, the tunnels revealed disused water cisterns the size of cathedrals, intricate designs on the walls, fascinating artefacts such as 1940s vehicles impounded by the police and underground pools of an ancient aqueduct.

He wasn't the only one enthralled. The whole party hung on Davide's every word and Matthew asked interesting questions which led their guide to go deeper into the history of this remarkable feat of construction. The tour overran, precisely because of this particular dynamic. Davide returned the party to the entrance and accepted their thanks and tips, before turning to Matthew.

"You are very well informed, *signor*. You should see *Napoli Sotterranea* also. I think you will find much of interest. I would like to discuss further, but my next party is waiting. I wish you all an excellent stay in Naples."

Adrian stepped in and shook Davide's hand first, palming him a five-Euro note. Matthew should not have to do the tipping for all of them. Davide thanked him, saluted Matthew and winked at Luke before hurrying off for his next job.

"*Grazie mille!*" called Luke.

Davide looked over his shoulder with a surprised smile. "*Prego!*" he said, with a nod.

Matthew crouched down to address Luke. "You really did pay attention to my impromptu Italian lesson."

"Yes, I did. Maybe we should go somewhere so I can practise ordering a pizza."

Matthew laughed and looked up at Adrian. "I'd say a pizza and a glass of red should fortify us for the next set of tunnels. And if I'm not mistaken, the rain is letting up. Shall we?"

They walked along the narrow streets for at least five minutes, hunting for a pizzeria they liked the look of until the heavens opened once again.

"There's one up there!" yelled Adrian and led the charge. Luke kept pace with him, splashing through puddles and giggling. They reached the shelter of the awning and waited for Matthew to catch up. When he did, his hair was plastered to his face and he needed a minute to regain his breath before he could speak.

"Wet. Bathroom," he gasped and Adrian pushed open the door.

While Matthew went to dry himself off, a waitress showed Adrian and Luke to a table. She gave them menus and patted Luke's cheek. Adrian's laughter at Luke's startled expression died in his throat as he saw a familiar figure shaking an umbrella outside. The man with the beret stood under the awning and lit a cigarette.

Luke followed his gaze. "That's the man who was taking pictures of us."

"What? Where was he taking pictures?"

"When you were trying to get a taxi this morning. He took pictures of me and Granddad on his phone. And I saw him before when we were on that ferry. Do you know who he is?"

"No. I don't know. Although I've seen him a couple of times too. Yesterday, outside our apartment and also on the Isle of Capri. Listen, Luke, I don't think we should say anything to your grandfather about this. I really don't want to worry him."

"OK." Luke helped himself to a breadstick. "I won't tell Mum either. But maybe we should tell Beatrice."

"Yes," Adrian replied. "That's a very good idea. We should definitely tell Beatrice." He scanned the exterior, searching for their unsubtle tail. The man in the black beret had disappeared.

Preoccupied by the fact someone was following their small party, Adrian paid little attention to the tour of *Napoli Sotterranea*. Neither did he notice Matthew's reticence, absorbed as he was in terrifying imaginary scenarios. Someone kidnapping Luke and sending them body parts until they paid a ransom. Matthew shot by a hitman in a case of mistaken identity. Another religious obsessive hell-bent on punishing Adrian for his 'deviant' lifestyle. Again. Why couldn't people just leave them alone?

It was only when they emerged from the tunnels into weak spring sunshine that Adrian spotted his companion's wan pallor and unsteady hands.

"Matthew! Are you all right?"

The older man's lips were blue and his pupils dilated. "Feeling a bit off. Could we hail a taxi?"

"You don't look well at all. Let's get you to the hospital."

"No need, medication back at base camp. I know the drill."

The journey to their lodgings was twice as nerve-wracking as usual. Quite apart from the hair-raising wildness of the traffic, Matthew appeared to be seriously sick. Three times Adrian asked what was wrong and on getting a mere shake of the head in reply, he suggested a doctor or hospital. Matthew refused, saying he just wanted to get home to the apartment. Luke curled his arm around his grandfather's and leaned against him, in a touching gesture of reassurance.

The cab pulled up outside their building and Adrian thrust a bunch of Euros at the driver, before assisting Matthew through the front door. With one last glance over his shoulder for anyone wearing a beret, he shepherded his charges up the stairs.

Matthew made straight for his room and closed the door.

Luke and Adrian stood like spare parts in the hallway for several seconds until the front door opened and Beatrice Stubbs burst into the apartment, hot and breathless. Her fractious expression lifted at the sight of them and darkened the moment she saw their faces.

"What?" she demanded.

"Granddad's not very well," said Luke.

She dropped her bag and ran down the corridor to the master bedroom. Luke and Adrian took off their coats and shoes, and sat together on the sofa to wait.

"Adrian?" whispered Luke.

"Yes?"

"Should we wait a bit before telling Beatrice about that man? She's already got a lot to worry about."

Adrian forced a grin. "Very good idea. Let's keep this a secret from everyone else for the moment."

"OK." Luke turned an imaginary key on his lips. "Maybe we should start making dinner for everyone. When Granddad feels better, he'll probably be hungry. He might like some garlic bread."

"Between the two of us, we might be able to rustle up some pasta to go with it. Go and wash your hands, and let's get started." Adrian could hear tones of Tanya in his voice, which he considered a good thing.

Beatrice emerged over an hour later. Luke had made his garlic bread and gone to find his iPad, leaving Adrian to assemble the meal.

She came into the kitchen and sat down with a thump. "Chest pains. Could be any number of things so the bloody-minded old sod is going to a doctor tomorrow or I'll drag him there by his britches. He's prescribed himself aspirin. I ask you! Aspirin! This is precisely the age where he's susceptible to all manner of conditions. I would shout and rant at him for keeping this to himself but that would be the pot calling the metal black. Maybe I should take him to his GP when we get home. Dr Haring has all his records and could refer us if this really is something to worry about. Oh damn and hell blast, why is this happening now?"

Adrian looked up from the sauce he was stirring and shook his head.

"Who knows? Health doesn't wait till it's convenient for you to get sick. You know, it might be best to go home. He'll feel more comfortable with his own doctor and we can always do Naples another time." Adrian could feel her eyes on him as he chopped up some basil.

"He needs to see a doctor first. If it is his heart, there's no way I'm taking him on a plane. Anyway, I didn't mean you should leave. He's not your responsibility. You should explore the city, show Will the sights, and enjoy the freedom of not having an elderly gentleman and young child as your responsibility. Why else would you want to leave?"

It took several seconds for Adrian to take control of his temper and urge to blurt out the truth. He set the sauce to simmer and sat down at the kitchen table, facing a frankly stroppy Beatrice Stubbs. He poured them both a glass of Nero d'Avola and met her eyes.

"Right, you can shut up for a minute and listen. Not for a single second have I thought of Matthew and Luke as a responsibility. I gate-crashed this trip, remember? I am the freeloader here. I love every minute I spend with Luke and Matthew. They are great companions when it comes to enjoying new things. Luke because of his innocence, Matthew because of his experience. Plus, they both have enormous appetites. Today wasn't the first time I was concerned about Matthew's health, but I put that down to his getting older rather than a specific condition. If we decide to go, we all go. If we choose to stay, we all stay. All I care about is Matthew's well-being."

Bravo! Bravo! A virtuoso performance from the loyal friend. I almost believed it myself. What about Luke? What about your black beret shadow? Tell her! She should see the full picture. Don't be such a coward!

Apart from the noise of the street outside, the only sound in the apartment was Luke's high-pitched chatter as he Skyped with Tanya in the living room and the bubbling of Adrian's Puttanesca sauce.

"That is a very nice thing to say. Thank you. I would prefer Matthew to go home but at the same time, I want to finish this job. He refuses to leave without me, so I have no choice but to give up this fallacy of private detection as a bad idea. I must see if he's well enough to travel and take him home. Agusto and Isabella will just have to work something out themselves. It's just, I really thought I was onto something. Given a bit more time ... oh what does it matter?" She swilled her wine around her glass.

Her unruly hair, morose expression and familiar frown sparked a surge of warmth in Adrian. He loved this awkward, intractable female and recognised several of her characteristics in himself. She needed validation and would butt her stubborn old head against any obstacle until she got it.

He reached across the table and clasped her hand. "Why don't I take Matthew to a doctor here and you go back to the job? Will arrives tomorrow evening, which will be a relief for all of us. Depending on the doctor's opinion and your progress on the case, we could make a family decision over dinner. I'll cook."

Her hand squeezed his. "If you wouldn't mind, then yes please. That's a very kind thought and he'll be much more likely to accept it coming from you."

"That's settled, then. What do you think, spaghetti or tagliatelle with this sauce?"

"Tagliatelle. I always make a dreadful mess with spaghetti. May I make a request for tomorrow's dinner? Could we have something plain and simple? I feel in need of traditional British stodge."

Adrian grinned. "Beans on toast?"

Beatrice drained her wine glass and grinned back. "Fish and chips?"

"Why not?" He got up to supervise the sauce. He stirred black olives into the condensed tomato, chilli, caper and anchovy blend. In his mind, each represented a beret.

Chapter 15

That Englishman was sick. Nobody healthy has skin that colour. Pietro waited for a few minutes after the three went into the building, deciding if this was worth calling the boss. What would he say? 'The kid is still alive, but the old guy is a funny shade of grey.' No. His task was to keep an eye on the kid. The rest of them were not his problem. He stepped further back up the alley, watching where he put his feet, and once concealed by the shadows, he lit a cigarette.

The air was damp and cool after the torrential rains of the morning. He would finish this cigarette, make sure the young dandy didn't come out again, then call it a day and head for the bar. The sedan arrived. He knew that car well, after watching it bring the British chef back from Ecco. The woman got out, said something in English and shut the door. The driver waited until she had gone indoors. After a couple of minutes, the sedan purred along the street, feeble sunlight reflecting from its windows so the driver was nothing more than a silhouette. Pietro made up his mind. If all the English were safely inside, his work was done for the day. Time for a beer.

He dropped the cigarette into a puddle and smelt something foul. He checked his shoes. Both muddy and wet but no dog mess. A door opened between him and the street and he flattened himself against the wall. A young man slammed the door behind him, still talking on his phone.

Pietro caught a few words although the Italian was heavily accented Sicilian with a confusing amount of slang. "They are all inside now ... yeah, the detective just got back from the restaurant ... No, no chance. She has a driver who waits till she goes into the building ... What? ... I guess I could try ... OK, see you at the boat."

Coincidence? He would have assumed so but for the words 'restaurant' and 'detective'. Was someone else watching? He followed the young man in the denim jacket as he paced along the street, intent on his phone. Pietro crossed over three times, but the guy didn't look behind once. He walked in a straight line, directly to the harbour. At the gates to the port, he stopped, looking around, bouncing with impatience. Pietro bought a slice of pizza and a beer from a street stall, although he wasn't hungry, and turned his back on the other punters. A Vespa buzzed down the street, the guy in the denim jacket got on and to Pietro's surprise, they swiped their way through the harbour gates and rode along the cobbles towards the private marina, where expensive yachts gleamed in the weak sunshine.

A security guard patrolled the barrier to the marina and Pietro forgot all about his pizza, intent on the story playing out below. The Vespa slowed and a few words were exchanged. A burst of laughter from the guard and the Vespa was permitted access. Pietro watched and counted. Seven boats in, they parked the moped and walked up the access ramp to a small yacht. He couldn't see the name of the boat from his position. He drank his beer and left. Tomorrow, he would bring binoculars.

Chapter 16

Ettore was waiting at the kerb, as usual, a strange scowl on his face as he scanned the neighbourhood. His disapproving expression smoothed into a welcoming smile as Beatrice clattered out of the apartment building.

"*Buongiorno*, Beatrice! Ready for work?"

"*Buongiorno*, Ettore. Not really, but I have no choice. How are you today?"

"I am very happy, Beatrice, and I will tell you why. Today is a special day for my family. Two of my daughters are part of the Santa Maria festival. It is a great honour. My wife and I made the hairdressing before they left for school."

Beatrice threw her bag into the back seat and got in beside Ettore. Despite the terrifying nature of Neapolitan traffic, she was much more at ease beside her driver than aloof and distant in the rear. Nevertheless, she made sure to belt herself in. "OK, I'm *pronto*! What do you mean by the hairdressing?"

Ettore wound down his window to hurl abuse at a man weaving his way through the traffic. The man retorted with a jab of the finger. After both had finished insulting each other's mothers, Ettore drove on.

"*Pronta*. You are a female. This is a special occasion for my beautiful girls. The costumes are ready for tomorrow, but my wife must practise the hair. Beatrice, it is ..." He shook his head, kissed his fingers and met her eyes. "*Bellissima*! Even better, the girls can wear their hair like this all day. Elegant and practical. I do this for them since they are very small. I am expert."

As they drove onto the main street, Beatrice watched a dog tear open a rubbish bag, scattering papers and pizza crusts all over the pavement. "How did they get to be part of the festival?" she asked Ettore, with as much interest in the answer as the contents of the bin bag.

"Every year, we ask the organisers. Always no, too young. This year, they are thirteen and fourteen. They say yes! My wife and my sister make costumes for months and the girls exercise the singing. And the make-up. Today, I help with the hair. Beatrice?"

She dragged her gaze from the morning sea to Ettore's enquiring expression, his forehead echoing the ripples on the shore. "Yes?"

"You want me to do *your* hair?"

Ettore had missed his vocation. His gentle hands, deft combing and nimble fingers combined with non-stop monologue on everything from climate change to film festivals soothed Beatrice more than any massage. Outside Ecco, she sat in the passenger seat and allowed him to work his magic. In less than five minutes, he had tamed her unruly hair into a sleek and classy French plait. She flipped down the sun visor to admire herself in the mirror. It was neat and elegant and perfect for popping under a chef's hairnet.

She thanked him profusely and pressed ten Euros into his hand. "For your daughters!" she insisted and overcame his protestations.

He gave a gracious bow and she got out of the car. He beeped the horn in farewell and she trotted away to the restaurant, waving goodbye.

As soon as she opened the kitchen door, she saw Suhail and

caught her breath. The man had a bandage around his lower jaw and neck. A fight? A work-related accident? Instinctively, she looked at his hands but he had already donned the blue plastic gloves they all wore when preparing food.

Isabella caught her arm and pulled her into the office before Beatrice could ask any questions. She closed the door and slumped into a chair, her blue hair falling over her face.

"Isabella, what's happened?"

The younger woman looked up, her mouth a downward arc. "Suhail was attacked last night on his way home. This is how it starts. They make life difficult for you, and offer you a chance to make the harassment stop. They 'protect' you from the violence they are paying for, IF and only if, you do them a favour. If you refuse, you end up like Rami."

"Is Suhail badly hurt?"

"They cut him. Just a surface cut across his throat to show what could happen next time. But he fought back and got slashed across the chin as well. He wanted to come to work, even after spending half the night waiting to be treated at the hospital. No matter what I say, he shuts his mouth and tells me nothing, but he might talk to you. What happened to him is relevant to your case. Agusto and I agree he must go home after the lunch shift. Ettore can drive you to your apartment then take him safely back to his place. He needs to rest as Easter is going to be extra busy for all of us."

Beatrice winced at the thought of Suhail's injuries and then let out an enormous sigh at the concept of 'extra busy'. She simply couldn't work any faster and with Suhail under the weather, he would be unable to pick up her slack.

"What about this evening's service? Do you want me to cover that?" she asked, praying Isabella would refuse.

A half smile spread across Isabella's face. "Thank you, but that's not necessary. No offence, Beatrice, but we have a reputation. Agusto will take over desserts tonight, with Chantal's assistance. What I want you to do is talk to Suhail. He knows you're a detective. You must persuade him to tell you what happened last night and whether he knows who they are working for."

"I'll do my best."

"Thank you. Oh, and your hair looks nice. Adrian did a good job." Isabella flashed her smile and picked up the phone before Beatrice could contradict her.

Holy Thursday was hellish. As everyone had predicted, the restaurant was frantically busy. But the one advantage of the traditional nature of the religious festival was that everyone wanted to eat the same thing. *A Fellata* for starter, which seemed to be an ornately arranged plate of meat and cheeses to Beatrice's untrained eye. Next course was mussel soup, which Agusto presided over himself, followed by Ecco's take on cannelloni – a Jenga-style construction of stuffed tubes around a pyramid of tomato sauce. The main course was roasted kid with rosemary potatoes, filling the kitchen with a blissful aroma. Suhail and Beatrice had three jobs to do until dessert orders came in. Prepare the *pastiera*, the cake that would be the centrepiece of next week's Easter menu. Bake individual *Colombe*, the dove-shaped little cakes that had their own unique tins. And make the *cassata*, a liqueur-soaked marzipan, sponge, chocolate and ricotta confection, decorated with candied fruit and nuts.

It had become obvious during the last few days that Beatrice's culinary skills, such as they were, tended more towards the beating, whisking, folding and mixing elements of kitchen techniques. The fine details of decoration and plating were best left to Suhail, whose delicate fingers wielded tweezers and piping bags with surgical grace.

The one thing she had learned was the precise arrangement and timing of her *affogato*. Two dinky scoops of brown bread ice-cream tilted diagonally against a honey pourer in a cocktail glass, one hot, fresh *ristretto* and a brandy snap on the saucer either side of the glass and then bellow 'Service' at the top of her lungs so someone would come and take the thing away to the service counter for inspection by the chef. If only the damn dessert wasn't quite so popular.

She must have made at least fifty of the things by three o'clock and Agusto had only sent two back for sloppy presentation. All the cakes were baked and decorated and their workstation looked relatively clean in comparison to the previous two days. Suhail tried to send her away while he cleared up but Beatrice refused.

"The more hands on deck, the sooner we can leave. I understand we're taking the same car."

Suhail gave a sad nod and began cleaning the surfaces. Instinct told Beatrice now was not the time to ask questions. Then again, the car wouldn't be ideal either. He was unlikely to open up in front of a driver, no matter how amiable Ettore could be. Perhaps if she invited him for a cool drink, hinting that it was Isabella's suggestion he should talk to him? She could do no more than try.

Beatrice made her proposal as they left the restaurant. Suhail accepted the invitation but didn't look too happy about it. She asked Ettore to wait for half an hour and so it was that Beatrice and Suhail sat on the roof terrace with a glass of lemonade and gazed out at the scenery.

"I don't want to pressure you, please understand that. But if your attack last night was anything to do with the death of your friend or the espionage at the restaurant, it would help me a lot to form the bigger picture."

Suhail looked at her for a second and turned his eyes back to the colourful rooftops of the city. He sipped at his lemonade and the pain of swallowing was visible on his face. "He wasn't my friend."

"Oh. I assumed ..." She stopped. "Sorry. Making assumptions is a terrible habit and in this case, unforgiveable. Let me start at the beginning."

"It's OK. I know what you want to ask me. Yes, we both come from Damascus in Syria. No, we were not related. Neither of us was a refugee; we both came to Europe with a work permit. We knew each other, yes, because we went to the same hospitality college in Milan. That is why I can speak Italian and English. Rami got a job in Napoli and encouraged me to apply. I was working as a pastry chef in Bergamo and wanted to see more of Italy. Agusto gave me a chance and liked what I could do. He employed me. That was one and half years ago. Rami helped me find lodgings and at first, we spent a lot of time together."

He took another drink and squeezed his eyes shut as he swallowed.

"Are you in much pain? Would you like a painkiller?" Beatrice asked.

He held up a palm in refusal. "Thank you, no. Taking pharmaceutical products is against my beliefs. After a few months, Rami's other 'activities' became impossible to ignore. Chefs at Ecco are relatively well paid, yes, but Rami had a luxury apartment in a palazzo, bought an expensive motorcycle and he wore designer clothes. Both of us have families still in Syria and we often discussed how to send money home. How is it I live in a one-bedroom apartment in a cheap area and his lifestyle is so glamorous?"

"He had another source of income?" said Beatrice, her mind scurrying. But if Rami had been the one to sell recipes to some shady buyers, why would they kill their cash cow?

"Maybe more than one source?" Suhail shrugged, glancing at her sideways.

Beatrice examined that idea and found it had potential. She looked at Suhail in the hope he would elaborate.

He stood up. "I should go. The driver is waiting and I am

tired."

"Of course, I completely understand. I'll walk you out. Please can I ask one more thing?"

He sighed and his hangdog expression drooped lower as he pulled on his jacket.

"Last night. Do you have any idea who it was that attacked you? Or who they might be working for?"

"No, I don't know who they are. But I know their methods. They frighten me three, four times and then take off the masks. They won't stop until I do what they want. Isabella is kind to offer me a ride home, but these people know where I live. I cannot hide."

From below, a male voice called out. "Is there a Beatrice Stubbs in the house?"

"Up here!" she shouted and got to her feet.

It was such a fillip to see Will, his strong and capable persona an instant reassurance. Clearly, his arrival had a similar effect on the rest of the group. Adrian was wreathed in smiles, Matthew appeared relaxed and comfortable and Luke capered around trying to show him the delights of the terrace. Beatrice remembered her manners.

"Suhail, let me introduce you. This is Matthew, my partner. These are my friends, Adrian and his husband Will. And last but not least, this is Luke, Matthew's grandson. Everyone, this is Suhail, who works with me at the restaurant."

Suhail shook hands with everyone, his face sombre until he got to Luke. "Hello, Luke. It is a pleasure. How old are you?"

"Six years old and I can order my dinner in Italian."

"That's very impressive," Suhail replied, his face softening into a rare smile. "Thank you for the drink, Beatrice, I will leave you now. Goodbye, everyone, and have a nice holiday."

The sound of farewells echoing behind them, Beatrice walked her visitor down two flights of stairs. She opened the front door and watched him get into Ettore's car, more than a little worried for his welfare. The vehicle drove away and Beatrice trudged back up, wondering if her whole mission at the restaurant was a case of closing the stable door after the mole had bolted.

After a lively chat on the terrace, Beatrice suggested everyone freshen up before dinner. Not least because she wanted to buttonhole Matthew.

She closed their bedroom door and turned to face him, placing her hands on her hips. "Did you see a doctor?" she demanded.

"Yes, I did. She can't find anything wrong but suggests I should avoid over-exertion and certainly not subject myself to any stress. I toyed with the idea of asking her, 'Have you tried living with Beatrice Stubbs?' but thought better of it. The upshot is, I intend to spend the rest of our time here taking it easy. I still want to see the sights, but perhaps one excursion a day will suffice. Now that Will has joined us with an extra pair of sensible hands, I won't feel bad about excusing myself and stretching out on the sofa, reading books and eating olives. Talking of which, how was your day?"

Beatrice kissed his cheek. "It's a relief to hear you're approaching this with such a mature attitude. If it's all the same to you, I'd rather keep you around for a bit longer. My day was bloody knackering, if you must know. I was actually planning a nap after Suhail had gone. I'm also wondering if this whole situation is more complex than it first appears. I need to talk to Isabella and Agusto tomorrow, if at all possible."

Matthew sat down on the bed, kicking off his shoes. "Why wouldn't it be possible? They are your clients."

"Yes, and under normal circumstances, I'd insist on a meeting. The thing is, Easter Friday is such an epic event here, the restaurant will be swamped and attention spans short. What do you intend to do tomorrow?"

"We considered the Sorrento or Procida Easter parades. My concern is that the first has hooded, robed figures singing Gregorian chants and the latter uses effigies of Christ's Via Cruci, some rather graphic. I'm not sure either will be conducive to a good night's sleep for Luke. Therefore our plan is to stay in the city and follow the local processions along the streets, not straying too far from home."

Beatrice wrapped her arms around him and pressed her cheek to his chest. "I am so glad to hear it's nothing serious. I do love you, you know."

He kissed the top of her head. "Me too, on both counts. Will's arrival vastly reassures me and there is one more bright spot. I spoke to Tanya this afternoon. She and Gabriel are taking excellent care of our animals. I confess that was an added worry."

"You're an old softie, Professor Bailey. Right, I'm going to get in the shower. I still pong of mussel soup."

"Ah, that's what it is! I thought you whiffed of fish. Go ahead, Old Thing, I plan to sit here quietly and peruse *The Times*."

At eight o'clock, the party convened for cocktails on the roof terrace. Adrian and Will had prepared a thick mulligatawny soup for dinner and Beatrice was suffused with a sense of relief. If she could just tie up the job within a couple of days, she would be able to enjoy her favourite people in a beautiful location. Best of all, she had a fellow copper, DS William Quinn, with whom to share ideas. She raised her gin and tonic. "Cheers, everyone, I'm so pleased we're all together again!"

"Cheers, Beatrice!" The clinking of glasses and familiar smiles warmed her.

Easter would start tomorrow and although she had yet to get through the next two days, she had the whole of Sunday and Monday free to spend with her menfolk. Things could only get better.

Chapter 17

Interesting. Another man had arrived. This should certainly be reported to the boss. What if they now split up? He answered his own question. Follow the kid, obviously, those were his orders.

He waited in the alley for another few minutes, looking up at the lights of the apartment and the shadows of movement within. There was no sign of the guy in the denim jacket this time. Just as he was beginning to think he was wasting his time, a door opened. The same youngster as last time emerged except now he wasn't on his phone. Pietro waited a full minute after he had exited the alley and then headed towards the port.

He kept his distance and stayed on the opposite side of the street, with the guy in his peripheral vision. Once at the port entrance, Pietro kept walking until he overlooked the private marina. He got out his binoculars and scoured the horizon, making a long sweep from right to left. At first he thought the young man had gone, but when the Vespa approached, he saw him emerge from behind an advertising billboard. As before, the guy jumped on as a passenger and the rider swiped them into the port. The Vespa buzzed its way down to the marina, Pietro's binoculars following their progress.

The guard lifted the barrier and the rider saluted him. Pietro moved his focus ahead, counting the boats till he found number seven. It was a relatively small yacht, around 25 metres long, with the name *Naiade* painted in gold on its navy hull. The Vespa came to a halt right in front of the gangway leading onto the deck. The two riders went aboard. A blonde woman, her right hand shielding her eyes from the sun, was waiting at the top to meet them. She shook hands with each of them and they retreated inside.

Pietro put down the binoculars and lit a cigarette. He wandered back in the direction of the pizza stall and bought a Peroni. The old man behind the counter indicated the binoculars and asked if he'd been birdwatching.

Pietro replied that he'd been admiring the yachts. "If I had a million, that's what I would buy. When you get sick of a place, you can just go somewhere new. That's my idea of freedom."

"You'd need more than a million," said the man, shaking his grey head. "Those boats are a money pit and I should know. My youngest son used to crew on one of the charters. One of the respectable ones, mind you. Damned expensive things to run."

Pietro swigged at his bottle and swallowed. "One of the respectable ones? What do you mean?"

The old man used one finger to pull down an eyelid, a gesture to signify he wasn't fooled. "They look the part, all shiny and glamorous, but most of this lot are involved in shady stuff, like drugs, prostitution, arms dealing. The security they've got down there? It should be the other way around. Keep them away from us, that's what I say. The stories my son used to tell ..."

Pietro's attention was drawn by the Vespa emerging from the marina and leaving the port. Once they got outside, the guy he had followed jumped off the bike and with a clasped forearm handshake, said goodbye to his partner. Pietro finished his beer and wished the old guy a nice evening.

"So you don't want any of my pizza tonight?" asked the man. "You seemed to like it yesterday."

Pietro stared at the man. Was he that memorable?

He shook his head and made a decision not to come back to

this joint. He didn't like people being overfamiliar and anyway, he had to report to the boss.

Chapter 18

The driver of the Fiat Cinquecento had obviously checked nothing was coming in the opposite direction when he overtook the bus. Unfortunately, he didn't see the Piaggio scooter coming up behind him on his left. He pulled out sharply, knocking the scooter over and sending both riders crashing into the street.

Ettore and Beatrice saw the whole thing as their vehicle was directly behind the Fiat. Ettore was out of the car instantly, rushing to the aid of the young couple lying on the tarmac. His jacket flapped back for a second as he reached in his pocket for a handkerchief and Beatrice noticed the holster and handgun. She didn't have time to question why a driver needed a gun as she hurried to offer assistance. After a great deal of shouting, tears and gesticulation, it was established that the couple on the Piaggio had sustained cuts and grazes, but thanks to their helmets, no serious damage had been done. Ettore and Beatrice left them to exchange insurance details and insults and continued on their journey to Ecco, which gave nowhere near enough time for all of Ettore's opinions on the standard of driving by young people these days.

When Beatrice eventually arrived, Agusto was ranting in Italian, slamming his palm on the stainless steel worktops and wagging his finger at the ragged semi-circle of chefs around him. Through the window in the swing doors, Beatrice could see

Isabella pacing the restaurant, having a heated conversation on her mobile. Beatrice closed the door behind her and turned to see all eyes focused in her direction.

Chantal, whose eyes were red and tearful, pointed at Beatrice and asked Agusto an aggressive question. The only words she could make out in the stream of impassioned Italian were '*lei*' and '*ricetta*' – 'she' and 'recipe'. Beside her, Suhail was shaking his head, his expression more sorrowful than ever.

"NO!" yelled Agusto, making everyone freeze. "*Non è possibile!*" He switched to English but the volume and tone remained at thermonuclear. "It cannot be Beatrice! Don't ask me why I know, but believe me, I KNOW! Someone in this kitchen is responsible and when I find out whoever it is, they will be very, VERY sorry! Now get to work!" He stormed through the swing doors into the restaurant, leaving the kitchen team looking shaken and miserable.

Marcello was kind enough to bring her up to speed. "My cousin ate at *Ristorante della Nonna* last night. They have a new dessert on the menu: *Affogato di Colazione*. Your speciality. Someone has stolen our recipe."

Beatrice stared at him. "That's not possible. Only Agusto, Suhail and I know how to make that."

Marcello shrugged and gave a sideways glance at Chantal. She broke into a volley of Italian of which Beatrice understood none of the words but all of the tone.

Beatrice held up a hand. "No, it wasn't Chantal. She helped us with service but not the recipe. It definitely wasn't her, it wasn't Suhail and it obviously wasn't Agusto. You have every reason to suspect me but I promise on everything I hold dear, I did not give away any of our secrets."

Agusto's brother Gennaio gave a deep sigh. "People come here all the time to copy our food. The dessert is popular, why not try to do something similar? A good chef can eat a dish, comprehend the contents and replicate it. I will talk to Agusto.

He must not blame our staff. The only way we stay ahead of the competition is to innovate. He needs to invent a new dessert. Today, we must cook. *Andiamo!*" He clapped his hands and everyone moved off to their respective stations.

As Beatrice crossed the room, she patted Chantal's shoulder. The girl gave her a watery smile and squeezed her hand.

Suhail was peeling clementines, a clean bandage around his neck. He didn't look up but said, "Thank you."

Beatrice replied in Italian, "*Prego.*" She pulled a plastic bag of dough from the fridge and eased it into a piping bag. So intent was she on her task that Suhail's voice startled her. He wasn't normally one for conversation.

"The young man I met yesterday, at your apartment. You said he is your partner's grandson."

"That's right. Matthew has two daughters from a previous marriage. The youngest, Tanya, is Luke's mother. He's a very sweet little boy."

"Yes, he is. If I understand correctly, your friends are homosexuals, yes?"

Beatrice's radar twitched and her defences rose. "That's right. They got married at Christmas. It was a beautiful ceremony. Luke was the ring-bearer."

They worked in silence for several minutes, Beatrice filling cake moulds and Suhail picking pith from golden pieces of fruit.

"His mother is not concerned about the little boy? Do you think it is a good thing for him to spend time with such people?"

"His mother is certainly concerned about him. This is his first holiday without her. But when she learned Will and Adrian would be joining us, she was relieved. Luke adores them both. Who wouldn't want their child to spend time with such role models? Kind, smart, interesting, responsible and fun to have around, I think they are an excellent influence. Would you like to check these cakes before I put them in the oven?"

That put an end to that conversation.

Friday lunchtime was an absolute misery. Among the kitchen staff, latent suspicion and hostility towards each other made cooperation complicated, everyone finding fault with everyone else. Agusto, in the foulest temper, sent back dish after dish, refusing to accept anything less than perfection. The waiting staff, who came under rising pressure from impatient diners as delays grew longer, shouted shriller and more irritable demands. The hours wore on. Beatrice and Suhail sent out one dove-shaped cake after another with clementine cream and angelica jelly spots until Beatrice knew she would relive the process in her sleep.

They made no *affogati* whatsoever. Agusto instructed staff to tell clients it was no longer on the menu. Over Easter, only traditional desserts. A new signature *dolce* from the *inglese* would appear on Tuesday. Beatrice hoped she would not be called upon for inspiration. The only other pudding in her repertoire was jam roly-poly with custard. She'd like to see Ecco's five-star version of that.

In a browbeaten silence, the kitchen crew cleared up the leftover food, storing what could be used and binning the remainder. Hobs polished, surfaces sanitised, floors mopped, the Hieronymus Bosch scenes of an hour ago were nothing more than unpleasant memories. The swing doors opened and Isabella called to them all.

"Agusto wants to speak with you. *Tutti!*"

They threw their kitchen whites into the laundry basket and made their way into the dining room. Agusto stood beside the bar, pouring Prosecco into a dozen glasses, laughing with Gennaio. In what had recently been a packed restaurant, only one family remained at table and they were evidently friends of Isabella's.

The team stood awkwardly outside the swing doors, waiting for instructions. For the first time, Beatrice saw a face she didn't recognise. A young African man with a pleasant face was dressed in a black tunic with the typical black and white headgear of the kitchen. She was convinced he had not appeared on the list of kitchen staff.

Agusto waved them closer. "Come! We drink a toast to Easter and to the best team in Napoli!"

Isabella and Gennaio distributed glasses of fizz while Agusto continued his speech. Suhail murmured in Isabella's ear and she summoned a waitress with a bottle of sparkling water.

"In every family, there is a balance. Me? I am fire. Sometimes the sparks, sometimes the ashes. My brother Gennaio? He is the earth. He speaks good sense and he tells me there is no spy in my kitchen. It could be any one of the diners who tries to repeat a dish. My team are loyal, hard-working and the best in the city! I want to thank you, all of you, for managing a stressful day and delivering a dining experience to make me proud. You are Ecco! Thank you all and *saluti!*"

Echoes of his final word rumbled around the room, the sense of resentment not entirely quashed. *Fire and earth is all very well,* thought Beatrice, *but Prosecco may not be enough to soothe troubled waters.*

Obviously of the same mind, Isabella got to her feet, her electric blue hair shining like a petrol spill in the afternoon sun. "These last months are very hard for us all. Questions of trust, safety and reputation affect everyone. Here at Ecco, we are family. An international, diverse, multi-talented family. There is no room for doubt. Someone is trying to damage this family and we will not survive unless we unite. Agusto and I make a promise here and now: we trust every single one of our employees. As Gennaio says, we must leave the competition behind. We innovate! We create! As fast as they steal our ideas, we create new ones. Ecco leads the way! *Saluti!*"

Responses to her toast were considerably warmer and smiles crept over some of less sullen faces.

"New ideas!" said Agusto, brandishing his glass like an Olympic flame. "We need new ideas! Tomorrow, we offer the normal menu and then we close for Easter weekend. Spend the time with your families. Relax. Feed your imaginations! On Tuesday morning, I want every one of you to bring me an idea for a top-class Ecco dish. I don't care if you are the fish expert, Marcello, think of an amazing salad or a completely different kind of soup. Chantal, you understand vegetables. Suggest a *secondo piatto* without meat! Why not? Suhail, think about something exciting we can do with pasta. Something with a Middle-Eastern twist, huh? All these dishes need a story. Personal, local, global, I don't mind. Bring me new ideas and I will work with them all. We are not only a team, but the winning team!"

Everyone found a space to put down their glasses and applauded Agusto's rallying call. Beatrice could see by the light in their eyes it was genuine. Chatter broke out in smaller groups and Beatrice caught Isabella's eye with a supportive smile.

Isabella beckoned her, and the two women sat at a table for two near the front door. They clinked glasses.

"My husband. Drives everyone crazy then makes them all love him again."

"He does inspire devotion. I shall be worrying all weekend about how to create a brand new bowl of brilliance to satisfy his standards."

A mobile phone trilled somewhere behind Beatrice, playing the James Bond theme.

Isabella lifted her glass to the light, admiring the bubbles. "If you could make this in edible form, that would satisfy me. You don't need to worry, Agusto doesn't expect anything from you. The role you are playing is much more important."

"I'm not finding it easy to observe the staff but I do think I'm making progress. By the way, the young black man over there? Why haven't I seen him before?"

"Benoît? He does the washing-up in the back room. He's a sweet kid but can only speak French so most of our communication is like this." She waved her hands about. "He comes from Cabo Verde and the only person who speaks French is Bruno which means that ..." She broke off, her eyebrows drawn together in concern.

All round the room, conversations withered into silence as Gennaio's urgent tone caught everyone's attention. He barked questions into his phone, his face pale.

Frustrated at her lack of comprehension, Beatrice scanned her colleagues' expressions for some kind of clue. Every employee displayed wide-eyed concern, pity or even fear. Whatever the person on the other end of the conversation was saying, it was not good news.

Gennaio grabbed his jacket and ran out of the front door, Agusto on his heels. Isabella caught her husband's sleeve and a rapid conversation ensued. She released him and sank back into her chair, her eyes fixed on the figures of the two brothers disappearing around the corner.

"What happened?" asked Beatrice in a low voice.

"Gennaio's warehouse is on fire."

"Oh my God! Is anyone inside?"

"No. On Easter Friday, almost no one is working. The problem is that Gennaio is our main supplier, so most of our produce is stored there. Next week could be a disaster. We can devise and imagine a million exciting ideas but what if there are no ingredients? Thousands of Euros' worth of goods sit in that place. What is going on? Why is this happening to us?" She covered her face with her hands and wept silently.

Beatrice noticed the bitten fingernails and dark roots of her hair. Aware of people filing out through the kitchen, she stood up, came round the table and gave Isabella a hug.

She held her for several seconds until the heaving shoulders stilled. The restaurant was completely empty save for the two of them. For no apparent reason, the hairs on Beatrice's neck rose. With a reassuring pat, she left Isabella's side and double locked the entrance to the restaurant. She shoved open the swing doors to the kitchen and listened.

Nothing. She paced quietly around the room, seeking out this hitherto unknown 'back room'. No more than a cubby-hole, with two sinks, four bins and an industrial-sized dishwasher, it must be incredibly hot and steamy to work in. Now it was empty and quiet. So what was bugging her?

Tutting at her own paranoia, she nevertheless picked up a knife-sharpener the size of a poker and opened the back door as cautiously as she could. The courtyard was empty, devoid of smokers but a movement attracted her attention in the garage. A hooded man was scraping a key along the paintwork of Agusto's beloved Ferrari.

She roared with outrage and pelted across the yard towards him. The man took off in the direction of the street, leaving Beatrice outpaced. Furious, she hurled the knife-sharpener at his fast disappearing back, surprising herself as it hit its target. The blow knocked him off balance and he stumbled sideways, falling onto his hip, but recovered himself and in one fluid movement, got to his feet and continued running into the next alleyway.

Beatrice gasped for breath, bent over with her hands on her knees. She was far too old for this sort of thing.

Once the police had taken statements, Beatrice was allowed to go. Gennaio and Agusto were still at the docks when the evening shift arrived for work. Maître d'hôtel Alessandro assured Beatrice he would take care of Isabella.

"Please, don't worry. I will make sure she is fine. Did you read my paper?"

"Yes, I did. To be honest, I am amazed how much thought goes into it all. I have a lot to learn. One thing I spotted, the author shares your name. Is it you, under an alias?"

His expression was wary. "The paper was written by my brother. I am only the translator. He used to be a professor at the university and he has a brilliant mind. Everything Ecco is today came from his work."

"I can see that. Extraordinary thinking. He doesn't lecture at the university anymore?" she asked, with a feeling she might be on sensitive ground.

Alessandro's face closed down. "No. He left. Agusto employed him here for a while, but it didn't work out. My brother is meant for greater things. Would you like me to call a taxi for you? You must be tired."

"Thank you, but I think my car is outside."

Sure enough, when she went into the street with them, Ettore was still waiting.

She deflected any questions about the police presence by saying it was a restaurant matter and asking about his daughters' Easter parade. That tactic got her all the way home without having to do anything more than smile and nod.

At the apartment, her first priority was Matthew. He seemed in excellent spirits, doing something on the computer with Luke.

"Old Thing! You're awfully late. Is all well at Ecco?"

She dumped her bag and came to kiss him. "No, all is not well. Hello, Luke!"

"Hello, Beatrice, do you want to learn how to download pictures and make a slideshow? I'm teaching Granddad."

"Thank you but I need a shower right now. Have you two had a nice day?"

Matthew looked up at her, concern in his eyes. "We certainly did and can tell you all about it over dinner. Just wondering if you're all right."

"Dog tired and beginning to wonder if this case is far too gnarly and deep-rooted for one ageing crone to tackle. Where are the boys?"

"Hiking up a volcano. Luke and I are cooking tonight. How does lasagne sound to you?"

"Perfect. I've had nothing since breakfast apart from a glass of Prosecco and feel positively squiffy. Back in a minute. Matthew, are you really feeling well?"

"Never better. Although I am a bit peckish. Small Fry, do you think we can put this on pause then go and start dinner?"

Beatrice smiled to herself as she walked down the corridor to their room, listening to Luke explaining the difference between Pause, Save and Log Out to his troglodyte grandfather.

After a welcome dinner with far too much bread but no dessert, Beatrice tucked Luke into bed and kissed him goodnight. Then she returned to the dining room to explain to the men in her life what had happened that day and how she planned to tackle the problem.

"The only way of knowing if someone actually stole our recipe or made an approximate copy is to go there and taste it myself. In order to do that, I need to get a table at Ristorante della Nonna tomorrow night. It's fully booked, I already checked. So I need someone to call the place and tip them off that a top critic is in town and looking for a last-minute table. Adrian, might that be your forte?"

Matthew, Will and Beatrice all burst into laughter at Adrian's hand-over-mouth, hand-on-heart Oscar winner expression of delight.

"It most certainly is! I would be honoured. Are we all going or just you?"

"See if you can get a table for one or at most two. Any more is pushing it. Meanwhile, you can take Luke to Ecco."

Now it was Will's turn to gush. "You can get us in there? Wow!"

"Of course I can, I'm the bloody pastry chef. But you're not going on a jolly. This is reconnaissance. I will give you detailed instructions as to what to order and how to evaluate everything on your plate. That's not to say you won't have a fabulous dining experience, just one that is highly analytical. Matthew, if Adrian can blag us a table for two, you have no instructions whatsoever. I want you to go into this blind. What you must do is give me full and comprehensive feedback on everything you eat."

Matthew took a sip of coffee. "I daresay I can manage that. Will we have the usual driver?"

"No." Beatrice folded her arms. "This is a private mission. One Isabella and Agusto know nothing about."

Chapter 19

The following morning, Adrian practised his speech in the mirror until he'd got completely into character. Only then did he pick up the phone. Someone answered after the first ring.

"*Ristorante della Nonna, pronto?*"

"Ah, *buongiorno*. Can I speak English?"

"It certainly sounds like it to me, but I don't have much to go on."

Adrian stopped, wrong-footed by the woman's caustic response and the plummy British accent. He instantly dropped the transatlantic twang and spoke in a clipped Home Counties voice. "I'm sorry; I meant *may* I speak English. My name is Adrian Harvey and I'm personal assistant to Mr Matthew Bailey. I'm calling to see if you might have a table for two for dinner this evening."

Her response was immediate. "Afraid not, we're fully booked tonight. Would you like me to check availability for tomorrow?"

"Oh dear. That is a pity. No, we have to fly back to London in the morning. Never mind, we understand it is dreadfully short notice but we only heard of your establishment yesterday."

"Can I ask where you heard of us?" The woman's voice had a hint of curiosity.

Adrian affected vagueness. "Um, good question. I believe it was from our concierge at Hotel Romeo. We've tried all the other

Michelin-starred fine-dining experiences and this chap recommended your establishment. Mr Bailey's curiosity was piqued. He loves to discover hot new locations ahead of the crowd."

The sound of a mouse clicking came down the line. "Did you say two people?" she asked.

"That's correct. We're quite flexible as regards time."

"In that case, I might be able to free up a table by nine o'clock."

"Why, that would be marvellous! Most kind of you. He will be very pleased. Shall I give you my number?"

Adrian was sending Beatrice a triumphant message when Will came back from his run, sweaty and panting.

"Guess what!" demanded Adrian, before Will had even closed the door.

"You got the table."

"Yes! It was a total piece of cake. Turns out the maître d' is a British woman. So it should be maîtresse d'hôtel, I suppose. Although that has a whole different ring to it. Anyway, they have a table for nine tonight, thanks to my exceptional performance. How was your run? Your face is very red."

"It's already warm out there. On top of that, dodging scooters and dogs and unpredictable old folk who stop suddenly in the middle of the pavement keeps you on your toes. Are Matthew and Luke still in bed?"

"No, Luke's just come out of the bathroom and Matthew is scrambling some eggs. He says he does want to come to Herculaneum with us, so long as we take it slowly."

"I'm glad to hear that. As an ex-Classics professor, he'll be fascinating on the subject of Roman ruins. OK, I'll have a quick shower, let's eat and get on the road."

Will was quite firm about protecting themselves and their valuables. Everyone donned hats and applied sunscreen, packing extra sun protection along with water bottles and fruit in their rucksacks. The Circumvesuviana trains attracted lots of distracted tourists and, as a result, a certain number of thieves. Will used a body belt to keep his wallet and phone safe. Adrian tucked his personal items into a bum bag, which he wore underneath his shirt. While Adrian assisted Matthew in concealing his wallet in what he referred to as his Action Man vest, Will sat Luke down for a serious talk.

"The train and the station will be very crowded and we will probably have to stand for the journey. I want you to stay very close to me. It's not dangerous so long as we don't get sloppy or split up. We must stay together at all times. Where is your iPad?"

"Inside my jacket, zipped in."

"That's what I like to hear. If you get too hot and want to take it off, I'll carry it in my backpack. Matthew, the ruins are quite exposed and the sun can get strong, so whenever you feel like a sit in the shade, let us know."

"Absolutely. I wonder if Isabella would mind my borrowing a walking stick. Not that I actually need one, but it might come in handy for leaning and perhaps even getting a seat on the train."

"Excellent idea. Right, team! Are we ready for the next adventure?"

Will's predictions turned out to be right. The graffiti-covered train consisted of three coaches for a crowd which could have filled six. Once everyone had crammed themselves in, Adrian thought he might as well have been on the Northern line in rush hour. A young woman stood to offer Matthew her seat, Will and Adrian formed a protective cocoon around Luke and they all watched the scenery. Colourful washing flew from balconies in the crumbling suburbs of Naples, with flashes of green from gardens with orange and lemon trees or plots of beans and peas. The bay spread out to the right with the sun twinkling off the sea. Perhaps his imagination was working overtime because of their destination, but the presence of Vesuvius loomed large to their left. The fact that many passengers had extinguished their cigarettes moments before boarding made the air feel stale and the atmosphere muggy. Adrian was relieved to get off at Ercolano Scavi and breathe a lungful of fresh air.

Without verbalising the arrangement, Will took charge of Luke, leaving Adrian to assist Matthew. The system was perfect. Luke's curiosity and energy were matched by Will's and the two of them dashed down the hill, heading to the ruins to buy tickets. Matthew and Adrian followed at a sedate pace, both wearing panama hats to deflect the sun and dismissing eager taxi drivers with a shake of the head.

The fact that the ruins were so much lower than modern-day ground level took Adrian by surprise. Much like Pompeii, the Roman town had been obliterated by the same eighteenth-century eruption of Vesuvius. Yet the level of preservation at this smaller, lesser-known site was extraordinary. They wandered from ancient house to house, temple to marketplace, marvelling at the brightly coloured friezes, the ovens, the columns and arches of the 'sacred place', all testaments to a sophisticated, advanced, artistic civilisation destroyed by the lethal volcano.

Luke and Will had grabbed an audio guide each, but Adrian had no need of such a thing. His guide was Matthew, who slipped into his professorial role as if it were born for it.

"The most dreadful thing about this disaster was that the people were completely unprepared."

"How so? They must have known they were living beneath an active volcano."

Matthew leaned his forearms on a stone wall and surveyed what used to be a busy little port on the Bay of Naples. "On the contrary. They saw the mountain as a rich and fertile benefactor, providing green slopes on which to cultivate grapes for wine-making. You are undoubtedly familiar with Lacryma Christi."

"I am. The tears of Christ. A very decent wine indeed."

"Isn't it? For the people of this region, Vesuvius was benign and the only geographical threat was from earthquakes. Those arches where all the skeletons were found? They were built as a refuge. The quake of '63 was recorded in some of the reliefs and not all the damage had been repaired by the time of the eruption sixteen years later. Seneca himself said there was no point in fleeing the region as earthquakes could happen anywhere."

"But not volcanic eruptions," said Adrian. "You need a volcano for that."

"With millennia of hindsight, that's obvious. Consider how much more we know about our environment. Not that we have learned any more respect for it. What I mean is that it's almost impossible to put oneself in the minds of the four thousand people who called this place home. We have only hints of the cultural, historical or geographical context. What one must remember, however, is that Vesuvius had not erupted in living memory. There was simply no reason to expect what happened and no preparations made. Some ten per cent of the population sought refuge in the arches or attempted to flee from the surrounding beach. They fled to their waterside bunkers, which of course were no use against an ash fall hotter and deeper than that of Pompeii."

Adrian imagined the scene. "What a horrible way to die."

"Yes. They were quite literally cooked. That human tragedy must always be foremost in our minds. Yet for the modern-day historian, the preservation of buildings, furniture, mosaics and even documentation carved on wood or stone makes this site an extraordinarily rich source of information. Far more so than Pompeii, in fact."

"If that's true, why is Pompeii so much better known?"

"In time, Herculaneum will outshine it. Scientists and archaeologists have uncovered less than half the information it holds. Pompeii holds a grim fascination due to the casts of the bodies. It's like seeing the dead. The problem was when they made those casts; they did not preserve the skeletons. Here, the bones of the ancients have revealed many more secrets. We can prove what a sophisticated society this was. Their sewage system and clean water supply, their legal records on slaves becoming free men, the fact they kept pets and even their diet. Thanks to contemporary scientific methods, we know they ate a huge variety of fish, fruit, herbs, spices and even black pepper."

Adrian became aware of two tourists standing behind them. "I'm sorry, we're hogging the view."

"Not at all," said the man in an American accent. "We were just eavesdropping. You sure know your stuff, sir. We couldn't tear ourselves away."

"Thank you, you're very kind. I taught Classics for many years, so the history of the Roman Empire is one of my passions. Have you seen Pompeii yet?"

As Matthew engaged the Americans in enthusiastic chit-chat, Adrian wandered out into the street, searching for a glimpse of Will and Luke. Tourists thronged the thoroughfare, all with cameras and phones held aloft. He could see nothing of his husband or their young charge and the sun made him squint. He turned to go back inside. Just then he saw a face he recognised. Black Beret Man, without his beret, was leaning on a barrier, looking down to the level below. Adrian followed his sightline. Luke and Will were pacing across a courtyard with a military bearing, playing Roman soldiers. Any warmth Adrian might have experienced at the sight was cooled by the fact he was not the only observer.

Someone was following them. No, not true. Someone was following Luke. Sweating, footsore and uncomfortable in direct sunlight, Adrian sensed a chill creep through his whole body. He went to find Matthew, searching for any kind of plausible excuse for why they should leave. Before he could even interrupt, Matthew spotted him and raised a hand.

"Ah, here is my friend. I must leave you now. It was lovely

meeting you and I hope you enjoy the rest of your stay. Goodbye and bon voyage!"

Adrian smiled and waved as the happy American couple watched them leave. He offered a forearm to guide the ex-professor, but Matthew was moving off at some speed, with the aid of his stick.

"Are you feeling all right?" asked Adrian, taking long strides to catch up.

"Yes, yes, just need the bathroom with some degree of urgency. I know where it is. Why don't you round up the other two and we'll meet at the café for something cold?" He hurried away, intent on the visitors' centre.

Eyes peeled for any sign of their tail, Adrian made his way along the street, unable to forget the thousands of people whose mountain protector turned on them and left them no escape. He looked up and saw Luke running towards him, with Will a few paces behind. Mr No-Beret-Today was nowhere in sight.

After a modest lunch of salad and *panini* at one of the many restaurants lining the road to the station, the party boarded the return train to Naples. Luke was visibly flagging and a pair of wiry older women insisted Matthew and Luke take their seats. That was the moment Adrian had been waiting for. As grandfather and grandson dozed against each other, first Adrian scrutinised the carriage then murmured into Will's ear.

"I haven't said anything before, because I wasn't sure and anyway I wanted to tell Beatrice first. But it just seemed another worry on top of her restaurant job when Matthew was poorly as well. The thing is, I noticed a man watching Luke when we were on Capri. Then I saw him again, that same evening, outside our apartment. The next day, when we were running to get out of the rain, he was there again and just to prove it was not my imagination, Luke recognised him too. He said the same man had been photographing them while I was trying to hail a taxi.

Today, I saw him again, in Herculaneum. He was watching you and Luke playing soldiers."

Will stared into his eyes. "How can you be sure it's the same bloke?"

"The first couple of times I saw him, he was wearing a black beret, you know, like the fishermen wear. He's in his late fifties, I'd guess and looks typically Italian. Other than that, he's average height and very slightly built. Today, he's wearing a yellow shirt and a leather bomber jacket which is frankly unflattering at his age. I've only seen his face twice before today. He has a moustache, sunken cheeks and leathery skin, as if he spends his life outdoors. It's the same guy, Will, I am one hundred per cent convinced. And I think he's after Luke."

The train rattled to a halt at a suburban platform, allowing more passengers to exit and board. Will glanced over at Matthew and Luke, a frown tensing his face.

"If this guy knows where we're staying, it's unlikely he'll follow us home again. Unless he wants to learn our routines. OK, listen to me. When we arrive at Porta Nolana station, you three get a cab back home, lock the doors and stay there. We'll tell Matthew I'm going shopping for dinner ingredients. I'll hang around the streets and see if anyone is watching our apartment. If someone matching your description shows up, I'll take pictures. We need evidence in case we need to go to the police."

Adrian clutched his arm. "Promise you won't do anything dangerous? I mean, that's the one man I've seen, but there might be others. I'm worried for you, Will."

"Don't be. I'm trained for this shit. All I need from you is to make sure Luke and Matthew get back safely. Can you lend me your hoodie? Oh, and give me that cap you bought at the gift shop. You and Matthew keep wearing your panamas. Makes you easy to follow."

Once the train pulled into the Porta Nolana terminus, Will

slipped out onto the platform, disappearing into the crowd before Luke and Matthew had even opened their eyes.

Tucked into the shadows behind a staircase, Will watched the occupants of the train disembark and grimaced at the pungent stench of urine emanating from the filthy corner. He narrowed his eyes, on the alert for a yellow shirt or black bomber jacket, especially when he saw Adrian and Matthew in their distinctive panama hats, walking down the platform either side of Luke.

The crowds surged and flowed around the trio, making it a challenge to keep them in his sights. He tugged the cap down over his eyes, pulled up his hood and shuffled into the flow.

He waited till he'd seen Adrian guide Matthew and Luke into a cab, then scanned the mass of humanity once more. The taxi drove away and a movement caught Will's eye. A figure in a brown leather bomber jacket, who had been leaning against a wall, straightened and made off into the Metro station. Will sped after him, hampered by suitcases, small children, groups of noisy teenagers and random people changing course as if to deliberately collide with him.

The man in the jacket had vanished and Will was faced with a dilemma. He could run back to the taxi rank and get home shortly after the others, or try to tail the tail. If the man was heading in the same direction, intending to observe their apartment building, he would get on Line 1 and travel as far as Università. Will made up his mind, bought a ticket and hunched along the platform, looking for his target.

The metro train screeched in, again covered in graffiti. Will had seen several brown bomber jackets, but none of the wearers was the man who had been idling by the taxi rank. The doors opened and Will took his place among the passengers, still yet observant, standing beside the door in case he needed to move quickly.

Two stops later, he was the first out of the doors. He made immediately for a bench, sat down and took out his phone. His position enabled him to watch his fellow travellers as they streamed towards the exit, all ignoring the phone-fixated hooded figure alone on the plastic bench.

Will's focus switched back and forth from mobile screen to station until he saw what he'd been waiting for. The brown bomber jacket moving with the flow, in no particular hurry. Will risked a glance at his face. Weather worn and grey whiskered, just as Adrian had described. After he'd passed, Will took a few shots of the receding back, making a note of the scuffed brown shoes and apparent lack of buttocks.

He waited till the majority of people had cleared the platform until he rose. If the guy was a pro, which Will doubted, he'd be just as aware of followers as those he was following. So the best thing to do would be to come from the other direction. Will set off at a jog, weaving to avoid the crowds. If Bomber Jacket went the shorter route, Will would have to hurry to find a safe place for observation.

Clouds had rolled over the bay, trapping the heat of the city beneath. The streets were humid and within two minutes of his gentle run, Will started to sweat. He unzipped the hoodie and took off the baseball cap, rolling both into a ball to shove inside his rucksack. He was stuffing the clothes into his pack when a shop doorway opened a few paces ahead of him. A man emerged, a brown bomber jacket over his yellow shirt and a packet of cigarettes in his hand.

Will saw his chance. "*Scusa!*"

The man's reaction to Will was a shocked double-take before taking off down the street like a rat. Will zipped up his bag and raced after him, pulling his pack on as he ran. He gained on the guy at first. A fit and well-trained detective sergeant, he was confident of catching him until the sneaky little rodent ducked into the traffic, causing a cacophony of irate horns. Will tried to follow suit and made it across the road after almost getting flattened by a truck. When he reached the opposite pavement, his quarry had gone, most likely into one of the myriad alleyways and side streets a local could use to lose a clueless foreigner.

Will stood like a statue, regaining his breath and allowing the shock of adrenalin to settle. The rat might stick its head out of the hole to check the coast was clear. And if he did, the cat would pounce. A full five minutes later, Will gave up and headed back to the apartment, already rehearsing a downbeat account of events for Adrian. He sent a quick message to stop him worrying.

No luck. Just doing a bit of shopping, back in an hour or so. Wx

Of paramount importance was a conversation with Beatrice Stubbs. He called her mobile and she answered on the first ring.

"Will? Is everything all right?"

"Fine. I just want a word, that's all. What time will you get to the apartment?"

She spoke to someone in the background. "Ettore says ten minutes. This traffic is the stuff of nightmares. Is something the matter with Matthew?"

Already on the street housing their apartment, Will saw a little corner café with a few tables and tired-looking cakes.

"Everyone is well and happy and full of stories to tell you. I just want five minutes to talk to you before they start. Meet me at Caffè Carolina just up the street from our place. It won't take long and you can still have a rest before dinner at Nonna's."

"OK, I'm on my way. Order me a peppermint tea. Unless they do Prosecco."

Chapter 20

Ettore dropped her at the apartment and Beatrice made as if to go inside, fumbling for her keys and waiting till he left. She liked Ettore enormously, but trusted no one. He waited too, making sure she was safely inside. She had no choice but to go indoors and peer out of the peephole till he'd gone. Once the car had driven away, she unlocked the door and walked further up the street until she spotted Caffè Carolina. The rangy figure of Will sat at an outdoor table. Furtive looks from a couple of young women sitting a few tables away made her smile. *You're out of luck, ladies, but I can't blame you for trying. He is a quite magnificent specimen.*

She grinned at him as she approached and he stood up to give her a kiss on both cheeks.

"A sight for four eyes," she said, with a pointed glance at the two glasses of fizz on the table.

"You'd better drink it before it gets any warmer. Ten minutes, you said."

She sat down and tucked her bag onto her lap. "Ten minutes, Ettore said. I can't be held responsible for all the traffic jams in this city. Anyway, I had to wait for him to leave before I could join you. Now tell me why we're having a secret assignation."

Will related the events of the afternoon and Beatrice listened intently.

"No one has mentioned this to Matthew?"

Will shook his head. "Adrian and Luke decided not to worry him, but they planned to tell you. I guess they just hadn't found the right time."

Beatrice rolled the stem of her glass between middle finger and thumb, pondering the facts. "Something about this is peculiar. How many surreptitious stalkers wear identifiable clothing and get so close so frequently that even a six-year-old notices? A black beret? He couldn't be more obvious if he'd added a scar, a limp and a pet monkey on his shoulder. Either this person is incompetent or they want you to know you're being followed. Whichever case it is, why follow a group of innocent tourists?"

"Adrian thinks the guy is after Luke. Of course that is always a possibility, but I'm sure he's still got the Portugal incident on his mind. My view is that someone is keeping tabs on us as insurance. If they suspect the real reason you are here, they might want to use Matthew and Luke as your weak point. Scare them enough and you will all leave. Adrian and I were not part of the plan."

Beatrice placed a hand on his forearm. "Another reason I'm glad you're with us. Who do you think 'they' are?"

"The same people behind the copycat restaurants, the warehouse fire and the damage to the chef's Ferrari. What do you think?"

Beatrice rubbed her eyes, forcing her tired brain to think. "It doesn't add up. If there is a spy in the kitchen selling recipes to a rival, why would they attempt to damage their cash cow? It's surely in their interests to keep the restaurant successful and popular so that their imitations bring in the punters. Why disrupt the supply chain and key a luxury car? That is threatening behaviour to coerce someone into doing what you want. Surely what they want is for Agusto to keep creating, getting great reviews and innovating. That's the honey pot."

The two women paid their bill and left, casting one more flirtatious look in Will's direction. He was oblivious, as usual, his entire attention focused entirely on the case.

"What if," Will tapped his fingertips to his chin, "the spy isn't giving 'them' what they need? What if they want more and are piling on the pressure? Look how fast your dessert appeared on a competitor's menu."

"You might have a point there. An American party came to Ecco this lunchtime and mentioned they'd eaten Agusto's signature veal dish at a restaurant in Switzerland. They did say the one at Ecco was superior, but it was called the same thing: *Vitello Vero alla Nonna*. I asked Alessandro – he's the maître d' – to get the name of the city, but the Americans couldn't remember. It had a monastery with a black Madonna was all they could recall. I'll wager my next Prosecco that wherever it is, there's a restaurant called Nonna's and it serves some familiar recipes."

Will chewed his lip and his leg jigged up and down under the table. "So it's not just a question of selling recipes to a rival. This is more like a franchise. These restaurants get the established name and the recipes and probably pay through the nose for the privilege."

"This sounds like a much bigger operation than one man making extra cash on the side. I think someone is making a lot of money out of this while blowing smoke in our eyes." Beatrice gazed into her glass of bubbles.

"OK, listen to this. Let's say you were stealing and selling recipes from a top-class restaurant and wanted to throw suspicion onto someone else. How would you keep operating but make yourself look innocent?"

Beatrice met Will's eyes. "Hire an investigator to find a non-existent spy and create a series of diversions to throw that person off the scent. Choose someone unsuited to the task and unproven in the field who might be easily frightened off."

They stared at each other for several seconds until Will's mobile rang. He made a mock face of alarm and answered.

"Adrian! We're just up the road ... What? ... Me and Beatrice. We were just having a chat ... OK, OK, be there in five minutes."

He ended the call and pulled out his wallet. "Drink up. We're in the doghouse."

She emptied the rest of her Prosecco. "Oh dear. I'd better think of lots of interesting questions to distract attention. Where did you go today? Vesuvius?"

Will handed the waiter a twenty-Euro note. "Vesuvius was yesterday. You won't make yourself any friends by forgetting where we've been." He took his change and left some coins on the table. "Ask Luke. He'll tell you every detail and then some." He lifted his rucksack and they strode up the street, both in thoughtful silence.

As Will unlocked the front door, he looked down at Beatrice. "One thing we haven't considered is the whole money-laundering angle."

"Case later, family now. Let's get indoors."

The presence of Luke was a godsend. Their mutual concern for the boy overcame Adrian's outrage and enabled them to communicate civilly, if not entirely naturally. He'd hissed his annoyance and frustration at Will in the privacy of their bedroom, stressing the fear and worry he had suffered. As ever, Will apologised for the concern but managed to imply that half the blame lay with Adrian's paranoia.

A truce, albeit hostile, meant the two men could prepare for the evening excursion to one of the most legendary restaurants in Italy. They showered and shaved, politely giving each other space, and dressed in their best. Adrian was adjusting his hair in the mirror when Will emerged from the bathroom. He stopped, just taking a minute to watch him.

"You look so damn sexy," Will said, his voice a husky

murmur. It was true, but his husband's expression showed he suspected a ruse.

"Apart from the extra grey hairs and worry lines I acquired this afternoon, I agree." Clearly Adrian wasn't about to forgive him, or Beatrice, quite so fast. "The car will be here in fifteen minutes. I'm ready and I'm going to check on Luke. He's probably still in his bathrobe playing computer games. Will you please hurry up and get dressed? I suggest that blue Paul Smith shirt I gave you for your birthday."

When Will had finished his preparations, Adrian and Luke were sitting on the sofa, both smartly dressed and laughing at some kind of Italian slapstick with the sound off. Beatrice sat at the desk, tapping away at her computer and Matthew was making a pot of tea in the kitchen.

Beatrice still hadn't finished giving them instructions when the doorbell rang, only eight minutes late.

"Have a lovely evening!" she exhorted them. "And notice everything!"

Matthew raised his mug and the party of three descended to street level to meet Ettore.

Chapter 21

With the youngsters gone, Matthew on the terrace with his book and a good two hours before their dinner, Beatrice knuckled down to work. First she added several more names to her spreadsheet of all relevant parties, drawing links between each person and filling in motive, means and alibi.

Her gut instinct was shut out of the process as she clinically assessed each member of the kitchen staff and marked their names as unlikely or possible spies. Even those who employed her.

Rami Ahmad had been the second chef, Agusto's right-hand man. He was part of the concept, observing the creation of each dish, learning the methodology and techniques. He had access to Agusto's creative mind and a great deal of disposable income. It was perfectly possible he had been the stooge, but why would his taskmasters kill him? And who had taken his place?

Marcello di Marco had stepped into Rami's job. Personable, keen, an excellent chef with a focus on seafood, he was right beside Agusto in the main kitchen. How could he have stolen the dessert recipe and why would he bring the copy to Agusto's attention? Unless he and Suhail were in cahoots.

Searching for a single spy would hamper her investigations. After this afternoon, she believed there could be a team. Beatrice sighed and moved on.

Bruno and Chantal could both be discounted. Bruno was Agusto's nephew and had only just started as an apprentice. His skills were more in the region of languages, not cookery. Chantal's abilities were limited to assemblage. She wasn't a chef and in Beatrice's opinion, had no desire to be.

Washer-upper Benoît couldn't see much from his cubby-hole and if he only spoke French, he would be unable to memorise and pass on kitchen secrets. If his monoglot status was true. She would have to check.

That left Suhail himself, who Isabella and Agusto said they 'had to trust'. Had he been in partnership with Rami and was now operating alone? Beatrice tugged at her earlobe, mentally turning every stone.

Other than kitchen staff, the next best informed individual would be the maître d'hôtel. Alessandro Bonardi was a closed book, polite and formal, who oversaw all front-of-house operations like a bird of prey. He must know the ingredients of a dish but would he be able to comprehend the techniques? The professor brother who had worked there for a while; where did he fit in?

Isabella and Agusto. They had chosen to include Suhail in the Beatrice Stubbs rising star chef deception – *we had to involve one other person, you understand*? – but it wasn't just one other person. There was Gennaio. No one apart from Beatrice had even questioned his inclusion. The supplier, the brother, the constant presence in the kitchen. The earth to Agusto's fire. A highly successful man who also drove a Ferrari.

It was hardly thinkable that he would set fire to his own warehouse to make himself look a victim, but it was also true that he was part of the inner circle.

Beatrice rubbed her eyes and checked her watch. Still over an hour until dinner and she couldn't see a clear motive, means or opportunity from any one of these individuals. She closed her laptop and decided to make herself and Matthew an aperitif. Her brain never functioned at its best on an empty stomach, but it might buck its ideas up after a gin and tonic.

Chapter 22

As the only member of the party who had previously eaten at Ecco, Luke gave his dining companions the benefit of his wisdom as they drove along the seafront. Buffalo milk was nothing to be afraid of and the risotto came highly recommended. Too much of the bread dipped in oil and vinegar could fill you up, which would be a shame. When ordering desserts, smart diners order three different things so everyone gets to have a taste.

Adrian took his advice on board, sharing a smile with his husband over Luke's head. Will reciprocated and reached his arm across the seat to squeeze Adrian's shoulder. Too much, too soon. He was not yet forgiven. Not only had Will taken it upon himself to tell Beatrice of the stalker, without asking Adrian's permission, but his explanation of their underhand private meeting was far from satisfactory. They were up to something and shutting Adrian out. He ignored Will and addressed the driver.

"Ettore, you don't need to hang around for us. We can catch a taxi home. You need some downtime as well."

The driver shook his head with some emphasis. "No, no. No taxi for you. Agusto's orders. I take care of you and make sure you go from door to door. That is my job. I give you my card. When you are ready to leave, call me and I collect. Here we are, everyone! Ecco!"

The entrance to the restaurant blew Adrian away. Blue and golden lights sparkled from the trees either side of an inviting walkway of blue carpet. The lower part of the walls were made of glass, so outsiders could see nothing more of the patrons than high heels, ankles and handbags, heavy hints as to the privilege within.

Luke caught hold of Adrian's hand as they walked up the carpet, while Will tried to persuade Ettore to accept a tip. A doorman welcomed them with a sweeping bow and glass doors opened into a beautiful, fragrant dining room of absolute perfection. Adrian wanted to move in and never leave.

The older man with hairy eyebrows behind the greeting podium smiled at Luke. "*Buonasera signori, avete prenotato?* Do you have a reservation, gentlemen?"

Luke looked at Adrian.

"I think so."

"Yes, a table for three, please. In the name of Beatrice Stubbs," Will had come up behind them and placed a hand on each shoulder.

The greeter man's eyes widened just a touch before he led them through the dining-area to a window table with a view to take one's breath away. They seated themselves and took in the scenery.

"Pretty!" said Luke, surveying the bay.

Pretty was an understatement. Adrian let out a long 'oh' as his eyes took in the sky and sea bathed in layers of indigo, pink and midnight blue, lit with thousands of sparkling lights from boats, islands and the spread of the city.

Will's hand snaked across the table and held his. "This is what I'd call a special occasion. What do you reckon, Luke?"

"I wish ... I wish Mum was here." His little eyes filled with tears.

Emotion welled up in Adrian. This young boy, who had

never spent more than a night apart from his mother, understood this moment of beauty and wanted to share it with the person he loved most in the world. Adrian was about embrace him and burst into sympathetic tears until Will spoke.

"Let's bring her here then. She can be with us via Facetime. Come on, we can't do it at the table, because the staff will think we're paparazzi. On the terrace, quick, before the sun sets. Adrian, will you order the drinks?"

The two of them ran off to the French windows and from his vantage point, Adrian watched them filming and cavorting and best of all, laughing on the terrace amongst the cocktail crowd. By the time they returned, he had composed himself, ordered two martinis and an orange juice, and decided that his husband was the most perfect man on the planet.

They were still browsing the menu when Isabella dashed out of the kitchen like a lit match.

"*Ciao, tutti*! Luca, I am so happy to see you again!" She placed her hands either side of his face and kissed the top of his head.

Luke took it in his stride. "*Ciao*, Isabella."

"Adrian! Will! So happy you are here." She kissed their cheeks and beamed her extraordinary smile. "Tonight, we have the tasting menu for you. Special people deserve special dishes. You will love it, I promise. What are you drinking? Not cocktails?! Alessandro! Come!"

The older man with hairy eyebrows approached, his uniform immaculate and smile prepared. Adrian realised this was in fact the maître d', not just a door greeter. "*Buonasera e benvenuti.* Good evening, gentlemen, and welcome to Ecco."

Isabella gestured to the man with an open palm, as if she'd magicked him out of the air. "Alessandro is our maître d'hôtel. His passion for wine matches mine, but his knowledge is far superior. It *is*, don't argue with me! Alessandro, these are personal friends. I want you to take special care of them this evening. We are very lucky to have this man in charge of our restaurant, you know. He comes to us from Rome, from the famous Spirito di Vino. But maybe after today you have enough of Roman ruins! Ha! Agusto and I will join you for coffee later. *Buon appetito!*"

They deliberated over the menu and accepted Alessandro's advice on the best choices of dishes according to personal preference. Adrian and Luke discussed why green and black olives appealed to them or not and Will folded and refolded his napkin, his face pensive.

"Everything OK?" asked Adrian.

Will refocused. "Yep. Just hungry."

Adrian knew that look. He was on a case.

Two hours later, after the most sublime meal in living memory, Adrian continued to make notes in his little book, under advice from Luke, who was still polishing off his ice-cream. Will sat back and folded his hands over his stomach, a contented smile on his face.

The kitchen doors opened, as they had done a hundred times that evening, but somehow the atmosphere in the room changed. Excited whispers rustled from table to table and anticipation electrified the air. A tall, greying man in chef's whites, good-looking in a silver fox way, moved from table to table, exchanging a few words with the patrons.

Two waiters brought extra chairs to the table, placed four shot glasses and petit-fours in the centre of the table and asked for their coffee preferences. Adrian and Will opted for espresso; Luke chose to stick with water. The second the waiters left, Isabella appeared beside them, like a genie with a bottle.

"Grappa. The only digestif after such a meal. Tell me quick, before he arrives," she said as she jerked her head at the big man making his way through the restaurant. "Did you enjoy your meal?"

"Yes!" said Luke. "Even better than last time."

Isabella's beam spread and she reached out to stroke Luke's cheek. "You are adorable. Such a wise boy. Adrian, tell me. Were the wines suitable to the food?"

Adrian was about to open his mouth when the spotlight hit their table. Agusto Colacino had arrived and stood with his hands on his hips, expecting the accolades he deserved. Will duly got to his feet and applauded.

"Bravo, Signor Colacino. That was a meal we will never forget. Thank you so much and many thanks to your expert staff, especially Alessandro. Your restaurant is exceptional. My name is Will Quinn and this is my husband, Adrian Harvey. And I think you've met Luke before."

Agusto took one of Will's hands and clasped it warmly. "Kind words, my friend, and I am very pleased to meet you. Yes, Luca and I are old friends. He has excellent manners. And what of your husband's opinion? You are a wine expert also, no, Mr Harvey?"

Adrian shook his head, modestly. "I wouldn't describe myself as an expert. But I am not exaggerating when I say that was the most delicious meal paired with the most thoughtful wines I have consumed in my entire life. Signor Colacino, I can now die happy."

Isabella roared with laughter and started pouring grappa into shot glasses. "Sit, let us relax and drink a toast to the Easter weekend! Thank God we have two days of holiday. I need to get outside, feel the sun on my skin, and breathe some sea air. Ah, the coffees! Luca, I asked the kitchen to make you my special hot chocolate. Tell me if you know what is my secret ingredient."

The boy's eyes lit up as a tall, elegant cup was placed in front of him, decorated with a whirl of cream, chocolate shavings and a *caprice* biscuit for dunking.

Inside Adrian's head, a grumbly voice was muttering: *What if he has allergies? Did she ask before presenting him with something full of sugar and chocolate? Has she put any alcohol in there? He's six years old and we are in charge of keeping this small person safe.*

"Enjoy, Luca! Tell me, young men, how do you find our city?" demanded Agusto.

Adrian and Will turned their attention to the man everyone wanted to meet, although Adrian was half listening to Isabella's bright monologue to Luke. Before Adrian could find a pithy reply, Will answered, "It's a sensory overload. I wish we had longer. There is so much to see in the city itself and we still want to visit the Amalfi Coast and explore the islands."

"Yes, we adored Capri," Adrian chipped in.

Will continued. "Are your family from this area, Signor Colacino? Your food suggests a deep understanding of this region."

Agusto reacted with genuine delight. "Thank you very much! Call me Agusto, we are friends. Yes, you are right. I come from a long line of Neapolitans. These ingredients, this place – they are in my blood. You have good taste. Do you work with food? Isabella told me your job but I forgot, I'm sorry."

With a glance around him, Will leaned in to communicate solely with Agusto. Adrian pretended not to notice but his ears were straining to hear what he would say. The chef understood the gesture and bent closer.

"I'm a Detective Sergeant with the Metropolitan Police."

Agusto's eyes gleamed. "You work with Beatrice!" he whispered, loud enough to be heard by at least three nearby tables.

"No, we're not partners, just friends. This is her case and I am not involved on a professional level. My husband and I have very different careers." He turned his gaze to Adrian, who affected interest in Luke's hot chocolate. "He's the one with the wine knowledge; I'm the one with police training. Not like you and your wife, whose specialisations seem a perfect match."

Agusto leaned closer still. "You have an expression in

English. 'The wind beneath my wings.' That is my wife. She has the ambition, the creativity, the understanding of how we stay ahead. Without her and my brother, I would be making *pizze*. Damn good *pizze*, of course!"

His laughter bubbled from his throat like lava, causing the rest of the table to join in, even if they hadn't heard the joke.

When they left over an hour later, with kisses, handshakes and a goodie bag for Luke, Adrian was full of bonhomie and goodwill, not to mention grappa. Agusto and Isabella were fascinating company, as was Agusto's brother, Gennaio, who joined them just before ten. Ettore was waiting as promised and the only delay was Will chatting to the maître d', having some kind of discussion about a flashy car parked on the pavement.

Luke was unpacking his goodie bag and inviting Adrian's approval, which he was happy to provide. When Will finally got into the car and thanked Ettore for his patience, Adrian had an inspired idea. He whispered in Luke's ear and got an immediate positive reaction.

When they got out of the car outside the apartment, Luke offered Ettore the bottle of truffle oil as a thank you. Ettore's instinct to refuse a tip could not overcome his adoration of children, so he accepted with effusive thanks.

Will's smile radiated approval and Adrian knew he'd made a smart move. He had a gut feeling and could sense Will and Luke did too. That strikingly talented family who ran Ecco were classy, talented and kind people they could trust. Naples was a truly extraordinary place. He wondered if they might be able to live here. Open a wine shop, join the right sort of social circles, attend opera and wine tastings, throw dinner parties on their roof terrace ...

"Are you getting carried away again?" asked Will, standing in the doorway.

"Not at all. Just keeping an open mind."

Chapter 23

Easter Sunday dawned bright and brilliant, which annoyed Beatrice no end. Matthew had failed to close the curtains properly and a shaft of sunlight wormed its way under her eyelids. With a grunt, she rolled over, dragging the eiderdown over her face. Eyes squeezed tightly closed, she attempted to return to sleep. She deserved a lie-in after the week she'd had. But Agusto's voice echoed through her mind, no matter how hard she tried to ignore it.

On Tuesday morning, I want every one of you to bring me an idea for a top-class Ecco dish. All these dishes need a story. Personal, local, global, I don't mind. Bring me new ideas and I will work with them all.

Matthew's breathing was thick and heavy, with stentorian snores. Beatrice rolled onto her back and stared at the ceiling, vaguely aware of church bells ringing across the city. A dessert with a story. A British classic with an Italian twist. Trifle? Eccles cakes? Mince pies?

She got out of bed and wrapped herself in a dressing-gown, closing the curtains so Matthew would not be disturbed by the sunshine. She padded down the corridor to the kitchen, poured herself a glass of apple juice and opened her laptop. `Classic British puddings`, she typed and began her research.

Forty minutes later, she had a shortlist of ten, none of which ignited any real excitement. Her feet were cold and her stomach was rumbling, so she decided to abandon the research, find her slippers and make some toast.

As she returned to the kitchen, Will opened the front door, sweaty, panting and glowing with exertion. "Morning!" he puffed.

"You've been out already? It's not even eight o'clock!"

"I know. Bells woke me. You?"

"Sun, snores and bloody Agusto with his ludicrous ideas. Shall I make us coffee and we can compare notes on last night? Are you peckish at all?"

Will grinned at her. "Starving. Right, I'll shower and join you in ten. Why don't you relax today? I'll make breakfast for us all. I'm a dab hand at pancakes."

"My favourite! I'd better help you by testing the first two or three."

The apartment was filled with the scent of fresh coffee by the time Will emerged. Beatrice had dressed in the dark to avoid disturbing Matthew and even by her own standards, the result could be described as eclectic. Pink pyjama bottoms with a jumping sheep pattern, an orange fleece and blue socks. She was warm, comfy and decent so who cared?

She peeked in on Luke as she passed his room. Sleeping with one hand under his cheek, he looked terribly vulnerable and small.

"Is he still asleep?" whispered Will from behind her.

"Flat out. Let's leave him to rest. It's Sunday."

In the kitchen, Beatrice heated milk and Will began making the pancake batter.

"Did Luke enjoy last night, do you think?" asked Beatrice.

"He loved it. He stayed up with us until almost eleven and we Skyped with Tanya and Marianne."

"Tanya and Marianne? Not Gabriel?"

Will cracked eggs into a pile of flour. "No, they were having a sisters' movie night. Luke raved about the restaurant. We all did. It really was a superlative evening. What about you? How was your meal?"

"Sub-par, I'm happy to say. Definitely falls short of your experience. Nonna's kitchen do some dishes very well, especially the copies of the veal and the ravioli. But my dessert was not the same thing. That wasn't brown bread ice-cream, more vanilla with some kind of caramel or maple syrup chips. Close, but no guitar. They serve it as an *affogato,* but whoever created that recipe does *not* work in the kitchen at Ecco. Here's your coffee."

"Thank you. Oh wow!"

"What?"

"You did the barista thing with a pattern on top. That is impressive."

Beatrice peered into his cup. "I didn't even realise I was doing that. See, that's what that man has done to me. Now I'm fiddle-faddling around with a perfectly decent cup of coffee. Anyway, let's get to the point because the smell of coffee and pancakes will soon be enough to wake the entire building. Apart from the fact that Agusto's food is divine, what did you find out?"

Will poured a puddle of batter into a pan and swirled it around before replacing it on the heat. "A couple of things I thought were worth noting, both regarding Isabella," said Will, his face reflecting internal thoughtfulness. "Firstly, the maître d' can't stand her."

Beatrice stared at him. "You mean Alessandro? How do you know that?"

Will shrugged. "I watch people. Alessandro is stiff and formal whenever he deals with Isabella."

Beatrice huffed through her nose. "He's stiff and formal with everyone. That's his style."

"But he doesn't shoot everyone daggers when he thinks no one is looking. His smile when she patronises him is almost painfully forced and disappears like elastic the second she looks away. I don't know whether it's relevant or not, but it's a detail I had to mention."

"Hmm. What was the other thing?" asked Beatrice, her chin in her hand.

"When we met in that café, you seemed under the impression we'd been up Vesuvius yesterday. So I'm pretty confident you didn't mention to Isabella that we'd been to Herculaneum." Will flipped the pancake.

"No, definitely not. The only words we exchanged yesterday lunchtime were about work and I didn't even see her after our conversation."

"So why did she joke that 'you've seen enough of Roman ruins today'? That was at Alessandro's expense, by the way. How would she know where we'd been?"

Stirring her coffee, Beatrice thought about it. "An assumption? All tourists in Naples would go to Pompeii at some point."

"She definitely said 'today'. And there's another thing."

The sound of a door closing and the shower starting up gave them pause.

"Quick now. Give me that pancake and tell me what other thing."

Will tipped the pan onto her plate. "It's about the Ferrari. You said some guy keyed the chef's car. His brother also has a red Ferrari Testarossa. This is at the same time someone sets fire to the brother's warehouse. Could it be that the wrong car got damaged? Was their target Gennaio, not Agusto?"

For several minutes, Will flipped pancakes while Beatrice cogitated.

Matthew walked into the room, yawning. "Good morning, early birds. Can I just say we really should buy a packet of peppermint tea? Eating late and drinking coffee in the evening plays hell with my digestion."

Beatrice finished her pancake. "The only things playing hell with your digestion are ravioli and saltimbocca plus a great fat slice of apricot pie with cream. Not to mention the grappa you had when we got back here. I did warn you."

"A man is entitled to a nightcap. You took me to a restaurant to test the cuisine. Of course I had to taste as many dishes as I could. It's only good manners. Is there any coffee on the go?"

Beatrice tuned out the morning chit-chat and stirred her coffee.

Time to accept it, you stubborn old coot. You need help.

In order to make any progress in the Ecco case, Beatrice had to kick ideas around with Will. By the same token, to have any hope of creating an exceptional dessert, she required imaginative input across three generations.

When everyone was at the table, she called a meeting and instructed her team.

"Now listen here, everyone, I'm afraid I need your help. All of you. Will, I want you to help me find the Swiss version of the Nonna chain and assist me on working the fraternal line of enquiry. Adrian, Matthew, Luke, could you think about classic British desserts I could suggest to Agusto? What special ingredients could I propose to add something new to the menu at Ecco? Would you please think it over for the next two days, discuss amongst yourselves and come up with a maximum of three ideas by Monday lunchtime? I'm aware we're all on holiday, but I have a job to do. Happy Easter! Pancakes first and then who's up for an Easter parade?"

The Easter Bunny, chocolate eggs and fluffy chicks of Beatrice's imagination were soon overpowered by heat, drums, song, prayer and religious iconography. Her nerves regarding Luke and his safety jangled constantly every second he was out of her sight.

Huge noisy processions drew crowds amid the narrow streets, becoming oppressive and in Beatrice's opinion, downright dangerous. She, Will and Adrian had agreed to keep a lookout for their stalker, all the while affecting a happy-go-lucky Sunday atmosphere for Matthew and Luke. It wasn't easy.

Just as her discomfort about being jostled by crowds and losing her sense of direction reached screaming point, Matthew caught her arm, motioning to a side street. At the end, she saw the most welcome sight. The beach! Sea sparkling in the sunshine, empty deckchairs and large beach umbrellas for weary tourists.

She raised her voice above the musicians and yelled, "Will!" waving an arm to point at their escape route.

He wasn't difficult to spot, as he had Luke on his shoulders. He acknowledged her with a nod and guided Adrian, who was still filming the event, between the throng to follow them. Gratitude for his intuition and understanding swelled in her chest. Whatever would they do without Will?

The moment they turned into the side street, the intensity of the music and claustrophobia of the crowd lessened. Beatrice took a deep breath and released Matthew's hand. Rotten oranges lay in the gutter, leaving a fetid smell which was almost comforting, like compost. They headed for the sunlit beach, like swimmers making for the surface, and burst out into the daylight with huge intakes of breath.

"That was special," said Matthew.

Adrian laughed. "Special is one word for it. Intense, scary and a bit alarming are just a few more. I'm glad we chose to avoid the more dramatic processions. Never mind scaring Luke, I would have wet myself."

The beach became their haven for the day. They paddled, dozed, chatted and read in the shade of a huge umbrella, shifting positions whenever the sun grew too hot. Will and Luke went beachcombing, Matthew and Adrian revisited their conversation on the wines of Puglia and Beatrice relaxed into a beach chair, just resting her eyes.

As the afternoon wore on, families began to descend onto the seafront, walking off their Easter Sunday feasts. The atmosphere was jovial and celebratory, entirely lacking in the religious intensity of the morning. Luke came dashing back with a hoard of shells and fishy-smelling pebbles, and announced he was hungry.

Adrian offered to cook for everyone that evening and Matthew placated Luke with the promise of an ice-cream. Will escorted grandfather and grandson to a *gelateria* down the harbour, while Adrian and Beatrice made their way back to their apartment in the late afternoon sun. Beatrice linked her arm in his and leant her head against his shoulder. "Despite the fact that no one has given me a chocolate egg, that was a rather lovely Easter Sunday," she said.

"No one has given you a chocolate egg *yet*," Adrian replied as they turned the corner into their street. "Yes, when we're all together, it's perfect. Although this morning was livelier than I expected, a few hours of sun and seaside completely relaxed me. I even forgot about the stalker. I checked with Will and neither of us has seen anyone remotely like him all day. Perhaps stalkers get Sundays off."

"He might be washing his beret," Beatrice suggested, causing Adrian to snort.

Their apartment block came into view, lit by spring sunshine and Adrian let out a sigh. "Italy and I were made for each other. This country embraces the good things in life with no apology. Which reminds me, we've had some thoughts about your dessert. Do you remember birthday parties when you were ... oh shit."

To Beatrice's surprise, Adrian shoved her up against a wall and pressed his body against hers, his hand forcing her head against his shoulder.

"Sssh!" he hissed.

Beatrice didn't move, her nose filled with the scent of aftershave and fabric conditioner. After a moment, he released her and leaned away to look up the street. Walking away from them was an older man, with grey hair and a brown leather bomber jacket. Neither moved until he had turned the corner.

"Was that ...?"

"Yes, it was. And he just came out of our apartment building."

They ran upstairs, careful to check every room. Nothing had been disturbed, no valuables were missing, no sinister messages had been scrawled on the bathroom mirror in lipstick or blood. Beatrice frowned. Had he got into the building but not the apartment? If so, what was he looking for? A thought occurred to her and she trotted downstairs to open the post box.

Stuffed with junk mail, the box contained no unsubtle envelope containing a cryptic threat made out of newspaper headlines. Nothing but pizza fliers and supermarket special offers. The front door opened, making her jump. Will, Matthew and Luke seemed equally startled to see her standing in the gloomy hallway.

"Beatrice?" asked Will, his face full of concern.

"Here you are! Just coming to look for you. How long does it take to get an ice-cream anyway? What flavour did you get, Luke?"

She led the way upstairs, with a discreet shake of the head at Will. *Not in front of the boy.* He said no more.

Once Matthew had retired for a rest and Luke took his games console into the living room, Beatrice summoned Adrian and Will to the roof terrace.

"The truth of the matter is that man came out of this building. Whether or not he'd been in this apartment, we have no way of telling. But in future, we set markers which only we know about. Then we can be sure only we come in and out of this place."

"I can take care of that," said Will. "My question is, if he did get into our apartment, how? Has someone given him a key?"

Adrian looked from one to another, his puzzlement clouding his features. "This place belongs to Agusto and Isabella. Surely they wouldn't give anyone else a key, unless it's a cleaner or concierge?"

"What reason would a cleaner or concierge have to follow us around the city?" asked Will. "You need to find out who has access to this place, Beatrice. I'm going to call Tanya and request we activate Location Services on Luke's iPad. We'll tell her it's just a precaution but I want to know where he is at all times."

Beatrice clasped her hands together and thought. "Good plan. The question is, how do I approach Isabella without letting her know I suspect her of having a part in this?"

Adrian shook his head with some vehemence. "Will told me your suspicions and I think you are both being ridiculous. Agusto and Isabella are lovely people, nice to children, friendly, talented and incredibly stylish. I cannot and will not believe she is double-crossing you. That is paranoia, plain and simple."

Beatrice made no reply. She had long since ceased to trust people on the basis of their appearance.

"My feeling is not to show our hand. Not just yet," said Will. "What we could do is lay a honey trap. How many people knew how to make your ice-cream thing?"

"Me, Agusto and Suhail. Maybe Isabella too, if Agusto told her."

"No one else?"

"To my knowledge, it would be only four people," Beatrice said. "Gennaio was away on business and no one else is privy to Agusto's creations."

Will cupped his jaw in his hand. "How about we create a dessert for the restaurant but when telling anyone what's in it, miss out a specific ingredient? You make it, get it approved and then ensure only you know exactly what's in it. You tell only

Agusto and Isabella the recipe, omitting the key ingredient. Then let's see how the Nonna chain picks that up."

"I couldn't do that without including Suhail. He's the one who actually makes the things; I just pretend to be a chef. But yes, if I ever think of a dessert, we might be able to pull that off," Beatrice sighed.

"We had an idea on that score," Adrian offered.

"One minute." Will placed a hand on Adrian's arm. "Beatrice, do you really think we can trust Suhail? I'm not sure the plan will work if we include another person. He could pass on the original recipe himself or tell Agusto and Isabella what we're trying to pull."

"I'm not sure. My gut tells me he's not been completely honest with me, but at the same time, I don't doubt his loyalty."

Will flipped open his notebook. "Loyalty to whom, that's the question. Anyway, before we leave the question of the Nonna chain, I wanted to tell you that I found the one in Switzerland. Chalet Nonna is in a tourist town called Einsiedeln. There's a big monastery and massive church which houses a black Madonna. The restaurant is pretty new but has a website and online menu. Their selection includes all the Ecco dishes we know have been plagiarised, including your *affogato*."

Seagulls screeched overhead and the sun grew pinker. Beatrice's brain buzzed, trying to make connections. "Then we're right about this being some kind of wider network. Someone is stealing recipes and selling them to new ventures. I'm guessing they pay a fee and get a certain number of recipes per month, per quarter, whatever. All of them have Nonna in the title, but the owners appear to have no connection. Unless the Swiss manager comes from Naples?"

Will checked his notebook. "No, the owner is Swiss. Stefan Kallin, thirty-eight years old and this is his first catering business. Previous jobs include journalism, travel writer, food critic and now he's opened his own place."

Beatrice pricked up her ears. "How do you spell his surname?"

"K-A with an umlaut-L-I-N," Will answered.

"In that case it's pronounced 'Kaylin', not 'Kallin'. I partnered with a Herr Kälin on a case in Zürich a few years back. I've no idea how common a name it is, but I might just give him a call. Can't hurt, can it? Adrian, you said you had an idea."

"Not on the whole fake restaurant thing, but I was thinking about desserts. Can you tell me again exactly what the chef wants?"

Beatrice interlaced her fingers and stretched her arms over her head. "I know this off by heart. It kept me awake this morning. *On Tuesday morning, I want every one of you to bring me an idea for a top-class Ecco dish. All these dishes need a story. Personal, local, global, I don't mind. Bring me new ideas and I will work with them all.* Isabella said I shouldn't worry about it as he expects nothing of me. Which makes me feel worse." She thought back to the afternoon in the restaurant, Isabella's hair in the sunshine, the golden bubbles rising to the surface of her glass. "She also said that if I could make Prosecco in an edible form, that would satisfy her."

Adrian clasped his hands together in delight. "Really? In that case, our idea is absolutely perfect. What special birthday treat do you remember from your childhood?"

"Pineapple upside-down cake," Beatrice said instantly.

Adrian rolled his eyes. "And how would the other ninety-nine per cent of the British public respond to that question?"

"Jelly and ice-cream?"

"Precisely!"

"Adrian ..."

"Wait, let me finish. You want a British dish with its own story, updated with a contemporary Italian twist. Our suggestion? Lavender and honey ice-cream, classic English garden-style, served with Prosecco jelly. Subtle, fragrant and designed around childhood memories of the chef - that'll be you. It's very spring-like and Eastery, and best of all, it looks simple but it's easy to cock it up."

A picture formed in Beatrice's mind. Her family garden in Gloucestershire, surrounded by dry stone walls and oak trees. Hollyhocks and roses, honeysuckle and clematis, filling the air with the fragrance of summer. A Labrador dozing on a freshly mown lawn, a wrought-iron table bearing plates of sandwiches, Scotch eggs and sausage rolls. Overhead, bunting blowing in the breeze. Half a dozen children singing 'Happy Birthday', her mother bearing a cake with six candles and her father recording it all on cine camera.

"I think that idea is quite brilliant! The only concern is that I have no idea how to make it."

Adrian gave her a knowing smile and withdrew a printout from the pocket of his jeans. "Nor do I. But the Internet does."

Chapter 24

Two days of holiday fed Suhail's soul. He spent his free time camping in the mountains. He meditated, prayed and recognised his place in the universe. Until that Sunday, he had not even realised how much was missing. Connected by his faith, cradled by the earth, he stared at the heavens and gave thanks for all his blessings. Over small camp fires, he heated water and the contents of random cans. His food was fuel, not an experience to be spun as a story or rated with stars. Alone with his thoughts, he found himself in the right place. Solitude was sustenance.

On Monday afternoon, he packed up his tent and cleaned away all traces of his presence, covering his fireplace with earth. That was when the memory ambushed him. He squatted down on his haunches and covered his eyes, all the better to see the images his mind offered.

Two little boys, the smaller one chasing his big brother in circles round a fire in the desert, their feet scattering sand as they ran. The smell of roasting meat and sound of childish laughter seemed real and present. A woman with a woven bag was unpacking bread. She called the boys and looked up at him with a smile like a caress. Her eyes reflected the firelight. And then she was gone. The velvet dusk, the warmth of the fire, the meat juices dripping into the pan below, the texture of the sand beneath his feet, the laughter of his sons, all gone. Instead, he was alone on an Italian mountainside.

He walked down the slopes and caught the little train back to Napoli, keeping away from people. For their sake and his own. He had not washed for two days and his body odour might offend his fellow travellers. His own reluctance to engage with society, on the other hand, could not be attributed to a single sense. People and their conversations, opinions, attitudes and judgements fractured his thoughts. Thinking, for Suhail, was an activity best practised alone. He rarely had sufficient time and space to indulge his favourite pastime in peace.

On this occasion, he had weighed silence and found it wanting. Dishonesty could take active forms, such as lying, cheating and deceiving. Or it could be passive, such as saying nothing. Suhail had sworn allegiance to silence ever since the one time he had spoken up and it cost him everything. He found it better to move quietly about his business, remaining distant and uninvolved. He was not responsible for what he knew and it was not his fault if people got hurt. He had done nothing.

Two days of examining his philosophy of disengagement brought him to a profound dissatisfaction. Retreating from the world and taking no responsibility was not living, but existing. If a man does nothing, neither good nor evil, which side is he on? Time to take action and speak up once again. If there was a price to pay, he had nothing left to lose.

Outside his apartment, he took a deep breath before unlocking the door, preparing to re-enter his everyday life, repeating his thanks for two days of purity and replenishment.

The key would not turn. He tried the handle and the door swung open. Suhail walked into the small bedsit and his peace vanished. He looked around at the broken crockery and torn clothes, read the graffiti on the walls and noted the stench of urine coming from his mattress. That was the last push. Time to leave. His most treasured possessions remained in their hiding-place behind the loose roof tile, which thankfully the vandals had not found. He packed them into a leather bag, threw the few remaining clothes they had not destroyed into his holdall and switched off the lights.

There was only one place to go. He sent one more prayer: *please do not let bad luck follow.*

Chapter 25

When the buzzer rang, Beatrice was mid-sentence. Everyone in the apartment looked to one another for an explanation. Luke's head lifted up from its habitual 45-degree angle over his phone, Will snapped shut his laptop and the discussion on recipes between Beatrice, Adrian and Matthew fell silent.

"Visitors on Easter Monday evening?" Will bounded out of his chair and picked up the intercom. "Hello?"

An electronic crackle came from the speaker. "My name is Suhail and I need the help of Beatrice Stubbs."

With a glance at Beatrice for permission, Will buzzed him in and ran downstairs to greet their unexpected guest. Beatrice waited in the hallway until they returned. Suhail's worried expression lifted just a touch on seeing her face.

"Suhail? Is everything all right?"

"I am deeply sorry to disturb you during your holiday. I find myself in an emergency situation and I must ask for your help. Also I beg your forgiveness. The last time we spoke, I was not truthful. I told no lies, but I omitted certain information. Can we talk?"

Beatrice considered the circumstances, Suhail's bulging holdall and the man's nervous stance. "Yes, of course we can talk. Do you need somewhere to stay? Because we have two spare rooms, you know."

He hesitated, with a glance at Will. Just then, Adrian and Luke came out of the living room.

"Hello, Suhail!" chirped Luke.

Suhail smiled. "Hello, Luke, hello, Adrian." He looked back at Beatrice. "Thank you. I would be forever in your debt."

"Come upstairs and let's take our conversation onto the terrace. And this time, we take our gloves off the table."

Beatrice took Suhail and a pot of mint tea up to the terrace.

"I apologise one thousand times for intruding."

"Yes, you said. And I said it's fine. I'm glad you're here and really don't have time to tell you so one thousand times. You and I are on the same side; at least I think we are. Can we be honest with each other?"

Suhail's eyes glowed with genuine warmth. "We are on the same side, Beatrice, I give you my word. This debt of gratitude I shall never forget. I am so sorry for my lack of truthfulness the last time we spoke. Even at the time, it was wrong to deceive you and in my heart, I knew it."

Beatrice sighed. It was going to be a long night. "Apology accepted. Can I make a request? Facts first and beat yourself up later?"

He bowed his head, his hand unconsciously touching his bandaged throat.

"Sorry, bad choice of phrasing." Beatrice poured the tea. "Where shall we begin?"

Suhail looked up and spoke in a flood of words. "Isabella and Agusto hired you to find the spy in Ecco's kitchen. You will never succeed because the spy is already dead. Rami was the one who sold recipes, this much I know, because he tried to persuade me to join him. I refused and our friendship was broken."

Beatrice observed this sad man's face, more animated than she'd ever seen it before. "You refused to cooperate and now they're applying pressure."

"That is correct. I am not a coward. I will stand up to these people. They offer me money, status, position, but what is that without honour? I refuse. Then they use physical violence, personal threats via messages in my locker and today my apartment was smashed. I repeat, I am not a coward. Neither am I stupid. I cannot stay there."

The man clenched his hands together and his eyes had a haunted look.

"You're safe here. I promise. But even if Rami was a spy, someone else is still active. The *affogato* recipe has appeared on more than one menu this week."

Suhail shook his head with a dismissive frown. "My belief is they don't have an insider anymore. So they try to copy the dishes but with no expertise, they will fail."

"Do you know who they are?"

"No. Rami never gave me any names. The people who approached me are nothing more than agents but their employers have connections. That is how it works. Beatrice, I want to do my job and protect Ecco. The problem is that I am afraid, for myself and also for you. These people are powerful and very dangerous."

Beatrice stared out across the twilight rooftops. "But not infallible. I have a rough plan. With your help, we can make it perfect. Why don't you unpack, freshen up and join me in the kitchen? We have work to do."

With the help of their curious six-year-old assistant, Beatrice and Suhail created eight individual desserts. Once in the kitchen, Beatrice was amazed to see Suhail's tension and trembles disappear. His focus was extraordinary, as was his patience with Luke. At one point Beatrice even suggested Luke go play on his device in the living room, but Suhail spoke up and suggested the task of peeling pistachios would be perfect for small fingers. Beatrice gave in and watched the interaction between the two with some curiosity.

The official tasting was a formal affair. Each taster at the dining table – Matthew, Adrian, Will and Luke – was given a piece of paper with A & B, C & D written as a column. Beside each letter was room to write a score out of 5 and space for comments.

Beatrice poured everyone a glass of water. "Don't forget; score the jelly and the ice-cream separately. Drink a couple of sips of water between the two dishes to cleanse your taste buds," she instructed. "Keep your opinions to yourself while tasting, just concentrate on the dish and write your notes on your scorecard. Please remember, the presentation is limited to what shops were open on an Easter Monday."

Suhail presented Dish One: four plates with a lilac-coloured ball of ice-cream resting beside a smooth dome of golden jelly, decorated with a few crushed pistachios and around the edge of the plate, some sugared almonds.

The chefs watched as the tasters took several mouthfuls and considered their verdicts. Once Adrian, the last to finish writing, had laid down his pencil, Beatrice removed the plates, hushing Luke's protest.

"If you like either or both, you can polish off the lot later. But first I need you to try Dish Two. Drink some water, please."

Suhail presented four cocktail glasses, frosty from the freezer. The ice-cream, a darker mauve this time, had set at a diagonal so the jelly settled into the remaining triangle, creating an asymmetric effect. Lying across each glass was a golden brown and blond *lingua di gatto* or cat's tongue biscuit and at the edge of the glass perched a purple and yellow flower.

Eyes widened as the glasses were set before them. "*Buon appetito*," said Beatrice. "The real thing would have edible flowers, but these are actually pansies I picked from the roof garden. Just set them to one side. Right, dig in."

The reactions were initially similar, thoughtful faces and expressions of approval. Until they took a spoon of the ice-cream. Luke's nose wrinkled and he took a sip of water. Matthew shook his head and bent to sniff his glass, while Adrian and Will put down their spoons.

Beatrice held up a finger to prevent any comments and pointed to the score sheets. All four heads bent to scribble urgently on the comments section. To her satisfaction, she could already see Adrian had written a zero next to section D and Luke gave it a minus 10. So far, so good.

She shared a smile with Suhail. "So, could you please give us your overall scores for Dish One, that is, jelly A and ice-cream B?" She totted them up and got a score of 37 out of 40, because Luke was not a fan of the Prosecco flavour.

"Now to Dish Two, which was evidently less popular. Scores please?"

Everyone spoke at once and Beatrice could only make out the words 'soapy', 'overly scented' and 'revolting' until Luke's voice was the last to fade.

"It tastes like Grandma's bathroom!"

After the laughter died down, Beatrice and Suhail took their seats.

"Right, your reaction was exactly what we'd hoped for. The jellies are in fact the same, just in a different presentation. The ice-creams have one important difference. The amount of lavender. The second one uses dried lavender and a significant amount more of it. Hence the overly perfumed, oppressive taste. Only Suhail and I know the exact measurements and it will stay that way. To everyone else, including Agusto and Isabella, we tell them the second recipe. Desserts at Ecco will be perfectly balanced and for those who like Prosecco, utterly delicious. If I'm right regarding our leak, those at the Nonna chain will smell like a grandma's bathroom."

Chapter 26

Maintaining Suhail's security was an issue that concerned them all. No one should know where he was staying, which presented an immediate problem on Tuesday morning. Ettore would arrive at his apartment to collect him for work and after finding no one home, would come to fetch Beatrice. They had to conceal their guest, for everyone's sake.

Beatrice woke early from bad-tempered dreams of crocheted toilet roll covers and lavender fields, feeling hungover despite the fact she'd drunk nothing more than water last night. She slipped out of bed and went upstairs to get some fresh air on the terrace. As she paced the perimeter of the huge space, a vehicle horn tooted, attracting her attention. She looked down to the car park behind the building. She'd hardly even noticed it before, as the view from the other three sides was so commanding. People were beginning their day. As she watched, a woman got out of a car and called something to the adjacent building. Finally a man came hurrying across the gravel, pulling on his jacket as he ran. Two teenagers called something to the harassed man who lifted his hands to the heavens. They laughed, she tooted the horn again and he got into the car. Before their car had even left the compound, two women got onto a moped, placing helmets over their glossy hair, and buzzed out of the gates into the street. Two more suited workers got into their separate cars and vacated their spots.

The car park was private, shared by three apartment blocks on the same street. Somehow, each vehicle that entered or exited was able to operate the large steel gates which closed after each arrival or departure. Directly below her, a man hared out of the same building as hers and straddled a silvery motorcycle. He threw the strap of his briefcase across his chest and fastened the chinstrap on his helmet. He blew a kiss back at the doorway. Curious, Beatrice leaned over the balustrade to see the recipient. Rather than a Gina Lollobrigida lookalike in a suggestive nightgown, there was a brindle cat sitting Sphinx-like on the doorstep.

Helmets. Gates. Privacy. Beatrice began pacing. Yes, on a moped, Suhail could leave and arrive at their apartment with relative anonymity, but at the restaurant? If people were watching him, they could follow the bike and put two and two together. How could they get the man to and from work without revealing the connection to Beatrice? It would have to be a team effort. Time to call on the cavalry. Again.

Will adopted the role of bodyguard with proprietary authority. "Today, Suhail and I can leave via the back gate and take a cab. Beatrice, you should stick to routine. Go with Ettore. We'll work out an alternative for this evening to get Suhail back here. Tomorrow, I'll hire a moped and helmets, drive Suhail to work and pick him up afterwards. Between us, we can handle this and keep you both safe."

Suhail, clutching a cup of coffee, listened to the conversation. A smile blossomed on his face, an expression so rare it stopped Beatrice in her tracks.

"Will, Beatrice, I cannot begin to thank you enough. Your kindness and the efforts you make for my safety are humbling. One day, I will repay such gestures of humanity."

"Hey, we're all in this together," said Will. "You're the chef;

we're your back-up team. I'll go tell Adrian the plan then we should hit the road. Beatrice, is that OK with you?"

Beatrice finished her coffee. "You two go ahead. I need a few minutes to brush my hair. Will, what would we do without you?"

"Stay out of trouble, I guess. You remember I thought this private investigation gig was a good idea, right?"

Ettore was late and when he did arrive, he was distraught.

"Suhail is gone! His apartment is a catastrophe!" He pronounced it Cat-Ass-Troff. "I don't know where he is, if he is alive, how to find him. His neighbours know nothing. This is bad, very bad. First Rami and now Suhail, what is happening in this city? We welcome everyone! Always. Napoli is a melting pot, we have all kinds of people and this is what makes the city special. If Suhail is gone or somebody hurt him, it is my fault. I am to protect him, bring him to work. This is very bad, Beatrice. Isabella will blame me!"

"Has anyone called the police?" asked Beatrice, disingenuously. "Or perhaps the restaurant should do that if he doesn't turn up for work."

"Yes, Agusto must call the police. This, all of this, is because somebody wants to destroy Ecco. It makes me sad in my soul. Good people, beautiful food, loyal employees and now, what happens to us?" He took his hands off the wheel for an empty-handed gesture and Beatrice's right foot hit an imaginary brake.

His phone rang and Ettore conducted a brief and urgent conversation in Italian. When he rang off, he reached over to shake Beatrice's leg.

"God be praised! Suhail is at Ecco!" he said, with a huge grin. "He left his apartment and he stays with a friend. Isabella cries and Agusto thanks God. I am so happy, Beatrice! And so are you!"

Beatrice played the game. She bent her head onto her clasped hands. "Our prayers have been answered, Ettore, and we should give thanks. Suhail has a guardian angel. This is going to be a very special week!"

Ettore closed his eyes and thumped a palm to his chest. Beatrice's toes clenched and she wished her passionate and emotional driver would keep his eyes open, at least while he was behind the steering-wheel.

The morning was as busy and stressful as ever, particularly as everyone had a new dish to prepare for Agusto's approval, yet the atmosphere had a celebratory feeling. Rather like a new beginning.

Suhail took charge of the daily duties, leaving Beatrice to create 'The English Garden' herself, under his supervision. The temperatures and timing had to be precise, so she used a thermometer and timer. Once diners began to arrive, the basic house desserts were complete, so they had around an hour to prepare all the extras – tuiles, biscotti, *lingue di gatto* and citrus crisps. There was always a brief hiatus for the dessert corner while the *primi piatti* were served and Beatrice seized her chance.

She ducked through the mayhem of the main kitchen and out into the courtyard, clutching her phone. Ensuring no one was in earshot, she dialled Herr Karl Kälin of Swiss Federal Police. She wasn't sure if he'd remember her from that serial killer case a few years back, but she had certainly not forgotten him.

He answered the call in the same brusque manner she recalled from their collaboration. "Kälin."

"Hello, Herr Kälin, this is Beatrice Stubbs. We worked together a few years ago on the D'Arcy Richter case."

"Hello, Frau B. Yes, I remember that case. And you are not someone I would forget. Are you well?"

Beatrice had a sense of déjà vu, the uncertainty of whether he was being friendly or simply dry. She chose the optimistic outlook. "Yes, thank you, just dealing with the onset of old age.

How are you? I hear you recently retired."

"Correct. And unless I am mistaken, so did you. I am curious what reason you have to call me, unless it is to compare pensions."

Beatrice's lips twitched. He really was a truculent old bugger. "Indeed I have retired from the Metropolitan Police, but I still do a little detective work on a private basis. I'm currently investigating a case in Italy and there appears to be a Swiss connection. Do you know of a place called Einsiedeln?"

"I do. It is in Canton Schwyz about one hour from Zürich. What about it?"

"Well, there's a new restaurant of interest to my investigation, and the chef and owner shares your name. Kälin. I wondered if it might be a relative of yours."

"Ah, I see. You find two people with the same name from the same country and assume they are related. Do you apply the same logic when investigating someone from England called Smith?"

"It's not something I would discount," she retorted, her jaw tensing. How could that irascible git still irritate her over so many miles and years? "Perhaps if I give you the full details, you can tell me if I'm chasing my own trail. The chef's name is Stefan Kälin and the name of the restaurant is Chalet Nonna."

There was a moment's silence at the other end and Beatrice paced the courtyard, spotting something on the ground. The knife sharpener she had hurled at the intruder who scratched Agusto's Ferrari. She crouched to pick it up and spotted something else a few paces away. It looked like a credit card. Beatrice's eyes widened, just as Kälin's voice rumbled into her ear.

"That is a coincidence. Stefan is the son of my cousin. His success as a chef has come as a surprise to all of his family. Until now, he has always been what you would call a 'quitter'. Stefan has begun many careers seeking fame and now finally finds himself a celebrity on the restaurant scene."

"Aha! So I was right to ask you," said Beatrice, with a certain smugness.

"I'm afraid you just got lucky, Frau Stubbs. Every third person you meet in that area is called Kälin. As I said, this is a coincidence."

Exasperated, Beatrice got to the point. "Very well. So that is one of those areas where cousins are still allowed to marry. My question is more about this restaurant, how well you know the owner and if you can tell me anything about the financing and creative impetus behind the venture."

The silence went on for much longer this time.

"Herr Kälin?"

"The older we get, the less we learn. I see you still cannot manage to moderate your opinions before expressing them, Frau Stubbs. Although I am a busy man, I will visit the restaurant. Perhaps I might learn something by using a more sophisticated approach. I wish you a good day."

He rang off before Beatrice could wish him the same.

After a hectic but more successful lunch service, Agusto was ready to try his chefs' new ideas. Each nervous cook had designed and prepared a new dish for his approval, presented to the Colacino trio in the restaurant. Nerves and a certain amount of friendly competition electrified the kitchen.

Agusto, in an excellent mood, made some changes and additions, yet gave the thumbs up to them all. Every chef who returned to the kitchen had positive news. Finally, it was time for dessert.

Beatrice used her hip to open the swing doors, gave them all a big smile and placed the single dish in front of Agusto. The script she had prepared with Suhail scrolled through her head. *Double cream, egg yolks, milk, honey, dried English lavender to create the delicate scent of summer in an ice-cream, with subtle*

*flavours of Prosecco in a sunshine jelly, with a light biscuit evoking
the classic birthday tea.*

Agusto tasted first, followed by Isabella and Gennaio.

"Yes," said Agusto. "I like. The birthday tea, the English
Garden, this is a good story. The jelly is too sweet, use a Brut.
The ice-cream is perfect but I don't like the biscuit. Too simple
for Ecco. Nothing we do is boring. Hmm. The birthday tea. Alice
in Wonderland. Tea party." He closed his eyes.

Beatrice wondered if this was a typically Italian habit. She
said nothing and kept smiling. He may well have dozed off.

"What happens at an English birthday party?" Agusto
demanded, his eyes now wide open.

"Oh, you know, singing, presents, cake. Sparklers in winter,
bunting in summer, maybe a scavenger hunt or pass-the-parcel.
At least, that's how we did it in my day."

Gennaio shook his head. "I understand nothing." He stood
up and took out his cigarettes, jerking his head at the door.

"Wait, Gennaio!" called Isabella. "What is 'bunting',
Beatrice?"

"Flags. Little triangular flags along a line. Very British symbol
of a celebration."

Isabella and Agusto spoke eagerly in Italian. Whatever was
said, both were pleased with the outcome.

"We will make the bunting," Isabella announced. "Agusto did
it many times before with edible paper. Lavender ice-cream,
Prosecco jelly and little flags you can eat. I LOVE this idea!"

Isabella clapped her hands and Agusto kissed her cheek.
Gennaio, still on his feet, flicking his lighter, looked back at the
table. "OK, I can vote for this English dessert. What about the
other guy's idea?"

Agusto shook his head. "Suhail's apartment was trashed this
weekend. We can't expect him to create a dessert in those
circumstances."

"Really? Everyone had the whole weekend to invent new

ideas, including the Arab. When he comes home to a burglary, all his ideas go ..." He flashed both hands as if to make something disappear.

Isabella got to her feet. "Gennaio, go smoke."

"I'm going. But listen to me, when even the fake chef can create something and that refugee cannot, we have a problem? He is useless."

Beatrice bristled. "Fake chef? That refugee? Just a minute ..."

"Out!" yelled Isabella, shoving Gennaio towards the door. She flashed a threatening look behind her, but it was not directed at Beatrice. Her husband cringed and retreated to the kitchen.

When both men had left the room, Isabella gave a dismissive shake of the head and an apologetic smile. "Ignore him. He's having a bad day. Problems with insurance at the warehouse. His office was destroyed and all his paperwork gone. Gennaio is not a racist, just quick to find fault."

Beatrice was not mollified. "In that case, he needs to moderate his language. I have a question regarding our accommodation. My guests want to hire a car this week. How do we get access to the car park at the apartment?"

"You already have access. In the kitchen drawer, there is a little grey device with a red button. Put that in the car and when you want to open the gates, press the button. Check it first. The batteries might be dead."

"Thank you."

"Beatrice? Please don't mention Gennaio's comments to Suhail. I will calm my stupid brother-in-law and make everything all right. Are you getting closer to solving our problem?"

"Yes. I don't want to give too much away, but I think I am closer to finding the source of the rot. Please tell no one. Everyone should carry on as usual. That is vital."

"Of course. I will say nothing. Thank you very much."

JJ Marsh

When Beatrice returned to the kitchen, most people had gone. Benoît was emptying the dishwasher and flashed her a wide smile as she popped her head around the corner.

"Hello, Benoît, I'm Beatrice. *Parlez-vous anglais?*"

"*Bonjour, Beatrice, ça va? Désolé, non. Avez-vous une cigarette?*"

"*Non, je ne fume pas. Bonne journée!*"

"*Bonne journée!*"

She retreated from a conversation which gave her very little, other than how much she loved the way her name sounded in French.

Behind the fridge in the dessert section, Agusto was talking to Suhail in Italian. From what she could understand, the chef was offering to help him find a new apartment. Deliberately dropping the used spoons onto a steel work surface, Beatrice announced her presence as subtly as a breeze block.

Agusto came around the corner. "Well done, Beatrice. I like your dessert very much. You know, I think you could be a very good chef. You have imagination."

"Not matched by my skills, I'm afraid. I am grateful for Suhail as my cover."

Isabella opened the kitchen door, her mobile in hand, beckoning Agusto with a fierce expression. "*Andiamo!*"

Beatrice didn't hesitate. "You best get on and so should I. Ettore will be waiting for me."

She waited till he had gone before saying her goodbyes to Suhail, with a whispered promise they would make a plan to collect him that evening.

The whispering was unnecessary. The kitchen was deserted. Benoît had finished his lowly task and left for the afternoon. She spotted him outside with Bruno, both lighting up.

Bruno saw her and waved. "*Ciao, Beatrice. A domani!*"

"*A domani!*" she replied, rather proud of her Italian accent. Then a thought occurred to her and she walked over to address

Bruno in English. "Sorry to disturb, but can I ask you something?" She felt in the pocket of her chef's whites and pulled out the plastic card she had found in the courtyard. "What is this?"

He took it and turned it over. "An access card, like in a hotel. Where did you find it?"

"It was lying on the ground over there. I think the man who scratched Agusto's car dropped it when I threw the sharpener at him. I wondered if it was worth taking to the police."

Bruno examined it more closely and showed it to Benoît, who pointed at the logo and spoke in rapid French.

Bruno blew smoke up into the air. "*Oui, d'accord.* Beatrice, we think this is a key card for the entrance to the docks. Benoît says this logo is ADSP, the people who manage the port. Gennaio has one exactly the same. Yes, maybe you should tell the police. It might be important."

"Thanks, you've been a big help. Have a relaxing afternoon. *Au revoir!*"

She spent a leisurely afternoon wandering the Centro Storico with Matthew and Luke, idly browsing all the various horns and masks at every street stall. She waited while Matthew took photographs of Luke: in front of towering monuments, posing with a double scoop of ice-cream, pointing at graffiti and fussing a small dog which looked like Huggy Bear. The sights and smells of the streets occupied only a part of Beatrice's mind. She turned the facts over and over, putting each person she suspected on an imaginary stand and examining their alibis. The more pressing problem of how to get Suhail home safely without being followed preoccupied her from piazza to gelateria. It was a good job Matthew took so many pictures, because she was unlikely to remember a thing about the day.

Around five o'clock, Matthew suggested they return to the apartment for a rest. She agreed with alacrity, her concerns for his health ever present. Not to mention the constant need to grab Luke and drag him out of the route of a moped. Her nerves were frazzled. The best place to keep Luke safe, let Matthew rest and give herself some thinking time was their beautiful, calm apartment.

On arrival at the front door, they met Will and Adrian returning from their expedition. They took afternoon tea on the terrace. To Beatrice's immense relief, Will had devised a plan.

Chapter 27

Adrian only had himself to blame. He wanted Beatrice to be a private detective. He wanted Will to come to Naples. He had encouraged her to take on the Ecco case. Now his husband had got all involved and enthusiastic about it and Adrian didn't have a leg to stand on when Will wanted to explore the area around the Porta Antica rather than going on a boat trip.

They found a restaurant within walking distance of Ecco and although they could not book – *no reservations, we'll fit you in if there's room* – they decided to eat there that night. As a party of five would not fit in a regular taxi, they would travel there with Ettore, and after dinner, Beatrice, Matthew and Luke would return home the same way. Adrian and Will would wait until Suhail left after his evening shift, when Will would meet him and insist he join them for a coffee. Once inside the bar, they would keep moving and leave through the side entrance where Adrian would be waiting in a cab. Anyone following Suhail would be waiting out front and by the time it became obvious their target had vanished, Adrian, Will and Suhail would be safely back inside their own apartment with their feet up.

Adrian thought the plan was relatively low on the risky side, apart from how he could explain his requirements to a cabbie in Italian. They walked the streets around the restaurant, checking escape routes, taxi ranks and parking places, while Will coached

Adrian in a few essential phrases. *Possiamo aspettare i miei amici?* Can we wait for my friends? *Mi dispiace, loro sono in ritardo.* I'm sorry, they are late. They practised till they were completely satisfied with the plan and began to look forward to the evening. Until they got back to the apartment and met Beatrice.

Her face pinked from their excursion that afternoon, she listened intently to their suggestions. "Very good thinking. Just a couple of points. I'm happy to use Ettore to take us there and bring Matthew and Luke back. However, I will stay with you two, for the following reasons. A, certain factors in this case need discussing but not in front of granddad and grandson. And secondly, it makes more sense if both of you meet Suhail from work. Strength in numbers. I will wait at the bar and when you send me a message saying you're on your way, I will find us a cab and explain the situation."

"In Italian?" asked Adrian, incredulous.

She gave him a headmistress-like look. "I think you'll find I can manage."

"OK," said Will, with a wry smile. "You're the boss. Just be aware that Il Capitano is a harbour café for fishermen and a far cry from the five-star joints you are used to. We're going local and eating street food. Rough and ready."

Beatrice laughed and ran her hands through her tangled hair. "I'd say me and Il Capitano are well matched."

The car eased up the Via del Porto and despite the views across the sea, Il Capitano had already drawn their attention. Coloured lights and striped awnings stood out against the dusky pink evening glow and the bustle and activity within would make any passer-by look twice.

"Here we are, everyone!" announced Ettore and stepped out of the car to open the rear door. He helped Beatrice and Luke out and gave a bow to Matthew, Will and Adrian. "Call me when you are ready to leave. I am at your service."

"Thank you, Ettore. It is possible that the boys might stay out later. But if you could come back at ten to take some of us home, that would be very kind."

"Buon appetito!"

Il Capitano was a restaurant with a difference. Facing directly onto the docks, what had once been a takeaway counter had grown up with delusions of grandeur. Long trestle tables formed canteen-style vertical lines away from the kitchen and marquees provided the walls, complete with plastic windows. Diners sat on benches, elbow to elbow with strangers. On a warm spring-like evening, it worked. Adrian dreaded to think of how the experience would change affected by winter chills and summer stink.

The waitress waved an arm at the tables, inviting them to seat themselves. Adrian liked the look of the one closest to the heater with no other occupants, but Will had already asked the people filling half a table in the middle if they could join them. So they had no choice but to cosy up to a bunch of total strangers on a hard bench and sit on their coats.

Adrian sighed.

"I know. It is awfully hard to choose," said Matthew, browsing the menu.

Luke tore off some bread and began the oil and vinegar routine. "I am REALLY hungry. Probably hungry enough for a starter and a main course and a pudding."

"Set menu!" said a fierce voice. A squat, dark woman in a pinafore stood at the head of their table with a notepad. "Salad or soup, *spaghetti alla vongole* and fish of the day. Very good. You want?"

Whatever it was, they wanted.

Dish after dish was plonked on the table with little ceremony, leaving the diners to shuffle plates around to the right owners, but the food was plentiful, the wine drinkable and the conversation lively.

Matthew's face glowed as he mopped up the caper sauce with a chunk of brown bread and he looked across at Adrian. "Tell you what, this ticks all my boxes. Those upscale establishments are fascinating, in a rare butterfly sort of a way. This, on the other hand, is how I should like to eat on a daily basis. Hearty, flavoursome and unfussy. Even the wine, if a tad boisterous, passes muster, wouldn't you say?"

It actually was. All Adrian's snobbery and judgement had disappeared as his appetite took over. A child in the neighbouring party managed to strike up a dialogue with Luke over some kind of puzzle and the nearest woman watched them converse in different languages with a fond smile.

She looked up and caught the adults' eyes. "English? *Turisti*?"

"*Sì, siamo turisti*," said Will.

To Adrian's ears, his accent sounded perfect and really rather sexy.

The woman asked another question. Will shook his head. "*Non ho capito.*"

She pointed at Luke and repeated herself. Adrian caught the word 'No potty' and wondered if she was asking if Luke was house-trained.

In the face of Will's blank look, Matthew responded. "*Lui è mio nipote. Adesso, l'unico. Ma ho due figlie. Forse ci sarà più bambini in futuro. Quanti figli avete?*"

"What did he say?" asked Adrian. Will shrugged.

They both stared at Matthew as he carried on a cheerful conversation with the kindly woman in what sounded like fluent Italian.

"I can't follow all of it," said Beatrice, "but they're discussing grandchildren. After spending most of his life teaching Classics, he's picked up a thing or two. You should hear him speak Greek."

As the evening drew on, Luke and his new friend said their goodbyes with gestures. Matthew wished everyone goodnight and kissed Beatrice before escorting his grandson to the car.

Beatrice gave a polite smile to the family and guided Will and Adrian over to the bar for coffee. She had just begun to speak when the door flaps opened and her driver strode into the room. Adrian nudged Beatrice, whose attention was elsewhere.

"What is it, Ettore? Are they both all right?"

"Yes, yes, but you must also come. I cannot leave you here. I am responsible for your safety and I will take you home."

Beatrice's expression hardened. "Thank you, but no. Please take Matthew and Luke back to the apartment. I will come later with Will and Adrian. They will take care of me, there's no need for concern."

Ettore side-eyed Adrian and gave Will the once over. "How long you want to stay? I can take them home and come back. It's not far and I wait till you are ready."

"Ettore! Please listen to me. I would like you to deliver my boys and then go home to your girls. You've worked long hours already and I am officially dismissing you for the night. Don't worry, I promise you we'll stay together. Goodnight and see you tomorrow."

Ettore stood for a moment, his face mutinous. "*Buonasera a tutti. A domani*, Beatrice."

They watched him shoulder his way out.

"Has he got a crush on you?" asked Adrian.

Beatrice snorted. "Just overprotective, that's all. Now listen to me. Three things I want to talk about. One, I found something in the courtyard outside Ecco. Apparently it's a key card to access the dock area. My theory is that when I walloped that bloke with the knife sharpener, he fell and dropped this. Why would someone trying to damage Agusto's or possibly Gennaio's Ferrari, have a key card to the docks? And why would that person be lurking around Ecco at the precise same time that Gennaio's warehouse catches fire?"

"If it is Gennaio they are targeting, it could be someone who works for him, someone with a grudge," Will observed. "My guess is that whoever it was lit the fire first, then came to the restaurant to damage the Ferrari. The idea being that Gennaio would get the alarm call, rush out to his car and find that it had been scratched. Message received: someone is out to get him. But for whatever reason, the fire took hold sooner than expected and the guy got the wrong car. Which tells me this person is an amateur."

"Interesting word, amateur," said Beatrice. "Our tail seems to be far from expert and I wonder ... what if the clumsy surveillance and half-arsed threats are either a double-bluff or poor performance from an outsourced contractor? Let's come back to that later. Point Two. The Spy. According to Suhail, there is no spy in the Ecco kitchens because he's already dead. Golden Boy Rami was selling recipes to some kind of powerful organisation. Perhaps that's true. But if he was the spy, how do we explain the fact that my dessert, albeit badly executed, appeared on a rival menu the next day? Nevertheless, Rami ended up dead and they are putting pressure on Suhail to step into his shoes."

Adrian gasped. He realised he was attracting attention so dropped his voice to a whisper. "So that's why they ..." He mimed cutting his throat.

Beatrice tutted, with a glance around the room. "Can we not conduct confidential discussions as pantomime?"

Abashed, Adrian sipped his coffee.

"You said three things," Will said, his focus intense. "The access card, Suhail's confidences and what else?"

"Gennaio has issues with Suhail. Today, he expressed little sympathy for Suhail's predicament and actually referred to him as 'the refugee'. This might just be casual racism. But I sense there is a strong antipathy between the two based on more than nationality. Suhail has never mentioned Gennaio by name, but I've seen how he avoids being in the same room with him. Then

Gennaio gave himself away by saying 'Everyone had the whole weekend to invent new ideas, including the Arab. When he comes home to a burglary, all his ideas go pfft.' Those were his exact words. He already knew Suhail's apartment had been turned over and when."

Adrian looked from Will to Beatrice, waiting for elucidation. Neither spoke.

After several minutes of staring into coffee cups, both heads rose and Adrian watched a silent communication which excluded him completely.

"What?!" he demanded.

Beatrice glanced around the glorified tent for eavesdroppers. "I believe we're being played. By whom I can't be sure. I think tomorrow will be the decider. Would you two drop into Ristorante della Nonna at lunchtime? Go late and act up till they fit you in. I'm pretty sure The English Garden dessert will already be on the menu. If it's the same as Suhail and I made, we know who's spilling secrets. It can only be Suhail himself, which is unlikely as he helped me lay the trap. If it's Grandma's Bathroom, things are a lot more complicated. Only Isabella, Agusto or Gennaio could be the leak and I know which one of the three I suspect." She checked her watch. "Shouldn't you be heading up to Ecco by now? Suhail usually finishes by eleven."

They drained their coffees and left PI Stubbs at the bar. As they reached the doorway, Adrian looked back to reassure her. He needn't have worried. Beatrice was busy collecting all the uneaten chocolates from each of their saucers. She saw him watching and affected an innocent look, unperturbed. She waved her phone as a reminder to call once they were on their way back to Il Capitano.

"Right, let's go get our man," said Adrian, his light tone belying his nerves. They were about to meet either a double-crosser who was playing them for fools or an innocent man being targeted by a corrupt gang of murderers. He made a vow to himself. If they survived this holiday, which was far from a certainty, their next vacation would involve nothing more dangerous than a peaceful canal barge along the Norfolk Broads.

Twenty minutes later, Adrian began to worry that Suhail had already left. Various kitchen and waiting staff exited via the courtyard, passing Adrian and Will on the street corner.

They had positioned themselves in that spot to be able to watch the front doors as well as see who emerged from the courtyard. As each person left, the tension in Adrian's shoulders increased. When his phone vibrated in his pocket and the ring tone trilled into the night air, he jumped as if someone had goosed him.

"Hi, Beatrice, we're still waiting … no, we're on the street outside … we can see the kitchen door from … oh hang on, here he comes. OK, we've got him. See you in a few minutes. Bye."

Suhail crossed the street and shook their hands. "Thank you for meeting me."

"Pleasure," said Will. "Let's go." He took the side of the pavement next to the road and strolled off, Suhail at his side.

The pavement wasn't wide enough for three abreast, so Adrian had to walk just behind. He was disappointed at the lack of performance involved. Surely they should put more effort into persuading Suhail to join them for a drink?

"Hey, guys, how about a beer?" Adrian said, adopting a hearty, masculine tone.

"I don't drink alcohol," mumbled Suhail.

"Great! All the more for me!" Adrian replied, bumping his fist against Suhail's shoulder.

"What *are* you doing?" asked Will, without looking back.

"Just in case we're being followed," Adrian hissed through his teeth. "I'm making it look authentic."

"Well, don't. Suhail is teetotal and we're not on a stag night in Brick Lane. If you want to be useful, when we get under the next street light, drop your keys or anything that makes a noise. Then stop and pick them up. Give me an excuse to turn around."

Adrian fumbled in his jacket pocket for some loose change and pulled out a tissue, releasing the coins onto the pavement. He cursed and bent down to retrieve them. "Hang on a second, guys!" he called. Will and Suhail stopped walking and turned to wait for him. He knelt under the pool of light, while they stood in the shadows.

"Sorry about that," said Adrian, as he caught up with them.

"Right." Will spoke in a low voice. "Do *not* look round. There's a guy about ten or twelve metres behind us who just crossed to the other side of the road. My guess is that he'll speed up and pass us. He's probably got a colleague further down who'll let us go by and then start following. Don't let them know we're aware we've got a tail. Just continue with a normal conversation and I'll keep watching him."

Adrian resisted the urge to check over his shoulder and followed Will's instructions. "How was your day, Suhail? Was it busy?" His voice came out louder than he'd planned.

Suhail, on the other hand, spoke softly. "Every day at Ecco is busy. We are always fully booked. People are curious about the guest chef and her British desserts."

Out of the corner of his eye, Adrian was aware of a young man in a white T-shirt walking briskly down the other side of the street, paying them no attention.

"So the experiment is a success?" asked Will, his gaze on a shop window beside Suhail, watching the man's reflection.

"Certainly. The reviews are very good. This has been an education for us all."

The lights of Il Capitano glittered ahead and Adrian's nerves increased. "How exciting for you!" he exclaimed.

"That is great news!" said Will, then dropped his voice. "When we get to the restaurant, I will gesture for you to go in ahead of me while I fiddle with my phone. Adrian, you lead the way straight through and out the other side. Don't run or hurry, keep all movements casual and get into the cab as normally as you can. I'll join you a few seconds later, after I've checked if anyone clocked what we're doing. OK?"

Adrian's confidence rose a notch as they approached the doorway. If Beatrice had managed to secure them a taxi, they could easily lose a juvenile pedestrian follower.

"You go ahead," Will said, his voice normal. "I just need to answer this."

It was the big moment. Adrian pulled back the tarpaulin 'door' and said in an equally natural voice, "No problem. We'll get the beers in."

With Suhail on his heels, he strolled along the length of the restaurant, projecting confidence and calm. There was no sign of Beatrice but the family they had met earlier were still at the same table. He gave them a friendly nod. Before he'd even opened the door at the other end, he could see the lights of the idling cab. They emerged onto the street and saw Beatrice's face pressed up against the rear window. They got in beside her and as soon as they had closed the doors, the passenger door opened and Will got in. He twisted to address Beatrice.

"The driver knows where to go?"

"Yes. Her name is Daria and I already told her what we want."

"*Ciao*, Daria. *Grazie mille. Andiamo?*"

The driver, who must have been in her sixties with curls every bit as unruly as Beatrice's, nodded and put the car into gear. They drove away from Il Capitano in a state of high tension.

Will spoke. "Suhail, Beatrice, it would help me if you got your heads down. Just so I can see what's behind us. Our tail has a mate on a moped that would have a certain advantage in this traffic."

Suhail leaned into the corner, shrinking himself into a hunch. Beatrice lay sideways, her head resting in the crook of Adrian's arm.

"But they'll still be waiting outside the front of the restaurant, won't they?" asked Adrian. "How would they know we've already left?"

Will's eyes scanned the scene behind them as the taxi waited at a T-junction. His voice was grim. "They know. They're right behind us."

They drove in silence for several minutes, Will constantly twisting to check out of the rear window. Adrian looked too but couldn't differentiate between the various headlights and mopeds that changed lanes and wove between the traffic at every stop.

Daria flicked her eyes at the rear-view mirror and then to Will. "Problem?"

Will's head snapped around. "*Sì. Gli uomini ...*" He stopped. Apparently his Italian vocabulary was not up to explaining the circumstances. He indicated their tail. "*Non sono buoni.*"

Even Adrian understood that one. Those men were not good indeed.

The driver gave Will a searching look, then nodded. "OK."

When the lights changed she took off at such a pace the force almost gave Adrian whiplash. He clutched the door handle as the taxi lurched from lane to lane, taking corners at speed and inciting a volley of car horns. Beatrice grasped Adrian's forearm so tightly it pinched. The taxi driver turned into a tiny alley, which Adrian feared might be a dead end, and switched off her lights. They crawled along in darkness, both Will and Adrian peering behind to see if anyone had followed.

The alleyway remained empty. The taxi driver pulled up the handbrake and waited. Nothing.

Will lifted his hand up for a high five. "*Brava!*" he whispered.

Daria flashed her teeth and reached up to smack his palm. Several seconds ticked by and nothing moved ahead or behind.

After a nod from Will, the driver started the engine and turned left into an even smaller alley, little more than a footpath, so that the car shunted bins and cardboard boxes as it progressed towards the lights of a main street. Someone shouted from a balcony above and Daria wound down her window to flip the finger.

They emerged onto a normal street, quieter than the main drag, but well lit and populated by frequent vehicles. Daria switched the lights on, indicated right and eased into the traffic. Will surveyed the area while Adrian patted Beatrice's shoulder.

"She lost them. We're OK."

They had travelled no more than half a mile when Daria released a vicious curse. Adrian recognised none of the words but the tone was unmistakeable. Her eyes were fixed on the wing mirror. Will spun round and stared past Adrian.

"Shit. They're back."

"*Ci sono due!*" spat Daria. "*Due!*" she repeated.

"Two? Two what?" asked Will, his eyes scanning the street behind them. "Oh, I see. The moped and the black sedan. Hellfire, we're popular tonight."

Adrian peered out at the dazzling blaze of headlights, completely bewildered how anyone could see who was trailing whom. As he watched, Daria changed lanes and one headlight did the same, immediately followed by a much bigger car, street lights reflecting in its black bodywork.

Without indicating, Daria swung into the right hand lane. The moped did the same. But this time, the big sedan stayed in the left lane, pulled level with the bike, overtook and swerved right in front. The bike slid sideways, throwing both riders to the ground. "Oh my God!" Adrian gasped.

"What is it?" asked Beatrice, elbowing her way to a sitting position.

"That car just rammed the moped! Who the hell would do that?"

Will's voice was urgent. "Daria, go!"

The taxi took off at speed and Adrian could see nothing but the commotion of people running from the café tables to help the stricken motorcyclists. The sedan had stopped but no one emerged to check the damage.

After several minutes of switching, doubling back and racing through back streets, Daria brought the cab to a halt behind some large steel gates.

Will leapt out. "Adrian! Here, use this remote and open the car park. Take Suhail and Beatrice inside. I will drive another block with Daria and then pay the woman with a handsome tip. You three get inside and shut the gates behind you. I'll come in the front door. Go, quick!"

They scrambled out into the night air and slipped between the gates as Daria's cab rattled off down the street. Adrian fumbled as he inserted the key to the back door, his nerves jangling and on edge.

Once they got inside, Beatrice heaved a huge shuddering sigh. "I need a large glass of something pungent and a lie down," she said, leading the way upstairs.

Suhail's voice floated up the stairwell. "Beatrice, this is not acceptable. I have brought fear and danger to your doorstep. That is wrong of me. I thank you for all your kindness, but tomorrow I will find somewhere else to stay. I cannot put you and your family at risk. I am ashamed and I apologise."

Much of Adrian's tension lifted as they approached the apartment, which already seemed like home. He tried to reassure their guest. "Let's talk about it tomorrow. This evening was scary, I agree, but tomorrow we'll be much more organised. Come on, I need a drink and so do you. Even if it is only a peppermint tea."

Beatrice opened the apartment door, marched in and dumped her bag on the nearest chair. "He's right. I don't have the energy to argue with you tonight, but we are a team and we must stick together. Adrian, put the kettle on. All we need now is DS Quinn to get home in one piece and we can ... Luke?"

Adrian heard the catch in her voice and rushed out of the kitchen.

In his pyjamas, tear-stained and exhausted, Luke stood at the end of the corridor. "Where have you been?" he sobbed.

Beatrice knelt to embrace him. "Luke, Luke, what is it? Did you have a nightmare? Where's Matthew?"

Through hiccupping sobs, Luke managed to say, "Granddad's not very well. He fell over and I couldn't wake him up."

Suhail was fastest and rushed down the corridor ahead of Adrian, Beatrice hot on their heels. In the doorway of the bathroom, Matthew lay on his front like a fallen tree. Suhail pressed two fingers to his neck and put an ear to his mouth.

His eyes met Adrian's. "He's breathing, but his pulse is weak. I think he's had a heart attack. You get some aspirin and I'll call an ambulance."

Beatrice crouched beside Matthew, her throat swollen tight as she stroked his hair. "Matthew? Matthew, my love, wake up. Please wake up."

Adrian ran for the aspirin, eyes flooded with tears. At the end of the corridor stood Will, white-faced and holding a weeping Luke in his arms.

Chapter 28

The corridors of the University Hospital were bright but silent. Beatrice sat in a low chair, staring at the array of highly-coloured magazines on the table in front of her. Her thoughts flew around her head, as black, uncontrolled and malevolent as a flock of Hitchcockian crows.

She hadn't been paying enough attention. She knew he was having chest pains. They should have taken him to a specialist the first time he'd complained. Had they taken out health insurance? Ten past four. They must have finished the tests by now. Why had she not listened when he wanted to discuss making a will? Him lying on the floor, Luke trying to rouse him, the idea was unbearable. If she were to lose him now, just after starting their retirement together ... she couldn't think like that. Matthew was the most important person in the world to her, the love of her life. He was her anchor, the only thing she could depend on. He was as strong as an ... older man who probably ate and drank too much, while doing very little exercise. If he pulled through, no, when he pulled through, she would personally take charge of his diet and exercise. Twenty-five past four. This was entirely her fault.

She got up and poured some water from the dispenser into a paper cup. Her mouth was dry and her breath stale. She drank it all and was refilling the cup when a nurse came along the corridor.

"*Signora Stubbs*?" She beckoned Beatrice with a gentle smile. Beatrice couldn't tell if her expression was one of deepest sympathy or nothing to worry about. She picked up her bag and followed the woman along identical corridors until they stopped outside a white door. The nurse knocked, listened for permission and gestured for Beatrice to enter.

The doctor sat behind a desk, typing notes into her computer. She looked up at Beatrice's worried face.

"Come in, please, sit down. My name is Doctor Farooqi. Your partner is resting. After we talk, you can go and see him."

Beatrice sat, not trusting her voice to express her relief.

"Mr Bailey had a minor heart attack and suffered a concussion as a result of his fall. We did some tests – an ECG and an angiography – and discovered he has a form of unstable angina. We need to keep him under observation for at least twenty-four hours, as much for the concussion as the heart issues, and we would like to perform further tests. There is a serious risk of further attacks or even a stroke unless we can ensure better blood flow to his heart. We injected him with blood-thinning medication and will watch how he responds. If that doesn't work, we may need to consider surgery to widen the problematic artery. His condition is treatable, I can assure you. I would like to know a little more about his medical history and lifestyle. Could you tell me how long he has had chest pains?"

With an overwhelming sense of shame, Beatrice told the woman all she knew. She was completely honest about Matthew's (and her own) fondness for rich dishes with buttery sauces, red wine, cakes and pastries and his only exercise being a stroll with the dog or a potter round the golf course on a Sunday morning. It all seemed blindingly obvious now and the more she continued, the more foolish she felt.

The doctor made no judgements but advised Beatrice to read up on the condition and take appropriate steps. Finally she permitted her to see the patient.

His eyes were closed when she entered his room. She sat in the chair beside his bed and watched his chest rise and fall. Some of his colour had returned, banishing that awful ashen look. She itched to reach for his hand, to feel warmth and life, but did not dare to wake him. Light seeped through the curtains as the first signs of dawn broke over the city. The terrors of the night retreated and for the first time since arriving back at the apartment the previous evening, tears welled in her eyes. Her beloved Matthew was still with her.

She sent Adrian a reassuring message and turned off the sound on her phone so his reply would not interrupt the peace. Then she gazed at Matthew's face, recalling his typical expressions of concern, amusement, exasperation, contentment and intense concentration. She patted a tissue to her eyes to stem the leaky tears.

By the time he woke up almost an hour later, her eyes were dry and itchy, the sun had risen and the usual street noises permeated the room. He gave her a weak smile and stretched out a hand. "Hello, Old Thing. Sorry about all this fuss. Must have given you a bit of a fright."

"That is an understatement." She clasped his hand, trying not to squeeze too hard. "How are you feeling now?"

"Fragile. Could I have some water?"

She lifted a glass to his lips and he levered himself gingerly up onto his elbows to drink. Once finished, he lay back on the pillow and smiled at her again.

"Thank you. This is all rather disconcerting." He blinked up at the ceiling. "I know I'm getting on and the chassis is a little worse for wear, but the engine has served me well for nearly seven decades. For the first time in my life, I'm not sure I trust my body. What if it conks out on me again?"

Beatrice dismissed the thought with a shake of her head.

"You're staying here till the doctor is sure that it won't. Once they let you out, you and I are going to make some lifestyle changes," she said, a bossy note in her voice.

He wrinkled his nose. "Can't say I like the sound of either of those things. I would vastly prefer to recuperate at home. Am I all right to fly, do you suppose?"

"Let's wait and see what the doctor says. Meanwhile, you get some rest and I need to get a few hours' kip before work. Would you like me to call your daughters?"

"I'd rather not worry them. Let's keep it quiet for now. Are you going back to the restaurant today?"

"Yes." Beatrice took a deep breath. "I'm near as dammit to solving this case and while you're in good hands, I'm going to tie it up. Please behave yourself. I'll be back to see you later this afternoon. Would you like to see Luke? I think he'd be reassured to see you're all right."

"Poor old Small Fry. Must have scared the wits out of the little chap. Please do bring him, if he wants to come. I shall make amends."

"Will do. Now be good and don't flirt with the nurses. I know what you're like when you start speaking Italian."

When Beatrice returned to the apartment to prepare for work, she expected to find everyone still in bed. Not so. Adrian and Luke were fully dressed and washing up in the kitchen.

"Beatrice! How is he?" Adrian dried his hands on a tea towel and embraced her.

She hugged him back, grateful for the contact. "He's awake and talking, but feeling a little delicate. They need him to stay in for tests. If you want to visit later today, he'd be thrilled to see you. Luke, you can go too."

"Can I take my phone so Mum can talk to him? She's worrying."

Adrian mugged an apologetic face. "I didn't have a chance to

JJ Marsh

intercept. Tanya sent a text and Luke told her what happened. We spoke to her and Marianne this morning after I got your message and they're a lot calmer now."

Beatrice sat down at the kitchen table with a sigh. "You can't blame them. They must be distraught. Oh dear, this really is a mess. Is there any chance of a decent coffee? Then I really should shower and change before Ettore arrives."

"You've got the day off," said Luke, reaching into the cupboard for the coffee grounds.

Beatrice rubbed at her eyes. "I'm sorry?"

"Isabella called just after nine," Adrian explained. "She heard what happened and said she doesn't expect you at Ecco today. She sends her best wishes and Ettore will deliver flowers to the hospital. When you have time, give her a call to update her on the patient."

"How the hell does she know what happened?" asked Beatrice, her eyes following Luke as he expertly filled the coffee pot with water, tamped down the grounds and screwed the device together. The child was growing up even as she watched.

"No idea," said Adrian, with a shrug. "But she knew what, who and where. Anyway, Will picked up the rental Vespa this morning and took Suhail to work. He should be back soon. Can I make you some breakfast? You look wrung out."

"Yes please. French toast with cinnamon and honey would do the trick because I'm going to start eating healthy foods as soon as Matthew comes home. You know, now that I have the day off, I could go to Ristorante della Nonna myself to check their desserts. How about you and Luke visit Matthew, take him his phone and let him reassure his daughters? After lunch, I'll go in to check on him and then we can have a team meeting back here."

Luke poured some milk into a pan and placed it on the hob. "What about Will?"

"What about me?" a voice called from the hallway.

Something about that man's presence acted as a tonic. Luke laughed, a smile spread across Adrian's face and Beatrice revolved in her chair to see the tall, lean man enter the kitchen.

He placed a hand on her shoulder, his eyebrows raised in enquiry.

"He's going to be all right," she said.

"When can we see him?" Will asked, planting a kiss on Adrian's lips and prodding Luke's shoulder. "Can you make me a coffee too, please?" He swung into a chair and faced Beatrice. "So, what's the plan?"

After a two-hour nap, Beatrice rose and checked her phone. One message from Matthew. `Doctors here are even prettier than the nurses!`

She chuckled, showered and dressed for her lunch appointment, feeling a whole lot better if not entirely rested. The apartment was cool and silent since Will, Adrian and Luke had left for the hospital. Beatrice sat in the roof garden for a few minutes, giving herself space to think. A breeze blew across her face, bringing scents of the sea, frying garlic, traffic fumes and a sweet hint of blossom from the trees in the backyard.

Ristorante della Nonna was two metro stops away, but Beatrice chose to walk. Something in her yearned for sunlight, people and open spaces. It was the first time she had ventured out into the streets of Naples alone and she clutched her handbag under her armpit, tense and alert. Chattering children ran past and a small dog barked from a balcony. A homeless man held out a cup and Beatrice scooped out some coins from her jacket pocket. The smell of drains hit her as she skirted some road works and ducked past some tourists holding a map. The further she went, the more comfortable she became, recalling her personal philosophy. The only way to understand a city is to walk its streets.

It was half past two when she arrived and stood back to allow a party to exit the latest Neapolitan culinary sensation. Fully in character as irritated businesswoman eager to get back to work, she enquired as to the availability of a table for one and how long service might take. The head waiter confirmed she could eat two courses in an hour and led her to a table for one by the window.

She chose not to go for two obvious copies. Instead she ordered fish of the day: stuffed red mullet with ginger and lime couscous, followed by the dessert labelled *La Dolce della Regina* - The Queen's Dessert – lavender ice-cream with Prosecco jelly. She ordered water and opened her laptop to make notes.

Her phone rang while she waited for her meal.

"Hello, Herr Kälin, thank you for returning my call."

"Frau B. Is this a good time?"

"Perfect. Just waiting for my lunch."

"At three in the afternoon? Of course, you are in Italy. They operate on southern time."

The waiter brought her water and Beatrice smiled her thanks.

"Southern Italian time but hungry British stomach. Do you have news for me?"

"Some. You asked me to visit the restaurant in Einsiedeln. My nephew and Chalet Nonna deserve their respect, it seems. Top quality food, a good reputation, expensive real estate and many good reviews. I am surprised."

She poured a glass of water but did not drink. "Surprised at the level of skill?"

"Yes, that was impressive. I ate one of the best veal dishes in my broad experience. My vital question was how he managed the business end. Stefan has no resources, nor does his close family. He told me the place is part of a high-end franchise. I asked him the terms. He did not answer the question."

Beatrice gnawed on an olive. "So he had funding for a prime piece of property and is making a name for himself. Can I ask if you had dessert?"

Kälin puffed into the mouthpiece. Beatrice couldn't tell if it was a laugh or a snort of derision.

"I had something called *Englishes Frühstück*. Ice-cream with coffee. Pleasant enough, if a little too crude for my taste. Most English things are."

A waiter approached with a plate of fish. "Herr Kälin, I cannot thank you enough. This is immensely helpful. I wish you and your nephew every success. I really appreciate your professional perspective. Have a lovely afternoon."

"Likewise, Frau B. *En guete*." He rang off.

So she was right. The Nonna chain was indeed a franchise. In which case, it was something far bigger than one rogue chef. The question was, which organisation was behind it? She quashed her assumptions and picked up her fork.

The restaurant grew less and less populated as the lunch service wore on and from her vantage point with her back against a wall, Beatrice could observe the floor and ensure no one could see her computer screen.

Twice she saw a waitress show a dessert to the head waiter as she returned dishes to the kitchen. *La Dolce della Regina* was not a success. Customers ate the jelly and downed the biscuit, but the ice-cream was left to melt into a lilac mess.

Beatrice's conviction grew and she left half the couscous. One, it reinforced the 'I'm in a hurry' image and two, it expedited the dessert.

Only she and Suhail knew the true recipe. Three others had heard the fake. Isabella, Agusto and Gennaio. Her gut feeling had become a conviction. Someone was lying to their faces and here was proof.

The jelly was light and sparkly with some gold flakes to add to the atmosphere. No issues with the biscuit either. But the ice-cream was like eating soap. Beatrice laid down her spoon and wrote rapid notes on her laptop, sent Will a message and called the waiter.

"Coffee, madam? Did you like your dessert?"

"No coffee, thank you. The dessert? A little too crude for my taste. Could you bring me the bill, please?"

She stared out of the window at the crowded streets and allowed herself a grim sense of satisfaction. In her first job as private investigator, she had been hired by the management of Ecco to root out the spy. It wasn't the easiest task, but now she'd worked it out. Her concern now was whether employers really wanted to know the truth.

The taxi driver wasn't at all happy at dropping her off outside the docks. His accent was impenetrable, but his gestures were clear. He wanted her to stay safe and this was a dangerous place. She assured him as far as she could that she was here for a business meeting, thrusting her briefcase in his direction.

The sun shone directly into her eyes as she got out of the taxi, making everything orange or an indistinguishable silhouette. She swiped the access card she had found behind Ecco on the security reader and the gate creaked open, allowing her in. Men working in the warehouses or loading ships stared openly as she passed. The best thing to do was to pick up her pace and give the impression she knew exactly where she was going and what she was doing.

It didn't take a genius to spot Gennaio's section of the dock. It was the only one cordoned off with tape since the fire damage. His Testarossa was parked at the side, along with several other less ostentatious vehicles. Beatrice released a small sigh of relief. Gennaio's movements rarely followed a routine but it was essential she spoke to him away from the restaurant. Surprise, her secret weapon, was unlikely to work if he wasn't actually here.

The warehouse was still operational, with pairs of shouty men loading vans from the mucky-looking bays. With a sharp move sideways to avoid a forklift truck, she wove her way through the parked cars to a Portakabin which acted as a temporary reception. Before she could reach for the handle, it jerked open and Gennaio came out, phone clamped to his ear. He stopped, staring at her.

"Gennaio, hello! Sorry to interrupt. Could I have a word?" she asked, keeping her tone light.

The big man said something in Italian into the phone, ended his call and spread his hands. "Beatrice! This is not the place for you. How did you get in here?"

"Detectives have their ways. Never mind that now. Listen, I need to talk to you and it will not wait. Can we go somewhere a little less noisy?"

His eyes darted about, alighting on his car. "Yes, of course. Come, I will take you back to your apartment. We can talk on the way. Is something wrong?"

Beatrice hesitated. She would rather talk in public but she did fancy a go in his car. Perhaps there was a way.

"In your Ferrari? Really? How exciting! Do you know, I've never been in one of those things? Can we stop at a café so I can pretend I'm famous?"

His face forced out a tight smile. "No problem. Let's go."

The Ferrari Testarossa was designed to attract attention. Bright red, low slung and incredibly loud, it turned heads as Gennaio revved his way out of the docks and into the never-ending snarl-up of Naples traffic.

"OK, Beatrice, you want to talk to me?"

"Yes, I do." *Play for time. Try the petrol-head distraction routine. Adrian uses it to great effect on Will.* "What I wanted to ask ... ooh, you can physically feel the power of this car, can't you? As if it wants to run."

Gennaio took the bait, nodding and smiling as he caressed the wheel. "She is a racehorse, built for speed. In the city, you cannot see her at her best. This weekend, we are going to the Amalfi Coast where she can run free."

Beatrice had never understood the male habit of referring to cars as female, nor had it ever seemed less appropriate than in this loud, attention-seeking, big red show-off. She asked several other questions as to performance and Gennaio was happy to explain. As they neared the university, Beatrice spotted a parking space opposite a busy café.

"Let's stop here! I'd like to buy you a coffee while we talk."

Gennaio's frown returned as he reversed, his big hand on Beatrice's headrest as he manoeuvred into the space. Two kids on bikes had stopped to watch. It must be dreadfully demanding to be the focus of attention all the time, even if you had spent over two hundred grand to achieve exactly that effect.

They ordered two *espressi* and sat outside in the sunshine. Beatrice lifted her face to the sun and smiled. "You are lucky to live here. The weather, the scenery, the food." She looked directly at him. "Isabella hired me to find out who is stealing recipes from Ecco and that is what I have done. Before I present her with my findings, I wanted to offer you the opportunity to confess."

His face showed the internal wrangling within. He considered denial, outrage, incomprehension and mirth, but eventually came to rest at defeat. Tearing open a packet of sugar, he nodded to himself, several times. "That was quick."

"Slower than I would have liked," Beatrice replied, watching every movement for an indication as to his potential reaction.

Gennaio looked around, ensuring no one was close enough to hear. "You are right, Beatrice. I started this. What you need to understand is that it was for very honourable reasons."

"Stealing recipes from your brother was for honourable reasons? I'm going to need some help understanding that."

He placed both hands over his eyes and breathed like a bull. After several inhalations, he faced her. "In the Colacino family, Agusto and I are both successful. Not everyone in our family is so lucky. We had an older brother, Giulio."

"Bruno's father?"

His eyebrows bounced upwards. "You are a good investigator! Yes, Giulio. He died in an accident. At the time when he should have been happiest with his young family, he lost his life to a careless driver who was writing a message on his phone. The two children were very little, young enough to adapt. The problem was their mother. When we buried Giulio, she lost her mind. Crazy with grief, she tried to kill herself and the children. Her neighbours smelt the gas and rescued the family. The children recovered but their mother died in the hospital." He sipped at the little glass of water beside his coffee.

"That's so very sad," said Beatrice, all her concentration on this man.

"What to do? Giulio's younger brothers were both making a career and could not adopt children. The neighbours were good people. They had a child the same age and took care of Bruno and Chantal like their own. Agusto and me, we paid for their education. We sent them away to learn languages and now Chantal and Bruno both have a job at Ecco."

Now it was Beatrice's turn to look surprised. "Chantal is your niece?"

"Yes. Such a smart girl. She trained in Berlin and has the head for business. She and Bruno have the enterprise gene. They won't stay in the restaurant for long. The sad thing was their adoptive parents had bad luck. The mama and papa had cancer and passed away in their fifties. Their son, Fabio, became, how do you say, a hooligan? Always in trouble with the police, drugs, bad friends, angry with everyone. He needed help. Somewhere to start." Gennaio's expression pleaded with Beatrice to understand.

"What did you do?" she asked.

"Agusto was not interested. Fabio is not family, he says, so why should we care?" Gennaio slapped his chest. "I care. Fabio is like a brother to Bruno and Chantal. They love him no matter how many mistakes. Not like them, he is a fantastic cook. I

214

offered to help. We found a place, made it a restaurant and I gave him some recipes from Ecco."

"You or Rami?" asked Beatrice, her voice sharp.

Gennaio's mouth fell open. "You know about Rami?"

"Yes, and about how you are trying to force Suhail to do the same."

"No!" he hissed. "That is not me. This is why I am in trouble. Beatrice, please, listen to me. I swear on my brother's life this is the truth."

Such dramatic language did not sit well with Beatrice but she said nothing and listened.

"I supported Fabio. I sold him fresh ingredients for the same discount as I give to Ecco. He needed more than just good quality food. That's why I suggested copying five-star recipes but doing something special. I asked Rami for help. He was already working for a bigger outfit which could provide financing for a whole chain of restaurants. We met one of their representatives and agreed on the idea of a franchise. They put up the money, we provide the recipes, the owners share in the profits. Everyone wins."

Beatrice rolled her eyes. "Gennaio, I may look like a little old lady to you, but until recently I was Detective Chief Inspector of the London Metropolitan Police. If this is such an honourable exercise in philanthropy, why was Rami killed?"

Gennaio shook his head with some vehemence. "I don't know! Listen, Rami was involved in other things, things I didn't like. He was a bigger fish in this network. He told me he was a provider. Whatever these people want, he would find it. I don't know, I really don't, but I suspect it was women, drugs, exclusive access to restaurants like Ecco. The restaurant franchise was a business idea we took to them and they liked it. The Nonna chain has fifteen branches in Italy and they are moving north, where the money is."

"Such as Switzerland?"

For the first time, Gennaio's face reflected real fear. "You know more than I do. That is very bad. Beatrice, for these people, it is not philanthropy. They want their return on investment. I don't know what Rami did, but it was enough to get him killed. Now I have no more access to the recipes and they are angry. They are threatening Suhail, they put fire in my warehouse, they scratched the car ... I am afraid of what they will do next. You know far too much about this situation and that is not healthy."

The sun's reflection glittered in their water glasses. Beatrice pressed her fingertips to her temples and thumbs to her chin and thought. Finally, she looked at her watch.

"Go to Ecco and tell Agusto and Isabella what is going on. Be honest and admit your part in all of this. We will find a way of standing up to this organisation. Did you ever meet one of their representatives?"

Gennaio paled. "Only once, on a yacht. We took a trip around the bay to celebrate the concept of Nonna. We drank champagne and ate Japanese food." Gennaio's expression told her that was the air-brushed version of events.

"Can I ask if he was Italian?"

"No, it was a lady and she came from Odessa."

"Odessa in the Ukraine?"

"Exactly."

Beatrice stared at him. "This is getting complicated. Go to the restaurant and tell your brother and sister-in-law everything. I must go and visit my partner in hospital then I will come directly to Ecco. The four of us are going to come up with a plan to get these people off your backs. I already have an idea. Let's go." She dropped some Euros on the table and stood up to leave.

To her astonishment, when Gennaio got to his feet, he embraced her warmly and kissed her on both cheeks. "Thank you, Beatrice. You are our saviour! Come, I will take you wherever you need to go."

"Very nice of you but that's not necessary. I'm going back to my apartment first and that's an easy walk from here. Five o'clock at Ecco, OK? See you later."

She extricated her hands from his and trotted off down the street in the direction of her apartment. Once the growly red beast had driven off with a toot of its horn, she crossed the street. Now to grab Matthew's pyjamas, underwear and books, then she would take a cab to the hospital. Time was getting on.

She unlocked the front door, aware of a strange pong in the gloomy hallway. As if rice had gone sour. She wrinkled her nose and reached for the light. That was when an arm snaked around her neck and pressed some fabric against her face, forcing the sour smell into her nostrils.

With a yelp, she kicked backwards and jammed an elbow into her assailant's ribs, loosening his grip for a second. They staggered backwards and she stamped her heel onto his foot, wishing she had worn heels. Her consciousness grew foggy, her limbs weak and she subsided to the floor in the arms of a stranger.

Chapter 29

The sky shifted from the Easter-egg pastels of a summer afternoon to a menacing steel on the way back from the hospital, threatening another spectacular storm. Raindrops battered the windscreen like a barrage of watery arrows and the taxi's wipers could not keep pace. Once outside the apartment, Will told Adrian and Luke to run for shelter while he paid the driver.

They ran as instructed, laughing under the feeble shelter of Adrian's jacket, splashing through puddles and shaking themselves off in the porch.

The taxi drove away and Will caught a glimpse of a man in a black beret running along the other side of the street. Another car passed and the man had gone. He decided not to mention it in front of Luke but to tell Beatrice just as soon as he could find the elusive woman.

Will unlocked the heavy wooden door and Luke took the steps two at a time, with Adrian close on his heels. They were both eager to find Beatrice. Will made out he was equally keen, but his true mood was one of concern, because she had neither made an appearance at the hospital nor answered her phone.

The apartment was empty. No sign of Stubbs anywhere. Two vertical lines appeared between Adrian's eyebrows

"She must have gone to Ecco after her lunch. Where else?" said Adrian, looking at Will for reassurance.

"Yeah, probably. She got distracted by the case and forgot the time. I'll call Isabella's mobile and check." He knew he didn't sound at all convincing.

Luke came running back from the bathroom with three towels for them to dry off the rain. "My trainers are wet."

"Oh no!" said Adrian. "That means they're going to stink out the whole place. We need to find some newspaper to stuff inside them. Can you have a look if there's anything in the kitchen?"

Luke ran off, dumping the towels on the floor. Will picked one up, dried his hair, unlaced his shoes and went into the living room to dial Isabella's mobile.

"*Ciao*, Will. How's Matthew?"

"Hi, Isabella. He's going to be fine. I was just wondering if Beatrice is with you."

"With me? No. I gave her a free day to be with Matthew. Maybe she is at the hospital or at the apartment, waiting for you."

"Unfortunately not. We just got back to the apartment and she's not here. She was meant to join us at the hospital after lunch, but didn't show up."

"You tried her phone, yes?" Isabella sounded concerned.

"Of course we called her. We've been calling her all afternoon. No reply."

There was a silence and a muffled conversation in the background.

Isabella's voice came back on the line. "OK, I send Ettore to collect you. Come to Ecco. All of you."

"What, you mean now?"

"Yes, now, Will. All of you come now. Together, we stay strong."

"What does that mean? Is Beatrice in trouble?"

"I don't know yet. Will, just get everyone downstairs and into the car. We talk when you get here."

"OK, OK. We'll be ready."

Adrian and Luke stood staring at Will as he rubbed the towel over his face in a gesture of exasperation. Those two lines on Adrian's forehead had returned and Luke was barefoot.

"Get changed into some decent clothes. Ettore is coming to take us to Ecco."

"Where's Beatrice?" asked Adrian.

"That's what I hope to find out."

For once, their voluble driver had nothing to say. Ettore greeted them politely and opened the car door but uttered not a single word on the journey to Ecco. The only sound was the rain drumming on the roof and the constant swish of the wipers. On arrival, he did not drop them by the entrance but drove into the courtyard at the back and parked outside the kitchen door. Will assumed that was to save them from getting wet, so was surprised when he got out and escorted them indoors.

The kitchen was full of people preparing for the evening service, who stopped and stared as Ettore threaded his way through the room, beckoning for his passengers to follow. He pushed opened the swing doors and held them open until Luke, Will and Adrian had entered the restaurant.

Isabella and Agusto were standing either side of a table, shouting at each other. They stopped abruptly when they saw the new arrivals. Sitting at the same table was Gennaio with his head in his hands and a thin man wearing a black beret. Adrian's mouth fell open. Their stalker stood up with an apologetic smile.

Will's voice was as thunderous as the sky outside. "Who the hell are you?" he demanded.

Isabella rushed to greet them. "Luca, *il grande ragazzo*. Will, Adrian, come here and let me explain." She indicated towards the table with her head. "And you," she added brusquely to Ettore, who took a seat next to Gennaio.

Will approached the party and folded his arms. He did not sit. Adrian remained standing and Will saw Luke's hand slip into his.

"You know Gennaio, Agusto's brother," said Isabella.

The man looked up, his expression sorrowful, and greeted them with a nod.

She pointed to the stalker. "This is Pietro, who maybe you recognise. He is part of the Ecco family and I hired him to watch you, to make sure you didn't get into any trouble. But he's not good at surveillance and I think he made you afraid, no? I am very sorry. So is he."

She said something in Italian and the man placed a hand to his chest. "*Mi dispiace*," he said in a smoke-roughened voice.

Agusto released a sound of infuriated exasperation and Isabella splayed a hand to shut him up.

"My husband knew nothing about this. But I knew nothing about what *he* was doing!" Her eyes flashed. "I thought Ettore was a new driver, but today I find he is a bodyguard, hired by my husband to protect Beatrice. His name is not even Ettore!" Her pitch rose to almost a shout.

Agusto's chin was defiant. "At least I chose a professional. Why would you employ *Lo Stupido*, of all people?"

The man in the black beret clearly couldn't understand English, but caught the insult and objected with some vehemence.

"Enough! Silence!" Agusto commanded, and everyone obeyed. "We can argue about who is right and who is wrong after we find Beatrice. She went to Ristorante della Nonna for lunch. Then she took a taxi to the docks to meet Gennaio."

The big man heaved his shoulders upwards in an expressive shrug. "She wanted see the damage to the warehouse. I showed her where the fire started and she asked if she could ride in my Ferrari. I drove her back and we took a coffee together. Then she went back to her apartment. What more can I say?"

Will's eyes narrowed. "Did you see her go inside?" he asked, his tone accusatory.

"No, he didn't." Ettore spoke, his voice startlingly different to the garrulous Italian gent they knew when he was behind the wheel. "But I did. I was watching her the whole time." His entire posture changed, his accent mutated to somewhere east of London and his manner became slow, precise and professional. "My name is Russell Lane and I'm a personal security specialist. I apologise for the subterfuge but it was for your own good. I follow Beatrice everywhere. Only when she goes home for the night do I clock off. This morning I watched her visit the docks, tailed her and Gennaio to the café and saw her enter the apartment block. I parked opposite the front door, waiting for her to come out. The only person who left the building that I recognised was him," he said, pointing at Pietro.

The thin man in the black beret immediately started protesting.

Agusto yelled at him, Isabella screeched at Agusto, and Pietro threw his hands in the air as if asking the heavens for help.

"SHUT UP!" Will bellowed. "Pietro was in our apartment building? Again?"

Isabella flushed. "He has a key. I told him to look around while you were out, to see if he could find anything."

"And did he?" Will's eyes bored into Pietro, who looked around as if seeking an escape route.

"No. He says he did his job. Wait till you are all occupied, access the apartment, check for anything relevant and leave."

"Hold up." Ettore/Russell leant his elbows on the table. "Beatrice went into her apartment while Pietro was there and he didn't even see her?"

Isabella relayed the question and Pietro repeatedly shook his head, saying the same phrases over and over, accompanied by various supplicatory gestures.

"There is a back door," said Will, addressing Russell. "If she thought someone was following her, she might have gone in the front door and straight out the back to give them the slip. Maybe she didn't even go up to the apartment at all. But why hasn't she answered her phone or called to tell us where she is?"

There was a portentous silence. Russell shook his head. "Maybe she did go out the back door. But not voluntarily."

"You think she was kidnapped?" Gennaio gasped and clutched at his heart. He was worryingly pasty and sweaty, a far from wholesome look.

"Will?" Adrian gave a pointed look at the little blond head beside him. The boy's eyes were huge. Will realised this was no place for a six-year-old, listening to stories of abduction and spying.

"Yes, right. You'd better take him back to the apartment. Listen, Isabella ..."

The kitchen door opened and Suhail emerged from the kitchen with a younger man, both in chef's whites.

"Sorry to interrupt," said Suhail. "We were talking, both of us worried about Beatrice. Bruno told me something. I think it could be important."

"Bruno, what is it?" Agusto's voice contained a tone of surprise.

The young man seemed mortified to have all eyes on him. "This is probably nothing. Beatrice found something in the courtyard. She thought the man who scratched Agusto's Ferrari dropped it when he fell. She asked me what it was. I recognised it because Gennaio has one. It was an ADSP key card."

A silence hung over the group and Adrian looked from one face to another, waiting for an explanation. Gennaio sat down with a thump, as if his legs had given way.

Will was not as patient. "What the hell is that and what does it mean?" he asked.

"It means," said Russell, his face thoughtful, "whoever keyed the Ferrari has access to the port. All right then. Someone starts a warehouse fire on Easter weekend. Shortly afterwards, another person, or perhaps the same one, comes here to key the car. The port is a good place to hide something, or someone."

"Then let's go there now! That's obviously where they've taken her!" Adrian exclaimed.

"Wait," said Bruno. "We need to think about this. The port covers an enormous area. Whenever I go there with Gennaio, I always get lost. Where do we start to look?"

Pietro started chattering to Isabella, his expressions as lively and exaggerated as a French mime. The frustration of not being able to understand drove Will to the point of despair.

"What? What is he saying?"

Slapping the back of one hand into the palm of another, Agusto commanded control of the conversation. "There is a boat. *Lo Stupido* is not as stupid as he looks. He saw other people, more than once, watching Beatrice's apartment. They ride a Vespa. He followed them to the port area. Every night, they go to the same place and leave fifteen minutes later." He pointed a finger at Russell. "These are the people you stopped chasing Beatrice's taxi."

"*Come si chiama la barca*?" snapped Russell.

Pietro answered immediately. "*Non so come si dice, ma è* N-A-I-A-D-E."

Russell scratched at his beard. "I asked him the name of the boat. He says it's called *Naiade*. No more messing about, we need the police. These people are counting on us trying to rescue Beatrice ourselves. That is not going to happen. This is a kidnapping and we know where they might be holding her. Will, do you want to come with me, off radar? You look like you can handle yourself. And we're taking him for directions." He threw a dirty look at Pietro. "*Tu vieni con me*."

The front door opened and Alessandro the maître d' stood staring, his umbrella dripping onto the mat. "Pietro?" he exclaimed, his tone incredulous.

"Alessandro, I can explain," said Isabella, her voice drowned by the movement of chairs, hurried instructions and phone calls.

There was no way Adrian was staying at the restaurant if Will was in the thick of things. At the same time, he couldn't possibly drag Luke into a hostage situation. Isabella and Agusto were distracted and everyone else was either a total stranger or busy with the business of the restaurant. He sensed a presence at his elbow.

"Luke, would you like to help me in the kitchen?" asked Suhail, his voice calm and low in direct contrast to all the yelling and drama in the restaurant.

Luke looked up at Adrian for permission. "Can I?"

With a pang of guilt, Adrian checked with Suhail. "Are you sure? I have no idea how long this is likely to take and you have a job to do."

"We will be fine. He can sit in my station and help till it gets busy, then play his games till you come back."

Adrian could have kissed him. "I really appreciate this, Suhail, thank you. Luke, do exactly as Suhail tells you and we'll be back as soon as we can."

"With Beatrice?"

"Yes," said Adrian, with false confidence. "With Beatrice. Oh, and please don't say anything to your mum or granddad. It's not fair to worry them."

Luke shook his head. "I won't. The last thing we want is another heart attack on our hands."

The maturity of his phrasing amused Adrian, who had a powerful urge to give the boy a hug. Rather than make the departure too dramatic, he squeezed his shoulder instead. With one last grateful smile at Suhail, he rushed to catch up with Will, Russell and the man in the black beret.

Chapter 30

The storm had moved inland, leaving the city cooler and wetter as the rain let up and hints of brightness glowed on the horizon. Will hoped the cloud cover would blow away before dusk. Sunshine equalled hope.

Even Russell's driving style was different to Ettore's. He propelled the car with a cool professionalism, his eyes assessing the environment from all angles. Will was fascinated as he spoke in Italian to Pietro without taking his eyes from the road. There was something of Jean Reno in that kindly face, steely nature combo. Will waited till they stopped talking.

"Russell? What's the deal here? Whose side are you on?"

Russell's eyes met his in the mirror for a second. "Mine, mate. I work for myself and my family, and that includes Agusto. Him and me go way back. When I came to Italy thirty years ago, a muscle-bound idiot looking for trouble, I got a job with the Colacino family. They trained me, taught me Italian, stopped me fighting in the streets and introduced me to my beautiful wife. I worked with them for twenty-eight years. Couple of years back, I retired to spend more time with my girls, but I still do the occasional job for Agusto. He can always count on me. Listen, I want Beatrice back every bit as much as you do."

Adrian squeezed Will's arm and asked a hundred questions with his eyes. Will had no answers. Other than meeting the police at the entrance to the yacht marina, none of them knew what would happen next.

Once Pietro confirmed they were at the right gates, Russell drove straight past, turned around in a side street and double parked. "We'll wait here for the police. Got to work together." He continued to observe the area as if committing the whole place to memory.

Minutes later, an unmarked car passed them and indicated right. Russell gunned the ignition, driving away smoothly and took the same route.

At the gates, he got out. "Will, come with me. You two, stay put."

Will watched as Russell bent to address someone through the unmarked car's passenger window. He introduced Will and pointing towards their car, indicated their passengers Adrian and Pietro. Russell straightened, gave the thumbs-up to the gatekeeper in his little cubicle and strode back to the car, Will right behind him.

"Right, this is a bit bigger than I thought," said Russell.

The gates opened and the two cars moved as one, easing along the harbour towards the boat called *Naiade*. "The cops have been watching this lot for a while. They're not saying why but the combination of forces involved says one thing to me."

"Drugs," Will answered. "Marine police, detectives and special force? It's either that or terrorism."

"Yeah, that's what I'm thinking. The restaurant chain is nothing more than a sideline for a drug network. These people have bigger things on their minds than a couple of puddings. Undercover uniforms are waiting outside the entrance and a marine police vessel is coming to do 'a routine check'. The police are going in, we're to stay back."

The last remnants of storm clouds billowed away from the port area, leaving the evening sky the colour of mouldy peaches. The police vehicle indicated once and Russell slowed, steering the car right to rest between some trailers, watching the car ahead continue for another hundred metres. Moments later, the reverse lights came on and it sped backwards to pull up beside them.

Four men got out and one shouted something which sounded urgent. Russell and Will got out of the car.

"*Dovè?*" asked Russell.

The man pointed at a two-tone yacht approaching the exit to the harbour.

Russell caught Will's arm and indicated the boat. "That's the *Naiade*. It left a few minutes ago. They must have seen the police arriving. We're going after them and we'll force them to stop. Come with me!" He yelled at the car, "You two, stay there! Don't move!"

Adrian's voice piped out, like a muffled squawk, but Will had no time to argue.

Shivering with a combination of cold and fear, he ran after Russell as they raced onto a jetty. The police speedboat drew alongside with much shouting and rope activity. Russell leapt aboard as if they spent his life jumping on and off dangerous things in near darkness, whereas Will needed a helping hand from the crew.

Once the newcomers were sitting on a damp plastic seat, the boat reversed and took off at a speed. Wind smacked Will's face like ping-pong paddles. An officer shoved lifejackets at them. Russell looped his lifejacket over his arm and stood up to watch their progress. Will decided to put his on. Falling overboard in the dark without a hi-vis lifejacket was a risk he couldn't take.

"There they are, the bastards!" Russell roared over the noise of the engine.

Will followed the direction of his finger and saw the bigger boat, white and gleaming in the fading light, clearing the entrance to the marina and heading out into the bay.

Their speedboat changed gear and bounced across the waves

as if it was a skimmed stone. Another police vessel sped in a horizontal line to their diagonal, also with a flashing blue light, heading right for the bow of the *Naiade*. The yacht would be trapped by the pincer movement of two police speedboats and have no choice but to stop.

The yacht increased its pace but clearly could never outrun two smaller vessels built for pursuit. Then a shout went up from the frankly suicidal cop leaning out from the police bow with binoculars. Will didn't dare ask for an explanation, but sat still and let the professionals do their job. The throttle slowed and lights swept the area around them, the cop pointing frantically at a shifting point in the sea. Amid all the shouts, a police officer in a wetsuit pulled on flippers and dived off the side into the cold, black waters of the Bay of Naples.

Will clenched his teeth against the cold. To his amazement, Russell climbed onto the bow, preparing to jump. "Russell, what's going on?"

He looked over his shoulder. "They threw something overboard. The police think it's Beatrice." With that, he dived into the sea.

Chapter 31

Beatrice could hear tinkling bells or wind chimes. A gentle rocking motion told her she was no longer on land. Her head hurt as if her scalp was too tight and she was roasting hot with a desperate thirst. She opened her eyes and took in her surroundings. A white-painted cabin with a single porthole, some storage lockers and the bunk she was lying on. Her eyes were so dry and scratchy, blinking didn't help. The smell of sour rice was still in her nostrils, her mouth tasted furry and an unpleasant pressure bore on her bladder.

She sat up with great care, every movement stiff and painful. No one else was in the room, waiting for her to wake and say, 'Finally we meet, Mrs Stubbs' while stroking a white fluffy cat. The room was overly heated, but to her great relief, there was a tiny sink in the alcove between bunk and door. Water! She ran the cold tap and sticking her head in as far as she could go, gratefully swallowed six or seven gulps of water. It could only aggravate the bladder situation, but if it came to the worst, she'd pee in the sink. She cupped her hands and washed her face. She needed to clear her muddled head.

She tried the door and was not in the least surprised to find it locked. Outside the porthole, she could see nothing more than the hull of another boat. There was no sign of her handbag, keys or phone in any of the empty storage units, nor could she find her shoes. Trying to ignore her bladder, she crossed her legs and searched under the bunk in case her captors had left her a potty.

Nothing. Things were becoming urgent. She looked at the mini sink. How could she even get up there, leave alone balance on such a fragile sort of affair? A sudden rumble of engines under her feet distracted her attention and in a few moments, the boat was moving. She peered out of the porthole, aware that the light was fading and whoever had taken her from the apartment block had every intention of taking her a lot further.

Her nerves already strung out, she gasped when there was a clattering at the door. It swung open to reveal a muscular man in a vest, whose features suggested he might be from China. He carried no weapon, clearly not concerned that Beatrice might pose a threat. With one finger, he drew a line from her to the door.

She didn't move. "I'm going nowhere until you tell me why you brought me here and where this boat is heading."

In two strides, he reached her, picked her up and threw her over his shoulder. She kicked and rained blows on his back to no avail. He ducked out of the doorway and paced along the corridor at speed, ignoring her protests. He clomped up a metal staircase and she inhaled sea spray and chill wind. Voices shouted and lights flashed as she struggled and fought with no effect whatsoever. He marched along the deck paying her no more attention than if she were a toddler having a tantrum. He was heading for the rear end of the yacht. There was a proper name for that bit of a boat but she couldn't recall it now, because she was convinced he intended to throw her off it.

There was only one weapon left. She allowed herself go limp and released her bladder. He roared his fury and yanked her away from his body. Five seconds later, she found herself flying through the air and with one almighty smack, she hit the sea.

From that height, the impact on water had the same effect as slipping on a sheet of ice. Winded and shocked by the cold, Beatrice instantly sank below the surface. Her body convulsed, desperate for air. Bubbles rushed past, heading upwards. Using every muscle she had, she kicked, clawed and wriggled herself after them, her lungs screaming. Her head burst above the water and she inhaled a mouthful of oxygen, then spluttered and coughed as a wave smacked her in the face. She trod water, using far too much effort in wet clothes, and tried to get her bearings.

Lights were all around her and she realised there was just as much danger of being torn to pieces by a propeller from one of these boats criss-crossing the bay as there was of drowning. She had no clue which direction was port or how to get there. It took all her energy to stay afloat. Never a strong swimmer, she'd been recently drugged, was fully clothed and no match for the choppy waters of the Mediterranean Sea.

Her only hope was to call for help. She bicycled her legs and flailed one arm over her head. "Help! Help!"

The cold penetrated to her bones. *Keep moving, woman, don't give up*, she commanded herself. The waves slapped her and submerged her again, making her breathing panicky and urgent when she broke the surface. Something else was in the water, coming in her direction, calling her name.

"Beatrice!"

Her vision blurred by seawater, she had no idea who it was and how he'd found her. With another huge effort, she paddled her feet and waved one arm. "Help me!" Her voice was barely audible to her own ears.

Arms encircled her from behind and lifted her shoulders above the waves. "Hold still, I've got you. Don't fight me, Beatrice. Look, here's a lifebuoy, can you grab that?"

Another man swam into her vision and she became aware of radios chattering somewhere nearby. The second man hauled her up so that her upper body was supported by the buoy. He grabbed the handle and kicked away, dragging her behind him. She looked up and saw lights shining in their direction from the deck of a boat.

The first man swam to her side and shouted a question. "Are you injured at all, Beatrice? Did you get hurt?"

Her freezing hands clutched the float and her teeth chattered. "No, I don't think so." Then she recognised the face. "Ettore? What are you doing here?"

"Just hold on tight, we need to get you out of the water."

Hands pulled and pushed her onto a small ledge at the back of another smaller boat. She vomited sea water all over her feet. They dragged her onto the deck where Ettore wrapped her in a big silver blanket. Someone gave her a warm drink which tasted like an Oxo cube. Will appeared out of nowhere and sat beside her, his face a mask of concern. A huge weariness overtook her as her body began to heat up. Her eyes closed and she leant against Will, who was asking someone else if it was safe to let her sleep. Safe or not, she couldn't keep her eyes open a second longer.

"Beatrice? Beatrice!" Will's voice sounded urgent.

Fingers pressed at her neck. "It's all right. She's just exhausted. They've called an ambulance so we'll have her in hospital in twenty minutes."

Beatrice smiled and tried to open her eyes. "You know ..."

Will bent close to listen. "What is it? Are you OK? Beatrice?"

She couldn't lift her head. She just managed to part her lips to say, "I peed on him," then succumbed to sleep.

Chapter 32

Adrian sat on a squeaky stool outside Beatrice's hospital room, waiting for the police to finish interviewing her. Will took the opportunity to cross to the other side of the building to see Matthew. He was the best person to play down the nature of events and reassure Matthew that Beatrice would be fine. Although Adrian was the better actor, Will's presence always tended to calm even the most agitated of spirits. Two detectives had taken Ettore and Pietro to the police station to give their statements while another two hung about till the doctor gave Beatrice the all-clear. That had been over twenty-five minutes ago, when they entered her room.

Without any real role to play, Adrian chose to 'guard' Beatrice. Against what, he wasn't sure. He glanced at his watch. Only nine o'clock? It felt more like midnight. He wondered whether to call Isabella but decided to wait for Will to return so they could choose what to say. His mouth was dry and he decided it would be safe enough to leave his post long enough to go to the water fountain by the lifts. He was just filling a paper cup when the lift pinged and Will came out.

"How is Matthew?" asked Adrian, as they walked back towards Beatrice's room.

"Health-wise, in good form. As for his emotional state, suspicious. I think he knows there's more to it than I let on. At least he accepted the fact that she's alive and in good hands. He was worried about Luke too, but I picked up a message from Suhail. They are both back at the apartment because the restaurant is closed."

"Ecco is closed? Why?"

Will shrugged. "Dunno. When I called him back, Suhail said it was something to do with Gennaio. Apparently there was a huge row between him and Isabella, and then Agusto sent everyone home."

"It must be pretty severe to close the restaurant. Is Luke OK?"

"Yeah, he's watching TV and eating spaghetti Bolognese. Have the police spoken to Beatrice yet?"

"They're in there now," said Adrian. "The doctor said we can take her home when they've finished. Or maybe she wants to go and see Matthew."

"She'll have to wait till the morning. Visiting hours end at eight. That's why they kicked me out."

They sat down outside Beatrice's room and Adrian remembered his plan. "We should call Isabella and let her know Beatrice is OK."

"Good point." Will got to his feet again. "I'll go outside and do that now. I hate hanging about in hospitals. You know what else? I'm starving. Right now, I could kill for some spaghetti Bolognese."

"Me too. Let's hope Suhail has catered for us all."

Spaghetti, Bolognese or otherwise, was not to be. When the three of them got out of the taxi outside the apartment, Agusto's Ferrari was parked outside.

Adrian looked at Will, arching his eyebrows.

"Oh. Right. When Isabella said they needed to talk to us, I assumed they meant tomorrow. Are you up for this, Beatrice?"

"Doesn't look like I have a choice, does it? I suppose that means dinner will have to wait."

"Are you hungry too?" Adrian unlocked the door and they trooped up the stairs.

"Famished. It takes more than being kidnapped and chucked off a boat to put me off my food."

As they entered the apartment, Suhail came out of the kitchen with some glasses and a carafe of water. He broke into a genuine smile when he saw Beatrice and indicated towards the living room. To Adrian's surprise, Isabella and Gennaio were sitting with Agusto at the dining-table. Isabella's eyes were red, as if she had been crying. Once Beatrice came into the room, she burst into fresh tears and embraced her in a hug. Gennaio and Agusto stood up, both looking like schoolboys outside the headmaster's study.

"I'm fine, I'm fine," said Beatrice, extricating herself from Isabella's arms. "Nothing to worry about. Where is Luke?"

"In his room," said Suhail. "He fell asleep on the sofa, so I put him in his bed."

"I'll go check on him," said Will.

"Thank you," said Beatrice. "Shall we all sit down?"

Isabella pulled a tissue from her pocket and dried her eyes as everyone took their seats. Suhail poured water for everyone and was about to leave the room when Agusto spoke.

"Suhail, please stay. This concerns you as well. Gennaio has something to say."

Gennaio leant his forearms on the table, his face a picture of remorse. He nodded his head several times without meeting anyone's eyes and swallowed. Will slipped into the room and gave Adrian and Beatrice a silent thumbs-up.

Gennaio looked up and released a long shaky sigh. "Beatrice, I want to apologise. You gave me the opportunity to do the right thing. You told me to confess that I was the person selling recipes stolen from Ecco. When I left you this afternoon, I planned to do it, I really did. Only after I saw my brother, I just couldn't say the words. I was too ashamed."

Adrian saw Suhail's eyes widen.

"Yes. I am sorry to you also, Suhail. I was the one putting pressure on you. I wanted to offer my protection in return for the recipes. I thought you would be like Rami. You are not. You are a different man."

Suhail said nothing, his expression frozen.

"Then Beatrice disappeared. I was afraid. These people do bad things if they don't get what they want. The warehouse, the car and now taking Beatrice? This is to force me to work for them. So I told my brother and Isabella everything and I ..." he struggled to speak, swallowing and rubbing his eyes, "cannot find the words to tell you how sorry I feel. I ..." He shook his head, unable to continue.

Adrian's head was reeling. He had more questions than he could articulate.

Agusto took over. "My brother is not a bad man. Stupid, greedy and a liar to his own family, yes, but in the first place he did this for a good reason. He wanted to help someone start a restaurant career. Instead of doing it properly, he cheated, asking Rami to steal my recipes to take a short cut. Then they saw they could make money and borrowed financing to begin a franchise. The people who loaned the cash wanted a cut of the profits and even worse, to use the Nonna chain to clean their own dirty money. Gennaio was in trouble. He couldn't say no. Then Rami got involved with these people and had an arrangement to sell ... other things. He got very rich and didn't need the restaurant job, but he stayed for the recipes."

Isabella was shaking her head in disbelief. "Rami. I still can't believe it. He was such a good man. My heart broke when he died."

"When he was murdered," corrected Gennaio. "They killed him because he was making his own profit from drug money. This was nothing to do with the restaurant. What was I to do? My kitchen connection was gone. I needed someone inside to help, so I made life difficult for Suhail. Some time later, I planned to offer him my protection. But Isabella hired Beatrice and everything became complicated. The financiers got angry and impatient and threatened me."

Adrian pressed his fingers to his temples, trying to comprehend the tangled knot of connections.

"So much deception," said Agusto, his voice half its usual volume. "Isabella hired Beatrice. I hired Russell to protect her but did not tell Isabella the truth. Meanwhile, she hired Pietro. God knows why. He is the brother of Alessandro, our maître d' and he also used to work for us. Pietro is a drunk and an idiot. He made too many mistakes and Isabella fired him. Then she felt sorry, so paid him privately to protect Beatrice and her family. She didn't tell me or Alessandro. More lies. A family of liars." He shook his head, his eyebrows arching in regret.

"You owe Pietro more than you know!" Isabella snapped. "Alessandro's great concept? The 'harmony of senses'? That is all Pietro's work. Yes, he is an alcoholic, but it was him who did the research, him that wrote the paper. Alessandro just translated it. When I found out about Pietro's work and heard he'd been fired from the university, I wanted to help. But as a waiter, he was useless. He was even worse as a private security guard."

Agusto looked thunderstruck but Adrian interrupted. He could hardly follow any of this.

"Wait a second," he said, turning to Beatrice. "You told Gennaio to confess? How did you know it was him?"

"The dessert Suhail and I made was on the menu at Ristorante della Nonna. Made to the wrong specifications. The only people who knew those false specifications were Isabella, Agusto and Gennaio. So I drew the only logical conclusion."

Adrian could hear the smallest hint of pride in her voice. He allowed himself a surreptitious smile. PI Stubbs had solved her first case.

Isabella sighed. "Now all our cards are on the table, what

happens next?"

"I'll tell you what happens next," said Beatrice. "You are going home to discuss your situation as a family. My job is done. After I've been to see Matthew in the morning, I will come to Ecco to say my goodbyes. Right now, I've had rather a trying day and nothing to eat since that foul dessert. I want a large plate of spaghetti Bolognese with extra cheese and then I'm going to bed."

Chapter 33

On Thursday morning, Beatrice woke from a profound and restorative sleep, stretched out in bed and blinked at the ceiling, recalling the events of the day before. With a yawn, she reached for her phone to check the time. Nine thirty-five on the twenty-fifth of April. Instantly she sat bolt upright.

Today was Matthew's birthday. She had completely forgotten about that in all of yesterday's shenanigans. Tomorrow they were due to fly home but she had no idea if he would be allowed to leave hospital, let alone get on an aeroplane. While he was all alone in a hospital room, worrying about why she hadn't visited, she was lounging around in bed till practically midday. She should be ashamed of herself.

She threw off the covers and padded up the corridor in her pyjamas to find the others. Voices came from the terrace above and she climbed the stairs to find Luke, Adrian, Will, Suhail and Isabella at breakfast.

"Good morning!" called Adrian. "Coffee?"

"I haven't got time for coffee. I must get to the hospital. Did you realise today is Matthew's birthday and the poor old thing is stuck on a ward hooked up to machines while we sit here enjoying the sunshine?"

"Come and sit down," said Isabella. "Everything is OK. I came round to invite you all to a party at Ecco today, but Will told me it is Matthew's birthday so I called the hospital and asked when he will be released. Good news! They said he can come home after the doctor is finished! Then I called Ettore, I mean Russell, but he will always be Ettore to me. He is coming here now. He will drive you to get Matthew and bring him home. Then we will have a triple celebration! Your first case, *Anniversario della Liberazione* and a birthday party!"

Beatrice accepted the coffee cup Will handed her, trying to take in the machine-gun fire of information Isabella was rattling off. "He can come home today? Did they say if he will be able to fly tomorrow?"

Isabella shook her head. "I didn't ask. You must check when you collect him. Your flights are tomorrow? So soon?"

"Yes, we have to get Luke home. He has school on Monday. I'm not sure Matthew will feel up to a birthday party when he's just out of hospital, to be honest."

"He is! Will called him after I spoke to the nurse. We all wished him Happy Birthday and sang down the phone, didn't we, Luca? He is looking forward to the party. And it will be a private event, just for us and the staff of Ecco. Today the restaurant is closed for Liberation Day but Agusto had a brilliant idea. Well, two brilliant ideas but I can't tell you the other one because he wants to make an announcement at the party. The first one was to invite all the staff and their families to lunch. Agusto will cook for everyone and you are our special VIP guests for solving the spying situation. When Will and Adrian told me it is Matthew's birthday, I knew that would be perfect!"

Isabella, unlike her husband, was definitely a morning person. Her bright chatter, vibrant hair and expansive gestures were all a bit much for Beatrice so early in the day.

"I'd better have a shower and get dressed before Russell gets here," said Beatrice, feeling as if events had rather run away from her.

"Yes, and I must go. There is much to prepare for the party."

"Do you need any help?" asked Suhail.

Isabella beamed at him and placed the back of her hand to his cheek. "Such a kind man! No. No work for you today. You eat, drink and enjoy a day off. You deserve it. Ecco at one o'clock, OK? *Ciao, tutti*!" With that, she bounced away down the stairs.

"I like her," said Luke. "She's full of beans."

Beatrice had to agree.

The weather was balmy and almost summery as Will and Beatrice emerged from the hospital with Matthew between them. Delighted to see Beatrice, demob happy and in high spirits about his birthday lunch, Matthew strode ahead, greeting the man he thought was Ettore with a cheerful wave. It was hard to believe that only two days ago, Beatrice thought she might lose him. If she lost Matthew, what was left of her life? She swallowed, determined not to give in to her worst fears.

The journey back was the perfect opportunity to bring Matthew up to speed but minimise the drama. Beatrice introduced him to Russell and explained his role in the scheme of things. With perfectly judged understatement, Will summarised the events of the previous evening, including Gennaio's confession. In the stunned silence that followed, Russell spoke up to inform them that six people had been arrested and charged.

"Four people from the yacht and the two local youngsters Pietro has been following. It doesn't get anywhere near bringing down the organisation that employs them, but it puts a stop to this particular operation. Job done."

Matthew stared at the back of Russell's head, wearing an expression of complete bewilderment. "Excuse me, um, Russell? Are you also a private investigator?"

"No. The detective side of things is not my strong point. I'm in personal security. Trying to keep people out of trouble. Most of the time, I'm pretty successful." He met Beatrice's eyes in the rear-view mirror. "But there's always one."

Matthew reached for Beatrice's hand. "My dear chap, you have my sympathies. I've been trying to keep her out of trouble for decades."

She returned his gentle pressure and smiled at them all. Meanwhile, she had a thought. A private detective really ought to have an assistant to do the heavy lifting.

Two hours later, scrubbed and brushed and in their smartest clothes, the party arrived at Ecco. Russell insisted on driving, even though he too was invited as a guest.

"Business as usual," he said, with a wry grin. "Let's not rock the ... er ... boat."

Isabella and Chantal greeted the guests and showed them to their seats. Initially, Beatrice was disappointed to find Suhail was seated at a different table to them, but when the laughter and jokes began from the kitchen team and waiting staff, she could see he was in the right place. Russell introduced Beatrice to his wife and daughters, his pride glowing. Rightly so, each of them was a classic Italian beauty. They seemed to fit right in, chatting in animated Italian to Marcello and his girlfriend.

The kitchen doors burst open and Agusto came out of the kitchen, followed by Gennaio and Bruno. Beatrice smiled. It really was a family business.

Agusto clapped his hands and the room fell into an anticipatory silence.

"*Benvenuti*! Thank you all for coming. I know it is your holiday and I am happy you can be here with your loved ones. Before we eat, I want you all to give yourselves a round of applause. The last few months have been difficult and you stayed with me. Your loyalty makes me so happy I could cry. Bravo!" His voice cracked and he began clapping. The room followed suit, with a few tears amongst the smiles.

"Second, with thanks to Beatrice Stubbs, who is not an

English chef but a private detective, we know who was spying." With an open palm, he gave the floor to Gennaio.

Beatrice caught a look between Chantal and Bruno. They didn't seem in the slightest bit surprised.

Gennaio made his confession and apology in the humblest tones, assuring everyone he'd had honourable motives but stronger forces had taken over. He didn't mention Rami or the bullying of Suhail. The staff looked confused and Agusto stepped back into the centre of everyone's attention.

"The idea of a franchise, supporting new restaurants, is a good one. But if we do this, we do it properly. No spying, no stealing, no financing from suspicious benefactors. Ecco is the best restaurant in Naples and with our success, we support others. We offer training and advice to new chefs. If they meet our standards, they can bear the name of Ecco. All of you, my loyal team, should know that you are the people I will consider above all others. You work, you learn, you innovate and then, you fly the nest!"

Isabella burst into applause and the whole room joined in, this time with real enthusiasm. Conversations started up and Agusto surveyed them with a paternal eye.

"Now, we eat! Isabella, Chantal, the champagne!"

They ate a four-course meal, each based on one of the new recipes Agusto's staff had created. It was a lovely way to repay them and each dish had been prepared with classic Ecco flair. All Beatrice could hope for was that her dessert was not on the menu.

A selection of vegetables, herbs and flowers *al brodo*, designed by Marcello, came as a shallow bowl of finely cut elements with a tea-kettle of herb-flavoured bouillon. The diners mixed the ingredients to taste, creating a fresh cross between crudités and soup.

Luke loved it and said he would make the same thing for his mum and Gabriel when he got home. Matthew and Beatrice shared a secret smile at the inclusion of Gabriel.

The pasta course had been designed by Chantal. Ravioli flowers filled with a cauliflower, walnut and black garlic crumble, topped with a mushroom and sherry velouté.

Will pored over the multi-coloured menu, clearly designed by Isabella. "This is gorgeous! Can't say I've ever had a vegan dish that packs as much punch. Beatrice, see if you can steal that recipe."

She laughed and showed a double thumbs-up to Chantal, who gave a giggly bow in return.

"Vegan? Is it really?" asked Matthew, taking another bite. "I'd never have known. It tastes like game."

His appetite seemed normal even if he had chosen water over wine and refused bread. Beatrice kept checking him for any signs of frailty and found none.

The main course had been awarded to Bruno, the most junior member of the kitchen. The adventurous nature of youth shone through. Bruno had created a Bug Burger, made of mealworms, crickets, grasshoppers with tomato, polenta and spinach, served with chopstick fries and all the trimmings. Its reception was mixed. Luke wouldn't touch the burger, but enjoyed the rest. Exclamations of delight and horror echoed through the restaurant, while Bruno stood at the kitchen doors, laughing.

"It may not make it onto the menu next week," said Adrian, "but this kind of chef is the future. It's got all the right textures and tastes divine. The Valpolicella complements it so well I wonder if Bruno shouldn't become a sommelier instead."

Finally, the three kitchen staff brought out the dessert, made by Agusto himself. A huge chocolate cake with candles and sparklers with the letter M right in the centre. The staff broke into song and Beatrice found her vision blurry as Matthew got to his feet. He blew out the candles, assisted by Luke, and sank into his seat. Isabella cut the cake and while she and the family distributed portions to all the guests, Agusto dragged over a chair to sit with them. He looked hot and happy as he grabbed Beatrice's hand and kissed it.

"Isabella drives me crazy. That woman has so many stupid ideas. But you? You were the best idea she ever had. You fixed this for us, not just the restaurant, but the family. I will never forget you."

His eyes glittered not with tears but an intensity Beatrice found embarrassing. She was British, after all.

"Thank you, Agusto. It was quite an experience. I hope to come back one day. We have all fallen in love with Naples."

"And we all fall in love with you. Hey, Luca, you like my chocolate cake? I made it light, especially for you, Matthew. After hospital food, you must be careful. I am happy you are well. Now I must get the coffee and a digestif for everyone. We have something special for you, Adrian, Will. For the connoisseurs." He leapt to his feet and loped off to the bar, leaving everyone at the table looking like they had just experienced a tornado.

Finally, at six in the evening, it was time to take Matthew home for a rest. They said their farewells, some more emotional than others, and Beatrice found her own throat swelling as she hugged Isabella.

Suhail chose to join them in the car, his face flushed and happier than Beatrice could ever recall seeing it. He sat on the pull-down seat opposite Matthew and patted his stomach.

"I ate too much," he said, with a suppressed smile.

"I drank too much," said Adrian, "but with all those different grappas to try, it's impossible to resist!"

Beatrice studied Suhail's face. She knew he didn't drink, but something had put a bloom in his cheeks. He met her eyes and that grin surfaced again.

"Today, Agusto promoted me to Head of Desserts. I start next week. And ..."

Whatever he had been about to say was drowned out by a cluster of congratulations. He shook hands, nodded his thanks and blushed.

"And what?" asked Beatrice, once the noise had died down.

"My apartment is fixed. Gennaio paid for all the repairs and I can go home tonight. For the first time in many months, I am happy."

"You deserve to be. As Isabella said, you are a very good man." Too far away to reach out and squeeze his arm, Beatrice made do with Adrian instead. He squeezed back and let his head rest on hers.

Altogether, it wasn't a bad way to leave Naples.

Chapter 34

Date: 6 June 2019
To: admin@beatrice-stubbs.com
From: russell@lanesecurity.it
Subject: Collaboration idea

Hi Beatrice and thanks for your email.

Many congrats on the launch of your own business. You will make a top investigator – I've seen the proof. As for joining your team as a permanent member, I'll be honest and say I couldn't commit to that. I've always run a solo enterprise and I go where the job takes me. That used to be South Africa for two years or Brighton for a couple of days. Nowadays, I don't leave Italy.

In any case, I've retired and only get back in the saddle on special occasions. The physical stuff is not as much fun as it used to be. You might want to consider a younger, fitter man. What about Will? He's smart and in peak form.

All that said, if a role comes up and our schedules fit, I'd jump at the chance to work with you again.

Unless I decide to become a hairdresser ;)
Russell

Date: 9 June 2019
To: admin@beatrice-stubbs.com
From: dawnwhit70@btinternet.co.uk
Subject: Collaboration idea

```
Hi Beatrice
Love the idea in principle, but I've got a
mission of my own. More women at the senior
level of law enforcement and I intend to be
one of them. You know I'm always keen to help
you in whatever way I can.
Let's discuss practicalities over a bottle of
Chablis when we come to Devon next month. God
knows I need to get out of London. Can we go
to that cream tea place again? Love, Dawn x

PS: Did you see himself in The Telegraph last
week?
```

Date: 12 June 2019
To: admin@beatrice-stubbs.com
From: ana@rockrabbit.pt
Subject: Collaboration idea

```
Hey Beatrice!
Great to hear from you and in answer to your
question, hell yeah! As a freelancer, obvs
because I still need to get my Pulitzer Prize
for Journalism. Let me know what you want and
when you want it, but count on me. Give my
love to the fellas and send Tanya a massive
kiss. Is her man a ride or what?

Love Ana xoxoxo
```

Date: 17 June 2019
To: admin@beatrice-stubbs.com
From: mxmioo9@bluwin.at

Subject: Enquiry

Dear Mrs Stubbs

My friend recommends you as a discreet and
efficient investigator.
I am in need of professional help in a very
delicate circumstance. This relates to a
contested bequest from a recently deceased
individual and her will.
My legal team oversee the aspects regarding
law. Where I require an alternative approach
is in observing the contesting party and their
behaviour, which I believe could provide us
with vital information.
I understand this is cryptic at this stage, so
would welcome a deeper conversation. If you
are able to fly to Salzburg in the next two
weeks, I can make all necessary arrangements.

With best wishes
Hana Maximilian

Date. 17 June 2019
From: admin@beatrice-stubbs.com
To: mxmioo9@bluwin.at
Subject: Enquiry

Dear Ms Maximilian

Thank you for your enquiry. I am certainly
willing to find out more about your
requirements to see if I can be of assistance.
Currently I am available to fly to Salzburg at
your convenience. I look forward to hearing
from you and wish you a good weekend.

Best wishes
PI Beatrice Stubbs

Chapter 35

"Take a break, Beatrice!" yelled Tanya, outside the French windows. "It's Bank Holiday!" She jiggled a cocktail glass and spilt some of the contents on her hand. Beatrice could lip-read the expletive even if she could not hear it.

Beatrice held up a palm, splaying five fingers. Just a few minutes more. Only a dozen more emails to read and reply to, then she would join the family in the garden. Gabriel and Matthew were barbecuing vegetable kebabs and corn on the cob, while Marianne arranged salads on the picnic table. Luke was nowhere to be seen, probably playing down by the stream with Huggy Bear. She wanted to be out there, in the summer sunshine, joining in the laughter. Only she and Dumpling remained indoors, her staring at a screen, him sleeping in a patch of sunshine on her desk.

Work could wait. She would log off and deal with the rest later. She ran her eyes over the senders, just in case.

A name stood out. Bruno Starieri. She remembered the young eager chef from Ecco and opened his mail. It contained one sentence and a link.

`I thought you should know. Baci, Bruno`

She clicked on the link, despite her better instincts.

It took her to a tiny piece on a news website.

Body in Danube now murder enquiry

Budapest Police confirm the grisly discovery of an adult male corpse in the River Danube is now under investigation as murder. The victim, identified as Gennaio Colacino, was an Italian national from Naples. In response to a question from our journalist, a police spokesman confirmed the man had died from a wound to the throat. Social media connects the victim to Michelin-starred chef and philanthropist Agusto Colacino, of celebrated restaurant Ecco. The chef has yet to comment. Reuters

Dear Reader

Wet, soggy and fished out of the Mediterranean, Beatrice has lived to tell the tale. Case over. Or is it? With Gennaio's body washing up in Budapest, there may be loose ends. PI Stubbs finds private investigating is a lonely job when visiting perfume houses in Paris, a chateau in Bordeaux or fashion shows at Versailles. Enter an assistant who won't take no for an answer. The next in the Stubbs adventures will be out in November 2019.

Acknowledgements

With enormous appreciation for Catriona Troth, Liza Perrat, Jane Dixon Smith and Gillian Hamer, aka Triskele Books, for editorial input and research assistance. Heartfelt and sincere gratitude to the staff at Hotel Romeo, Naples, who allowed me access to Michelin-starred restaurant Il Comandante. Special thanks to maître d'hotel Mario Vitiello, chef Salvatore Bianco and fixer Antonella Graziano. Respect and admiration to JD Smith (cover design), Julia Gibbs (proofreader) and Janys Hyde (Italian advice) aka The Jay Team.

Message from JJ Marsh

I hope you enjoyed HONEY TRAP. If you're interested in a taste of BLACK WIDOW, the forthcoming 9th Beatrice adventure, the first two chapters are included at the end of this book.

I have also written The Beatrice Stubbs Series, European crime dramas:

BEHIND CLOSED DOORS
RAW MATERIAL
TREAD SOFTLY
COLD PRESSED
HUMAN RITES
BAD APPLES
SNOW ANGEL

I have also written a standalone novel

AN EMPTY VESSEL

And a short-story collection

APPEARANCES GREETING A POINT OF VIEW

For more information, visit jjmarshauthor.com

For occasional updates, news, deals and a FREE exclusive prequel: *Black Dogs, Yellow Butterflies*, subscribe to my newsletter.

If you would recommend this book to a friend, please do so by writing a review. Your tip helps other readers discover their next favourite read.
Thank you.

BLACK WIDOW

JJ MARSH

Chapter 1

Temple Bar in Dublin was a drunken mess. Under-dressed girls cackling and falling over in the street, groups of men grunting like apes as they gulped down pint after pint, clashing music from opposing bars and neon signs inviting 2-4-1 shots to help people lose their faculties as fast and cheaply as possible. The whole scene repelled him.

He took a right up a side street and unfolded his map. No location services, no satellite data, no mobile phone. Not for Davor. A professional leaves no trace. If anyone needs to contact The Ghost, they know what to do.

The private club stood on Sycamore Street, just across from the Olympia Theatre. A small plaque announced its presence with nothing more than a number. He pressed the buzzer and gave his alias, as instructed. The door creaked open to reveal a staircase lit with green sconce lights between portraits of Ireland's literati. Of course.

He climbed the steps, ignoring sketches of Wilde, Yeats, Synge and Beckett, intent on the entrance above. Before he reached for the handle, the door swung open and a man welcomed him in, offering to take his coat. Davor refused and scanned the room for his host. With a jolt, he saw she was not alone. He recognised her companion and his significance. This meant one of two things: either a major job or a gold watch and lots of platitudes about many years of great service. He weighted up the pros and cons of both and found himself ambivalent.

She saw him approach and got to her feet for the greeting kisses, her green eyes reflecting the Art Deco table lamps. Even though it was obvious he knew the man beside her if only by sight, she performed the introductions. No one used their real names.

Davor sat, rolling his coat behind him, keeping his face impassive. One waiter brought champagne and another canapés. She began reminiscing. The first time she'd hired him. How long ago that was! He must remember the Algerian job, where they barely escaped with their lives. If it hadn't been for his piloting skills and that borrowed Cessna, she wouldn't be here today. Davor returned every serve with an easy lob. The years had gone by so fast! How was it possible she still looked so young and beautiful? Algeria was such a crazy mission! They used to be so naïve. She surely had not forgotten the incident in Oslo?

Her laughter and clapped hands drew discreet attention from the quiet tables around the room. They lapsed into silence, as if recalling more adventures from the past, while Davor waited for the inevitable. To his surprise, the man spoke first, his accent confirming his identity like a designer label.

"Mr Zola, I want to thank you. As an organisation, we are forever in your debt. You have been a loyal servant and we would like to offer you a token of our gratitude for your many years of service. Your most recent task was a masterpiece."

Davor lifted his chin, as if requiring clarification.

"You are too modest. I refer to the retirement of Mr Genet. That particular situation could have become very awkward for all of us. I am grateful you and Ms de Beauvoir for tying up all loose ends."

De Beauvoir shook her blonde hair in an affectation of modesty, but her green eyes flashed satisfaction. "That was all Zola. All I did was arrange the timing. He is a master of his craft.

And talking of craft ..."

He picked up his cue. These two were a slick team, slithery as a pair of snakes. Davor wondered if they were sleeping together. More than likely and sooner or later one would get bitten.

"We know you want to retire and we think now is the time. It would be better for all of us if you leave the scene. Go back to your country. Buy some land, keep chickens, grow vegetables." He handed over a slim envelope. "This is the code to access your retirement fund. Our only request is this: should you ever find yourself the subject of questioning by any authority, you have never heard of Ms de Beauvoir, Mr Genet and never in your life encountered Mr de Maupassant. Is that acceptable to you?"

Davor scooped up the envelope and shook the man's hand. He turned to his boss and clasped her hand in some semblance of gratitude. Her nails and jewellery pressed uncomfortably into his flesh. "It has been a pleasure working with you. My memory is now wiped and I will retire to the coast, go fishing and as you say, grow vegetables. I thank you both and give you my assurance you will never see or hear from me again. Good evening to you."

Outside, people hurried for shelter from the sudden downpour. Davor lifted his face to the sky, allowing the rain to wash him clean.

Chapter 2

"Can I ask what you do for a living?" asked the optician.

Beatrice opened her mouth, closed it again and settled on the simplest response. "I'm retired." She doubted she would ever be able to say the words 'Private Investigator' without getting an attack of imposter syndrome.

"Retired from what?" he asked, tapping the results of her eye test into his desktop computer. When she didn't respond immediately, he looked up. "I'm not being nosey, just wondering if your job involved a great deal of screen work. For a woman of your age, your eyesight is remarkably good."

"You just said I needed glasses."

"You do. But many people need glasses at a much earlier stage of life. Mostly those who spend much of their time looking at computer screens. People like me."

Beatrice grew less defensive. "I was a detective inspector until last year. There was a lot of screen time, but just as much was spent out on the streets."

"Ah, that may be why your long-sight vision is so strong. You'll only need low-strength corrective lenses for close-up work. Computers, reading and so on. Here's a prescription. Take that to any optician and when you've adjusted to your specs, you'll wonder what you ever did without them."

On leaving the surgery, Beatrice did not go directly to the

nearest optician. Instead, she stomped around the streets of Exeter, feeling beleaguered and out of sorts. It was tempting to stuff the prescription to the bottom of her handbag and forget about it, but then how could she read all the case files, spreadsheets and financial details of her new business? There was no escaping the fact – she was getting old. To cheer herself up, she stopped for coffee and cake at Pasticciera Fiorentina to indulge her recently acquired taste for Italian pastries. Finally, she succumbed to the inevitable and sought out an optician. At least she could choose a light frame which would not add still more years to her face.

The drive home to Upton St Nicholas did not fill her with her usual eagerness. In Exeter, like London, she could potter around, eat cake, browse a bookshop, buy a bottle of wine for her and Matthew or even attend a concert without meeting most of her neighbours. In the village, everyone knew everyone and observed the smallest adjustment to behaviour.

"Skimmed milk today? Are you and the professor on a diet?"

"Beatrice, will you put Heather straight? Friday's concert at the church hall was an operetta, not a musical."

"Hello, you two. Missed you on Sunday. Hear you went over to Crediton for a change."

It stifled her and she had deliberately begun to switch shops, pubs and routines simply to avoid the same faces, same comments and same dreary old habits. The imminent visit of Dawn and Derek would be a blessed relief.

Not even her new agency provided any real thrills. So far it was all suspected infidelity, benefit fraud and one neighbourly suspicion of vegetable sabotage. All within a fifty-mile radius. She was still awaiting all the emails saying 'you are urgently summoned to the island of Antigua for the most fascinating case of your career!' The disputed will job had already involved far too many unpaid hours of answering emails, and was yet to materialise. All because the tremulous creature who 'almost certainly' wanted to employ her, was still dithering about sharing confidential information. How can you expect a detective to investigate without giving her all the facts? Beatrice was on the point of telling her to find someone else to spy on her relatives, but she'd been looking forward to a trip to Salzburg. The Austrians did awfully good cakes.

She pulled onto their driveway, keeping an eye out for Huggy Bear. The little Border terrier had become adept at finding holes in the fence and escaping the garden to go searching for rabbits. Sunlight shone through the stained glass above the front door, throwing a rainbow of colour at her feet as she plonked her shopping in the hall. The house was silent. Matthew must have taken the dog out or she would have been barking and jumping up in delight at one of the family returning home.

Beatrice kicked off her shoes and padded into the kitchen. Empty, but crumbs on the counter and the smell of fried bacon suggested someone had made himself a snack. She opened the kitchen door to let in some fresh air and gazed out at the garden, with a certain amount of pride. To her left, the shrubbery shimmered in the breeze, as colourful as Rio at Carnival. The lawn was neatly mowed and her wildflower bee garden flourished, humming with winged visitors in the midday warmth. The stream bubbled and gurgled away, swollen with last night's rain. On her right, the brand-new winter garden, their new favourite room.

Her eyes narrowed. Between two large fig plants, she could see a human arm on the rattan rug. Panic seized her.

She raced through the house and into the conservatory, short breaths drying her mouth. On his back, snoring lightly, Matthew was dozing on a garden recliner. The newspaper and one arm had fallen to lie beside him and curled up on his stomach was a grey fur ball, observing her through eyes the colour of Dijon mustard.

Beatrice stood in the doorway to gaze at the comfortable pair enjoying an afternoon nap together. She really must stop panicking every time he dozed off. So if Matthew and Dumpling were both still alive and where they should be, where was the dog? The conservatory door was slightly ajar, leaving enough room for a terrier to slip through. The house phone rang from the hallway and she returned indoors to answer the call. Neither of the old chaps moved.

"Hello?"

"Hello, Beatrice. This is Lisa from Hazeltree Farm. Just wanted to let you know we've got your dog. She wandered into the yard earlier and I thought I recognised her. Jack checked her collar and sure enough, it's your Huggy Bear."

"Really? Oh thank you so much, Lisa. I've just got home myself. That animal is an escapologist. I'll jump in the car and come and get her."

"No need for that. I'm sending the girls round with a couple of jars of my homemade pickle. They'll bring the dog back to you."

"You are extremely kind, thank you. I'm sorry for the inconvenience."

"No need for that. I'd just be a bit careful. You know how these boy racers tear round the lanes and she's such a dear little thing. Give my best to Matthew and if I can have those jars back when you're done, I'd be grateful."

"Will do and thank you so much." Beatrice replaced the receiver, ashamed of her negative attitudes to village life.

While she awaited the return of the errant mutt, Beatrice set about preparing a ploughman's lunch to go with Lisa's homemade pickle. Bread and cheese were all very well, but it had to be accompanied by a decent salad. She was determined to ensure Matthew consumed his five a day, for the sake of his health. She washed some lettuce, chopped tomatoes, cucumber, celery and apple, fished out a couple of pickled onions and arranged everything around a slab of Cheddar. She heated the oven and while a crusty baguette was warming, she checked her emails. She was just printing one particular mail to study further when the doorbell rang.

Kayleigh and the other one whose name Beatrice could never remember delivered the dog and the pickle with shy smiles. They seemed reluctant to say goodbye to Huggy Bear, so Beatrice assured them they could take her for a walk whenever they liked. After they'd gone, Matthew came wandering into the kitchen, obviously woken by the doorbell.

"Oh I say, a ploughman's lunch. That looks just the ticket. I worked up quite an appetite doing the weeding this morning."

"Hence the bacon sandwich and the nap, I assume."

"Guilty as charged. Who was at the door?"

"The girls from Hazeltree Farm bringing Huggy Bear back. From now on, you can't leave her out in the garden unattended. You know what a Houdini she is."

Matthew looked down at the dog, who wagged her tail at him. "Did you run off again, you naughty girl?" The dog's ears softened into the canine equivalent of a smile and the tail wagged faster.

Beatrice suspected Matthew wasn't the only one who'd had bacon for elevenses. "She always ends up at one of the farms. Full of fascinating smells, I suppose. The problem is that means her crossing the lanes at some point, which is dangerous. Do you want apple juice or water?"

"Juice, please. The thing is, I thought she was asleep beside me. The three of us had a nice sit down with the paper and I must have nodded off. I apologise for not keeping an eye on her and I'll be sure to close the door next time. How was your trip to Exeter?"

Beatrice washed her hands and they sat at the kitchen table to eat. "I have excellent long-range vision for a woman my age, but I now need reading glasses. *Bon appétit.*"

"*Bon appétit.* Personally, I think it's remarkable you haven't needed them before. I had my first pair in my twenties. All that poring over textbooks as an earnest swotty youth took its toll. Though I wasn't asking about the optician. How did the client take your report? Was he satisfied?"

Beatrice watched him as he added salad dressing. Healthy vegetables would be a great deal less healthy if slathered with a oily sauce. He evidently sensed her gaze and limited himself to a modest drizzle.

"I wouldn't say satisfied, exactly. He accepted my findings and is prepared to pay me for my work. Yet he is still convinced his wife is deceiving him, no matter how many assurances I give. These infidelity cases are an awful bore, you know. Not just the lurking around watching people going about their daily business, but the unhealthy green-eyed monster that drives people to suspect their loved ones. It's all very depressing."

"I can imagine. This pickle is excellent. Very fruity. Well, you don't have to do those jobs if you don't want to. You're your own boss. Choose the fun ones and pass on the rest."

Beatrice seized her moment. "Funny you should say that. There is something rather more interesting on offer, in fact. Have a look at this." She reached behind her for a print out of the email and passed it to him.

```
To: admin@beatrice-stubbs.com
From: BrunoStarieri@mailshot.it
Dear Beatrice

I hope you are well. I don't know if you
remember me, the junior chef at Ecco in
Napoli?
Earlier this year, you discovered my uncle,
Gennaio Colacino, was the one selling recipes
from Ecco's kitchen. Everyone was very happy
you solved our problem and reunited our
family. Sadly, only a few months afterwards,
```

```
Gennaio was killed in Hungary. I forwarded the
news story, did you see it?
This is the reason for writing to you. The
police in Budapest are not pursuing the case
of my uncle's murder. Their opinion is that he
got into a fight and lost. We are convinced
the people he used to spy for arranged his
death. We have no proof but we owe Gennaio the
truth. We want to know how and why he died, so
we would like to hire you to investigate.
My sister Chantal and I left the restaurant
some months ago. Realistically, we were never
meant to be chefs. Now, we have our own
business as app developers. We are doing well
and can pay your fees and expenses.
Could you go to Budapest and see if you can
find anything the police missed? Just to be
clear, our intention is to use your report to
put pressure on the police to re-open this
case. We are not seeking personal vengeance.
I look forward to hearing from you and send
you warm regards from Naples.
Bruno & Chantal
```

Matthew's eyes roamed over the page as he absently ate some bread. Beatrice waited till he had finished before looking at him expectantly.

"More interesting, indeed, but a bit of a leap from stalking unfaithful spouses. This sounds like a rather dangerous assignment. One which is more than likely to stir up a hornet's nest."

"Yes, and with very little to go on, I'd feel bad about taking these young people's money. If the police aren't bothered, I really don't see why I'd be any more effective. But still ...."

Matthew's gaze rested on her, as he bit into a pickled onion.

"The thing is, it feels like unfinished business," Beatrice continued. "I solved the Naples case and found the spy in the kitchen. After the police arrested the people pulling Gennaio's strings, I assumed that was case closed. But what if we only cut down the weeds but left the roots intact? Or only routed half the rats' nest so they could regroup and attack the deserter later?"

"Can we manage to limit our metaphors to one theme at a time? Horticultural, zoological *or* military, if you don't mind. I would say your hypothesis merely reinforces my point. If you only caught the foot soldiers, there is a far more powerful general steering the troops. That would be a job for an entire opposing army, not a lone veteran without heavy artillery. Do you really want to engage with such people?"

Dumpling sashayed into the kitchen, sat at Matthew's feet and emitted a silent miaow. The signs were clear. A detective's powers of deduction could be honed at home as well as at work.

"Look me in the eye, Matthew Bailey, and tell me you have not been feeding these animals from the table."

Matthew busied himself with a forkful of salad. "There may have been one or two scraps which fell to the floor. By the way, what's the plan for the weekend and our visitors? Given Derek's enthusiasm for steam engines, I wondered if I might invite him along to the Devon Railway Centre. Take Luke with us, he loves it there. That way, you and Dawn could have a few hours to chat."

"That is a marvellous idea. Derek and Luke would enjoy that enormously and I'd appreciate some quality time with my old mate. But that deflection, deft as it was, does not address my question. Do we encourage bad habits and begging from our animals, or do we separate human and animal food, thereby giving ourselves peace at the dinner table?"

Matthew mopped up the remaining pickle with the crust of his baguette. "Point taken. Lax behaviour on my part. Won't happen again. I must say, Lisa's pickle is head and shoulders above anything else I've eaten. I hope she enters it in the village show. Now then, what about this case?"

Beatrice thought about it, watching butterflies flitter across the garden. It was a frightening prospect to go after some sort of criminal syndicate who would coerce, bully, threaten, kidnap and even kill. But she couldn't just ignore the situation. "At this stage, I'll think I'll just ask for more information."

Matthew shook his head. "I think we both know what that means. Thank you very much for lunch. I'm off to research the train place and ask if I can borrow my grandson."

Black Widow will be on sale in November 2019

Printed in Great Britain
by Amazon

87616915R00164